The Story of Henrietta

The Story of Henrietta by Charlotte Smith
First published as vol. II of *The Letters of a Solitary Wanderer* by
Sampson Low, London, 1800
First Valancourt Books edition 2012

ISBN 978-1-934555-54-5

Design and typography by James D. Jenkins
Published by Valancourt Books
Kansas City, Missouri
http://www.valancourtbooks.com

VALANCOURT CLASSICS

The Story of Henrietta

BY

Charlotte Smith

Edited with an introduction and notes by
Janina Nordius

𝕶𝖆𝖓𝖘𝖆𝖘 𝕮𝖎𝖙𝖞:
VALANCOURT BOOKS
2012

CONTENTS

CONTENTS

INTRODUCTION

The Story of Henrietta was first published as the second volume of Charlotte Smith's *The Letters of a Solitary Wanderer*, a work originally planned to include six volumes, but of which only five eventually appeared. At the publication of the first three volumes in 1800, Smith had long been established as a respected and popular writer, praised for her poetry and her gothic and sentimental novels, but also known for her liberalist political views and outspokenness on matters concerning the plight of women. The novella-length *Story of Henrietta* is among her least known but clearly most interesting works, for here Smith leaves the ruins and castles of Europe behind to make a significant foray into another, yet so far little explored field of gothic terror and brutality. Setting her story in the British colony of Jamaica, she expands her political concerns to embrace also the controversial issue of colonial slavery, a system supported by powerful financial interests in the metropolis but also increasingly criticized there by the growing abolitionist movement. In representing the slaveholding island as a location so fraught with horrors and anxieties as to chill the blood of the most seasoned gothic reader, Smith conjures up a parallel between women's disempowerment and the situation of the enslaved, while at the same time considerably radicalizing her critique of the West Indian slave regimes already begun in her short novel *The Wanderings of Warwick* (1794).

Charlotte Turner Smith: Life and Context

Charlotte Smith (1749-1806), whose transparent use of autobiographical material in her fiction has often been commented on by her critics, had close personal experience of many of the circumstances she related in *The Story of Henrietta*, even though she had never resided in Jamaica herself. Born Charlotte Turner, the eldest daughter of a well-to-do land-owner, she spent her childhood at her father's country estates in the south of England and, later, at his London residence in King Street, St. James's. She attended schools at Chichester and Kensington, where she received the education thought proper at this time for girls of her social standing, learning the social accomplishments she would supposedly need to secure a good marriage. In her memoir of Charlotte, her sister Catherine observes "that Mrs Smith's education, though very expensive, was superficial," and claims that later in life Charlotte "often regretted that her attention had not been directed to more useful reading, and the study of languages" (Dorset 24). When Denbigh (a character in *The Story of Henrietta*) commends Henrietta's aunt for making her niece concentrate on "useful acquirements, writing correctly her own language, understanding and speaking Italian and French" (7)—languages that Smith herself, whatever the shortcomings of her early education, apparently knew well (Fletcher 14)—he seems thus clearly to be giving vent to views held by the author herself. Having left school, young Charlotte was introduced into society as early as the age of twelve, and then swiftly married off to Benjamin Smith just a few months before her sixteenth birthday, presumably to be out of the way as her father, widowed since his eldest daughter was three, was arranging a new marriage for himself (Dorset 24-26).

Charlotte's marriage turned out a source of infinite regret to her. Benjamin, in his early twenties when they met, was the son of a prosperous West India merchant and director in the East India Company. He had been made a partner in his father's business, but neglected his affairs, and spent whatever money he could get hold of on his own personal

pleasures, caring little about his growing family. The financial situation of the family grew even worse after the death
in 1776 of Benjamin's father, whose will was so complicated
that, although his intention had been to provide for his grandchildren, it took almost thirty-seven years of legal wran-
gling until a settlement was finally reached in 1813. By then
Charlotte was already dead, having spent her last thirty years
fighting for the interests of her children and their families in
this drawn-out lawsuit (Stanton xxix). In the mean time, her
marriage had collapsed beyond repair. Constantly in debt up
to his ears, Benjamin had to spend seven months in a debt-
or's prison in early 1784—a situation whose dire effects on
the debtor's family Smith poignantly describes in *Henrietta*.
Charlotte accompanied her husband in jail for a time, and
also went with him to France the following winter when he
had to flee abroad to escape his creditors, but his constant
affairs with other women, the physical violence she had to
put up with at his hands, and his complete lack of responsibility for his family eventually made the situation untenable
(Stanton xxiii, 79). In 1787, after twenty-three years of marriage, she separated from her husband together with her children, determined to provide for them by her own writing.

By then she had already published a collection of verse,
the *Elegiac Sonnets* (1784), which had met with immediate success, and also a couple of adaptations from the French;* but
now she set herself to writing fiction, and published her first
novel, *Emmeline, the Orphan of the Castle* with Thomas Cadell
in 1788. Over the next eighteen years she published another
nine novels,† a longer poem (*The Emigrants*, 1793), as well as

---

* *Manon L'Escaut, or The Fatal Attachment* (1786), from the Abbé Prévost;
and *The Romance of Real Life* (1787), a collection of tales based on F. Gayot
Pitaval's "Causes célèbres et intéressantes."

† *Emmeline* (1788), *Ethelinde* (1789), *Celestina* (1791), *Desmond* (1792), *The Old
Manor House* (1793), *The Wanderings of Warwick* (1794), *The Banished Man*
(1794), *Montalbert* (1795), *Marchmont* (1796), *The Young Philosopher* (1798).

several books for children and two volumes of a *History of England* (1806), in addition to the novellas in *The Letters of a Solitary Wanderer*. In most of her fictional works she would dwell on the precarious situation of women under patriarchy, often using the gothic mode to drive home this and other concerns close to her heart. During almost all of her writing career she suffered from rheumatism, an illness which eventually made her unable to walk without help, and which seriously crippled her hands, a problem that her constant writing by hand did nothing to improve (Stanton 91). The pain and her incessant worries about money and the welfare of her children, of whom only six out of twelve eventually survived her, all took their toll on her health, and seem at least part of the reason why she never finished the sixth volume of *The Letters of a Solitary Wanderer*.

From the family she married into, Smith would have learnt a great deal about life and conditions at West Indian plantations, some of which information may well have gone into her writing of *The Story of Henrietta* much later. During the first years of her marriage, she and her family lived in the London house where her father-in-law, Richard Smith, conducted his business on the ground floor, and she saw quite a lot of both her parents-in-law. Richard Smith had resided for many years in the West Indies; he owned property in Barbados, and had married a widowed lady of that island. Charlotte's sister Catherine describes the elder Mrs Smith's "languid air, and sallow complexion," and her speaking in "the monotonous drawl and pronunciation peculiar to the natives of the West Indies" as being "wearisome" (28), apparently projecting part of her impatience with the woman onto the fact of her being Anglo-Caribbean. Charlotte may not have shared this penchant for caricaturing people from the islands, even though she would later make her Jamaican-born heroine Henrietta worry that her own looks might

resemble the stereotyped "cast of countenance" she ascribes
to "the creoles," whether white or of color (*Henrietta* 29).
The problems the younger Mrs Smith had with her mother-
in-law seem rather to derive from their different interests and
personalities. In a letter quoted in her sister's memoir she
relates how Richard's wife found her wanting in the domestic
skills expected of a West Indian mistress of a house:

> There are no women, she [the elder Mrs Smith] says, so
> well qualified for mistresses of families as the ladies of
> Barbadoes, whose knowledge of housewifery she is per-
> petually contrasting with my ignorance, and, very unfor-
> tunately, those subjects on which I am informed, give me
> little credit with her; on the contrary, are rather a disad-
> vantage to me; yet I have not seen any of their paragons
> whom I am at all disposed to envy. (Dorset 27-28).

As Loraine Fletcher observes, the last of the quoted sentences may indicate that Charlotte's "social life [. . .] was
spent with families who had made their money in the West
Indies, or with successful London merchants [. . .]" (Fletcher
29). Although she did not particularly enjoy the life she led
during these years, she would presumably have picked up
quite a store of facts and anecdotes relating to West Indian
life by socializing so closely with her in-laws and their circle.
The circumstance that "during the Eton and Harrow vaca-
tions," there came to stay with the family "four or five wild,
ungovernable, West Indian boys (sons of the correspondents
of the house)" (Dorset 29), would also most likely have added
to the picture she formed of plantocracy life and attitudes,
as we may assume from her including a similar episode in
Henrietta, in George Maynard's telling the story of his childhood (82).

   Although Charlotte at first seems to have found her father-
in-law as difficult to get on with as his wife, this changed over

the years. Especially after the death of the elder Mrs Smith in 1766, when Charlotte came to spend more time attending to Richard and helping him with his business correspondence, she won his respect and appreciation. Eventually they even became close friends. "Her father-in-law was in the habit of confiding to her all his anxieties, and frequently employed her pen in matters of business," we learn from Charlotte's sister; and he "frequently declared, that such was the readiness of her pen, that she could expedite more business in an hour from his dictation, than any one of his clerks could perform in a day" (Dorset 34). That the business she assisted him in and from which the family derived their income was largely dependent on Caribbean slave labor cannot have been unknown to Charlotte, but whether she was bothered by this or not we do not know. There is certainly nothing to indicate that she should have been overly critical at this early stage of her life (the late 1760s and early 70s), when voices against the inhuman treatment of Africans were just beginning to be heard in Britain, and the formation of the Abolitionist society was still more than a decade away. Perhaps George Maynard's sudden insight in *Henrietta*, as he finds some tracts on slavery among the papers of his dead friend, describes the process of Charlotte's own eventual awakening in the 1790s: "Accustomed to consider these people as part of the estates to which they belonged, I had never properly reflected on this subject before; and when I now thought of it, I was amazed at the indifference with which I had looked on and been a party in oppression, from which all the sentiments of my heart revolted" (131-132).

The *Society for Effecting the Abolition of the Slave Trade*, as it was officially called, was not formed until May 1787, and it took another twenty years of intense campaigning before the African trade was outlawed by the British Parliament in March, 1807, and still longer until the law emancipating the enslaved throughout the British Empire was finally passed in 1833. However, British intellectuals had begun to speak out against the indignities of slavery quite some time before the establishment of the Abolitionist Society. Importantly, too, writers of sentimental poetry and fiction—such as William Cowper in the 1780s, and novelists like Sarah Scott and Laurence Sterne as early as the 1760s*—appealed to the sensibility of their readers, asking them to sympathize with the sufferings of their enslaved fellow human beings. Yet although, as David Brion Davis has pointed out, this kind of sentimentalist writing helped to turn the tide in favor of abolishing the trade (473-474), many writers of fiction remained curiously biased on the issue of slavery itself. For even when adamant in their abhorrence of the trade, novelists writing about enslavement often tended to take an ameliorist view on the institution of slavery, arguing for improvement of conditions rather than for total emancipation. Or, perhaps even more frequently, they would vacillate:—between on the one hand praising what they conceived of as the humane treatment of the enslaved by benevolent slave owners—which in effect meant condoning slavery—and, on the other hand, condemning the institution of slavery altogether, on moral grounds.†

It is this kind of vacillation that marks Charlotte Smith's fictional treatment of the topic of colonial slavery, when she eventually begins to engage with it in her short novel *The Wanderings of Warwick* (1794). Around 1790, Smith had, as

* See e.g., William Cowper's poems "The Negro's Complaint" (1788), "The Morning Dream" (1788), and "Sweet Meat has Sour Sauce: or, The Slave Trader in the Dumps" (1788); Sarah Scott's novel *The History of George Ellison* (1766); and Laurence Sterne, *The Life and Opinions of Tristram Shandy, Gentleman* (1760-67).

† See for example Anna Maria Mackenzie's *Slavery, or, The Times* (1792), referred to by Smith's early biographer Hilbish as "the most popular of the anti-slavery novels" (501).

her sister Catherine disapprovingly puts it, "formed acquaintances with some of the most violent advocates of the French
Revolution, and unfortunately caught the contagion, though
in direct opposition to the principles she had formerly professed, and to those of her family" (Dorset 49). Even though
Smith like many of her radicalist friends would be disillu-
sioned with the Revolution after the Terror in 1793-94, her
political radicalization together with the upswing for the
abolitionist movement obviously made her reconsider things
she might have formerly taken for granted, and her concern
about the situation of the enslaved had not diminished when
she returned to the subject in *Henrietta* some five years after
writing *Warwick*. Although she was at that time still involved
in the lawsuit over Richard Smith's estate, trying to claim
for her children their fair share of the by then considerably
diminished fortune he had made from slave labor,* her treatment of slavery in *Henrietta* is far more critical, but also more
despondent than it had been in *Warwick*. But, above all, she
incorporates and uses her long experience in writing gothic
fiction to accentuate the horror and anxiety by which slavery
affects not only the enslaved, but also, ironically as we may
think, the gothic subject, whose role in this case is taken by
such British or Anglo-Caribbean characters as feel burdened
by their own complicity in the system.

The Story of Henrietta: Publication History and Narrative Structure

Charlotte Smith's last major work of fiction, *The Letters of
a Solitary Wanderer*, had a turbulent publication history. Smith
had agreed in late 1798 or early 1799 with the London pub-
lisher and printer Sampson Low to write six volumes, "each

* In a letter of 4 August, 1800, when discussing a sale of a Barbados
plantation belonging to the estate of her late father-in-law, Smith thus
makes an estimate of "the value of the Negroes" (see Stanton 353).

containing," as she says in her preface to the first volume, "a single Narrative, which the Solitary Wanderer is supposed to collect in the countries he visits" (*LSW*, 1.[v]).* Apparently there was some delay in getting the books out, for in the preface, dated October 1800, Smith claimed that the first two volumes had been printed and ready for almost a year.† The first three volumes were advertised in the newspapers in early November, 1800 (see *British Fiction, 1800-1829*), but as Sampson Low died late that year, his business was closed down. The remaining unsold copies of the volumes already out were bought by the publishers Crosby and Letterman, whereas the manuscripts of two more volumes, yet to be printed, were sold by Low's estate to Longman and Rees (*LSW*, preface, 4. iv). The latter published them as volumes four and five in February 1802, "being worse printed than an half penny ballad & on paper the very coarsest I ever saw," Smith comments in a letter to a friend later that spring.‡ Clearly displeased with the situation, she makes it rather clear in her preface to volume four that she has no intention of finishing the work as planned, and the sixth volume of *The Letters*, which was to have told "the story of the Solitary Wanderer himself," did indeed never appear (*LSW*, preface, 4. iv).

Making the Wanderer's correspondence to his friend serve as a frame tale for the stories included in *The Letters* allows Smith to work with multiple narrators in the tales her solitary traveler gathers on his journeys. *The Story of Henrietta* in the second volume is a case in point, as the whole novella is structured around a number of first-person narratives, retold

---

* In her preface to vol. 4 of *Letters of a Solitary Wanderer*, dated 1 Feb. 1802, Smith writes: "The work [. . .] was sold to Mr. *Sampson Low* more than three years since" ([iii]).

† "Since I began this Work almost two years have elapsed, and the two first volumes have been printed nearly half that time" (*LSW*, preface, I. [v]).

‡ Letter to Joseph Cooper Walker, the exact date being lost; see Stanton 416.

by the Wanderer in the same words as we are to understand
they were initially told to him. By employing varying per-
spectives to explore issues so obviously close to her heart as
the subjugation of women and the complicity of her supposedly enlightened compatriots in oppressing the African
enslaved, Smith at the same time underlines the urgency of
these questions and invites her readers to assess what they
are being told by using their own judgment and moral sense.
In addition to the Wanderer himself, who opens his frame
tale with some brief remarks on the story told in the previ-
ous volume, there are three major first-person narrators in
volume two: the young woman Henrietta, her fiancé and later
husband Denbigh, and Henrietta's uncle, George Maynard.
Of these Denbigh acts as a mediator, for it is he who, having
met the Wanderer in Liverpool on business, and told him of
his first acquaintance with Henrietta and subsequent adventures in Jamaica, also repeats to the attentive Wanderer the
stories he has heard from Henrietta and her uncle, and lets
him read a journal written by Henrietta during her voyage
and first stay in the island. All of these separate though inter-
related narratives are then reproduced by the Wanderer in
the first person, as he is supposed to have heard them from
Denbigh, or read them in Henrietta's journal.

The account of Henrietta's shifting fortunes that emerges
from these combined narratives is as full of suspense and
terrifying situations as the best-selling shockers of the 1790s,
although the setting and some of the problems engaged with
are rather far from the common run of gothic fiction at that
time. The daughter of a Jamaican planter, a Mr. Maynard,
Henrietta has been brought up in England by an aunt, but
was ordered back to Jamaica by her father a few years before
the Wanderer gets to tell her story. At the time of her return
to Jamaica, she and Denbigh have already met and formed
a mutual attachment, but when the latter follows her there

on another ship to ask her father for her hand, he is delayed
and arrives in the island six months later than Henrietta. This
separation exposes the lovers to a series of dire and terrifying situations. Henrietta's father turns out to be a tyrant of
the worst kind, who treats his daughter and the enslaved
under his power with equal unfeeling cruelty. Disregarding
Henrietta's affection for Denbigh, he plans to have her married to a friend of his whom she abhors; but during an uprising among the enslaved she escapes from this threatening
union, only to have fresh attempts made on her virtue and
integrity from various other quarters. Having for a time been
a captive among the Maroons, Henrietta eventually finds
refuge in the cave of a hermit, who by a strange coincidence
turns out to be her uncle, George Maynard. When Denbigh
arrives in Jamaica, he learns that Henrietta has been missing
since the outbreak of the rebellion, and sets out searching for
her. He is taken prisoner by an itinerant band of Maroons;
but when he is wounded and left for dead during a skirmish,
he too is rescued by the hermit, who brings him to his cave
where the lovers are reunited.

The narrative of George Maynard, Henrietta's uncle,
deals predominantly with his two unhappy marriages and
with the tragic fate of his only son. It is only at the end of his
tale that he records his sudden insight that the benevolence
and generosity he has shown to others during his relatively
wealthy life in England had in fact been made possible by
the enslavement of his fellow human beings, laboring on his
plantations in Jamaica. This insight, and his disillusionment
with his life in England, decide him to go and live in Jamaica
and try to improve the situation of the enslaved. But persecuted by the plantocracy for activities they see as subversive,
he opts out of the planter society as well and secludes himself in the woods.

To a present-day reader George Maynard may appear

rather patronizing in his attitude to his two wives, whose successive failures to create domestic happiness for himself and his son increasingly displease him. But this is clearly not the only role he is meant to play in the part of his story set in England, for he also acts as a corrective to such behaviors as Smith is known to have disapproved of. He deplores the shallow pleasures his first young wife finds among the fashionable circles of London society, and his regret at her frivolous life style and its disastrous consequences becomes the cue for one of his friends to deliver a more general disquisition on the roles commonly assigned to women at the time. In an openly didactic passage of the kind Smith so often includes in her fiction, George Maynard's friend claims it to be

> a melancholy truth, that women have no character at all; and what is called their education gives none: it only helps to obliterate any distinguishing traits of original disposition which here and there may rise by chance into higher styles of character. [. . .] If any of them venture even to look as if they had any will of their own, or supposed themselves capable of reasoning, how immediately are they marked as something monstrous, absurd, and out of the course of nature! while the most insipid moppet that ever looked in a glass is preferred to one of those reasoning damsels, especially by empty and superficial young men; who, such as the majority of them are, two-thirds of the younger women, desire only to please. (100-101)

The views expressed here could almost have been lifted straight out *Vindication of the Rights of Woman* (1792) by Mary Wollstonecraft, a writer with whom Smith shared many convictions regarding the systemic disempowerment of women in late eighteenth-century Britain. Yet the main inspiration for this diatribe would not have been Wollstonecraft's influence as much as Smith's own lived experience of having to cope single-handedly as a professional writer and sole supporter of a family. Nor was society's dismissive attitude to women's rational capacities the only personal grievance aired in George Maynard's narrative. Another example is the improvidence of his brother-in-law that ends him up in debtor's prison, leaving his family destitute—a blatant want of financial responsibility and consideration for the needs of others clearly modeled on the misconduct of Benjamin Smith. Against such behavior Smith holds up George Maynard, a paragon of upright morals and unfailing trustworthiness, who during his whole life in England prides himself on relieving even his less deserving relatives and dependants from distress by providing for their material needs. However, as it is George Maynard's role in the parts of Denbigh's and Henrietta's narratives set in Jamaica that is the most interesting in the novella's gothic scenario, these sections will be discussed in more detail later in this introduction.

The Gothic and the Colonial Setting

"You despise, as puerile and ridiculous, the fashionable taste, which has filled all our modern books of entertainment with caverns and castles, peopled our theatres with spectres, and, instead of representing life as it is, has created a new school, where any thing rather than probability, or even possibility, is attended to." When Charlotte Smith makes her letter-writing wanderer-narrator ascribe this scathing view of the gothic to his friend and addressee in the first volume of *The Letters of a Solitary Wanderer* (1.21), this is obviously not to dismiss altogether the genre on which so much of her own popularity as a novelist rested. Rather, by making the wanderer—a character apparently less keen than his friend to condemn the vogue for terror fiction—include a number of gothic stories among the "Narratives of Various Description" that make up the five volumes of the *Letters*, she provided herself with an opportunity to effectively divert this kind of negative criticism.

It is a commonplace in gothic criticism that the best gothic narratives tend to mediate urgent contemporary conflicts by situating them at some remove in time; hence, the caverns and castles of the allegedly "dark ages" were among the most favored settings in late eighteenth-century gothic for tales of barbaric practices and cruel injustices still haunting the present. Yet as we may infer from the remark made by the wanderer's friend above, these contemporary concerns of the gothic with "life as it is" were not always obvious to readers and critics at the time. In the case of Charlotte Smith, however, her commitment to real-life problems is always apparent, whether she is dealing with the vulnerable position of women or with the political issues of the day. Still, she might have felt called upon to justify her choice of dealing with such ultimately very serious matters in a genre whose very fashionableness was, by the time she wrote the *Letters*, beginning to be held against it. The "spectres" invoked against the wanderer's literary efforts by his friend and correspondent she needed not bother with; for in so far the supernatural occurs in her fiction it is only in the terrified imaginations of her characters, just as is the case with the "explained supernatural" of Ann Radcliffe, whose successful use of this technique some critics claim she owed to Smith (*e.g.*, Punter & Byron 166).

The "caverns and castles," however, presented a very different problem, and one which had troubled Smith before. Already in her novel *The Banished Man*, published six years earlier in 1794, she jestingly complains in an "Avis au Lecteur" about the "castles which frown in almost every modern novel," several of which she readily admits to be of her own creation (*BM* 2.iii). Pretending to be at a loss where to find further props for her writing, she then continues:

But my ingenious cotemporaries have fully possessed
themselves of every bastion and buttress—of every tower
and turret—of every gallery and gateway, together with
all their furniture of ivy mantles, and mossy battlements;
tapestry, and old pictures; owls, bats, and ravens—that I
had some doubts whether, to avoid the charge of plagia-
rism, it would not have been better to have *earthed* my
hero, and have sent him for adventures to the subterra-
neous town on the Chatelet mountains in Champagne,
or even to Herculaneum, or Pompeii, where I think no
scenes have yet been laid [. . .]. (*BM* 2.iv-v)

In locating her *Story of Henrietta* in Jamaica, Smith obviously found a more profitable setting for a gothic story than
those proposed above. To be sure, Smith was not the first
to situate a gothic plot in the West Indies; a notable prec-
edent is for instance Sophia Lee's Jamaican episode in *The
Recess* (1783-85). Yet to an even greater extent than Lee, Smith
exploits the awe-inspiring potential of the colonial landscape.
Although she had no first-hand experience of the vegetation
and wildlife peculiar to the Caribbean, she nonetheless knew
how to use what she had read and heard, presumably relying
on writers like Edward Long, William Beckford, and Bryan
Edwards,* all of whom had lived for many years in Jamaica
where they owned property, and had written extensively on
its history and natural resources. The latter she also knew
personally, as he had read and praised some of her first sonnets and thus implicitly encouraged her eventual publication
of the *Elegiac Sonnets* (Dorset 38). She would also have found
ample material in newspapers and magazines relating to the
more dire aspects of West Indian nature and climate, such as
hurricanes and floodings, and would thus have had plenty to

---

* In a letter of 3 January, 1798, apparently beginning writing *Henrietta*,
Smith mentions her attempts to "borrow Edwards or Long on Jamaica"
(Stanton 304), books with which she was evidently already familiar.

draw on as she depicted Jamaican nature as both ravishingly beautiful and unnervingly scary in *Henrietta*.

Hence, on arriving in Jamaica Henrietta remarks that she "could not help admiring the beauty" of the surrounding country (27). She is enthralled by the variety of "beautiful trees and shrubs" growing around her father's house, and by the mountains beyond, "which gradually increase in height to the distance of fifteen or twenty miles, where they seem to tower to the clouds, and of which many parts of them have, as I am told, never been visited by Europeans" (44-45). Yet her mood changes from rapture to terror as this almost Edenic scene is swept by one of those violent storms that figure so prominently in British fictions of the tropics, ever since the landslide success of Defoe's *Robinson Crusoe* (1719). As the thunder bursts over the house, "[n]o candle would remain burning," she says, and continues:

> I was involved in darkness; save only when the sudden glare of the lightning momentarily illuminated every object. [. . .] all at once there was a pause; a silence more terrific while it lasted than the fiercest rage of the storm. I thought I remembered to have heard, that such a dismal stillness preceded an earthquake, and I almost believed that I felt the ground opening beneath my feet. I listened, breathless; and then fear for the first time during this dreadful night took possession of me. (40).

Nor are the threats to the enchanting wilderness outlined by Henrietta above limited to the vagaries of the elements. Her eulogy on the beauty of the landscape ends with a passage tinged with ominous foreboding, as the vast forest covering the mountains and "the deep gullies with which those towering ridges are intersected" are also said to give shelter to the Maroons who, living there "sequestered from oppression" (45), often "issue from their sylvan fortresses, and retaliate on their oppressors" (45).

The Jamaican Maroons were the descendants of former slaves who had escaped from the Spanish at the British conquest of the island in 1655, and their number was later added to by runaways from estates owned by the British. After frequent conflicts with British troops over the years, the fighting escalated in the 1730s, ending in two separate treaties granting a certain limited self-government to the Maroon communities in 1739. But another war broke out in 1795, less than a decade prior to Smith's writing her story of Henrietta; hence, when Smith makes her heroine comment on the "alarm" recently caused by the Maroons (45) and places both Henrietta and Denbigh in the midst of the hostilities, she seems clearly inspired by these late events in Jamaica.

Bryan Edwards, by no means an impartial observer, referred to the Maroons taking part in the 1795 uprising as a "horde of savages [. . .] who, lurking in secret like the tigers of Africa, [. . .] had no object but murder" (Edwards, *Observations* lxiv). The alarmist tone adopted by Edwards here clearly reflects the fears of the white planters in a society where almost ninety percent of the population were slaves or the descendants of slaves imported from Africa, especially after the recent revolution in the French colony of San Domingo (now Haiti) in 1791. Unlike the Jamaican Maroons, the rebels in San Domingo had, to the horror of planter societies all over the Caribbean, defeated the planter regime and then successfully withstood the armies of both Napoleon and the British. It is hardly to be wondered at, then, that fear of rebellion was rife in Anglo-Caribbean circles, and when Smith's narrators adopt the same dehumanizing rhetoric as Edwards and occasionally refer to the enslaved as well as the Maroons as "savages," this fear is certainly part of the reason. But it was also a common discursive practice at the time to construct people of non-European descent as "Other" by using clichés such as the "noble savage" and the "bloodthirsty savage," both of

which notions occur in Smith's novella as the narrators vacillate between their xenophobic apprehensions of furious rioting and their basic sympathy with the victims of slavery.

Although Henrietta initially trusts to the moral nobility
of the Maroons and reasons that they "would not injure me,
for I have never injured them" (46), subsequent events show
that things are not quite that simple. Although no blood of
hers is actually shed during the rebellion, her intermittent
apprehensions at being isolated "in a remote house, of an
island, many parts of which are liable to the attacks of savages driven to desperation, and thirsting for the blood of any
who resembled even in colour their hereditary oppressors"
(35), are by no means shown to be far-fetched. Importantly,
though, while she uses the stereotype of the bloodthirsty
savage here, she never suggests that this assumed thirst for
blood is an innate disposition of the Maroons. Rather, she
makes it quite clear that their rage is a result of the treatment they and their fellow African-Caribbeans have been
subjected to by the planter society, and this understanding
of the motives behind the rebellion is indeed something
that permeates the whole novella. Yet it hardly diminishes
Henrietta's fright as she listens to "the strange yells as of
savage triumph" heard at the outbreak of the uprising (49),
nor her terror when having eventually become a captive of
the warring Maroons.

Seen in the context of the early literary gothic's preoc-
cupation with lurid stories set in pre-modern, "Gothic"
Europe, the alienating descriptions of the Maroons given in
The Story of Henrietta clearly serve to emphasize their roles
as representatives of a group of people not yet acculturated
into modern European and supposedly enlightened values.
To British middle-class readers, the alleged "savagery" of the
Jamaican rebels and the enslaved who joined them was likely
to be seen as typifying the moral ignorance and barbaric

behavior associated with a stage of civilization long since left behind by educated Europeans—at least ideally, if not always so in practice. Another example of the cultural backwardness that Europeans felt prevailed among African-Caribbeans in Jamaica is provided by the novella's many references to Obeah, or Obi, a religious tradition among the enslaved originating in West Africa. Castigated as dangerous superstition by Anglo-Caribbean planters, who believed its practitioners to be instrumental in fomenting rebellion among the enslaved, Obeah had by the end of the eighteenth century also become a popular motif in British plays and fiction, and hence a familiar scare to Smith's readers (Edwards, *History* 2.88; Richardson 174, 171).

Henrietta hears of the "Obeahs, persons who persuade others, and perhaps believe themselves, that they possess supernatural powers [. . .] resembling [. . .] those of the witches in Macbeth [*sic*] round the magic cauldron," when staying at her father's estate (47). The "Obi men and women" pointed out to her strike her as "horrid," and she shudders at the thought of their "wild rites of superstition" and the "sort of 'darkness visible'" which due to their influence seems to reign in the minds of the people of color around her (47-48). Even more frightening, though, is her creeping fear that, left with no other company than the enslaved on the estate, she too may have her reason infected with their superstitious notions. "I will not disguise my folly," she writes to Denbigh; "there are times when the hideous phantasies of these poor uninformed savages affect my spirits with a sort of dread, which all my conviction of their fallacy does not enable me to subdue." (47).

In beginning to suspect that her own mind might not be impermeable to such ideas as she finds utterly alien to her own self-image, Henrietta touches on the very core of gothic angst. For, as Jerrold E. Hogle observes, the gothic shows how

characters construct their identities on the basis of what they
wish to dissociate themselves from, whether this concerns
class, race, sexuality, or various kinds of aberrant behavior;
yet at the same time gothic texts also hold up the possibility
that what we thus define as Other may not be as far removed
from our own beings as we would wish it to be (Hogle 12).
Significantly, Henrietta's fears of resembling too closely the
people she meets at her father's estate are not limited to
what might happen to her judgment and common sense;
for surrounded by people whom she patronizingly defines as
"savage," and used to thinking in racial categories, she also
begins to worry about her own ethnicity. "Do you know," she
writes to Denbigh, "that there are three young women here,
living in the house, *of colour,* as they are called, who are, I
understand, my sisters by the half blood! They are the daughters of my father by his black and mulatto slaves" (29). Clearly
unnerved both by her father's intimate connections with his
female slaves, and by the fact that people on the estate "see
nothing extraordinary or uncommon" in this situation (29),
Henrietta does her best to press home her felt difference from
these new half-sisters by stressing their "odd manners" and
their "odd sort of dialect," the latter "more resembling that
of the negroes than the English spoken in England" (29). But
her desire to maintain her aloofness is frustrated as she is
overcome by doubts as to how far she really differs from her
sisters, even when it comes to outward features.

> The youngest of them who is a quadroon—a mestize—I
> know not what—is nearly as fair as I am; but she has the
> small eye, the prominent brow, and something particu-
> lar in the form of the cheek, which is, I have understood,
> usual with the creoles even who have not any of the negro
> blood in their veins. As I am a native of this island, perhaps
> I have the same cast of countenance without being con-
> scious of it (29),

she frets, frankly admitting that "the supposition is not flattering" (29). The remark is significant, for even though it is difficult to overlook the racial undertones implicit in Henrietta's comment here, she does in fact extend the category of people from whom she wishes to differentiate herself to include also white creoles, that is, persons of European descent born in the Caribbean. That white creoles might develop traits like those described above seems to have been a common notion at the time. Long and Edwards both remark on the deep eye sockets of the white creoles, which "conformation" they, in a pre-Darwinian spirit, ascribe to the climate: it protects the person "from those ill effects which an almost continual strong glare of sun-shine might otherwise produce" (Edwards, *History* 2.11; Long 2.261-262; see also Boulukos 95).

Yet Smith's readers would presumably have understood Henrietta's comments on physiognomy to refer not only to external appearance but, as was the common practice of the day, also to such traits of character as this particular cast of countenance was thought to encode. Henrietta is clearly disturbed by what she learns of her father, who is shown to embody all the negative aspects ever ascribed to the planter society by their critics in Britain. Mr. Maynard's sexual exploitation of his female slaves is just one example of behaviors branded as undesirable and frowned upon even in the writings of Anglo-Caribbeans like Long and Edwards, though less out of concern for the women than for reasons of "decency and decorum," as Edwards puts it (Long 2.328; Edwards, *History* 2.21-22). Smith does not make Henrietta dwell explicitly on the nature of his father's liaisons with her half-sisters' enslaved mothers, but her portrayal of the terrors of slavery, and her evident outrage at the disempowerment of women even when it comes to decisions over their own bodies (discussed further below), leaves her readers free to draw their own conclusions.

Gothicizing Slavery

Whatever the anxieties tormenting Henrietta in regards to her Creole ancestry and to the superstitious terrors that threaten to invade her mind when left alone with the enslaved, by far the most terrifying experience she faces during her stay in Jamaica is her brutal confrontation with the horrors of slavery. For whether it is the rebellious Maroons and runaway slaves that set her nerves on edge as they seek to revenge themselves on their oppressors, or whether it is her shock at seeing the way her father treats his slaves, these horrors are all ultimately shown to derive from the inhumanity of slavery.

The parallels between Smith's gothicizing of slavery in *The Story of Henrietta* and the exploration of personal and cultural anxieties that meets us in the period's more conventional gothic narratives set in feudal Europe are obvious. Most British upper and middle class readers at the turn of the nineteenth century wanted to relish the thought of living in an enlightened age when the barbaric customs of the past could no longer harm them; but far too many instances of continued or renewed oppression and brutality in their immediate present contributed to make this a less reassuring prospect. In addition, after the horrors reported from France during the Terror in the mid-1790s and other outbreaks of rioting and social unrest at home and abroad, modernity would have appeared just as grim;* and even political liberalists like Smith began to be seriously alarmed by the uncontrolled and indiscriminate violence let loose as the formerly oppressed sought to revenge their wrongs.

* For example, the Gordon riots in London in 1780, the United Irishmen rebellion in 1798, the San Domingo revolution in 1791.

In choosing the West Indian scene for exploring tensions like these between past and present, Smith knew how to reconcile her liberalist convictions with the writing of a spine-chilling story of suspense. We have no reason to question her commitment on behalf of the enslaved; but it is evident that the descriptions we get in *Henrietta* of the horrors resulting from autocratic despotism, together with the chaos and violence bred by the resistance to the planter regime, may also serve metaphorically as a comment on late events in Europe. For if we read the novella in this way as dealing with political oppression and attempts at liberation in general, Smith's strategy of putting the main blame for whatever horrors might occur in the process on the oppressors rather than the oppressed should clearly be seen as extending beyond the West Indian scene.

Importantly, though, in specifically making slavery the topic of a gothic story where all three narrators in various ways become the victims of the system and its repercussions, Smith also makes a far stronger statement against enslavement than what she had done in her novella *The Wanderings of Warwick* published six years earlier. In *Warwick* there is a rather long and clearly didactic episode set in Barbados, in which the eponymous hero unfolds his current views on slavery at some length, while also including, as a marked contrast to his present views, a flashback recalling a visit to Jamaica many years before. The younger Warwick is said to have reacted "with horror and indignation" (*WW* 45) at seeing "droves of black people going into the fields under the discipline of the whip" (*WW* 45), and reports how one of his friends witnesses "a mulatto girl of ten or eleven years old" being bound and severely whipped, until "her back [was] almost flayed" (*WW* 54). Yet the indignation felt by the young Warwick at these scenes is explained by his older self as "the feelings of a mind unadulterated by custom" (*WW* 45). For although he repeatedly "declar[es] against every species of slavery" (*WW* 66), he nonetheless maintains that "the subject seen nearer loses some of its horror" (*WW* 45) and in fact devotes the bulk of the Barbadian episode—a whole chapter—to arguing that the picture of West Indian slavery prevailing in anti-slavery circles in Britain may be partly exaggerated or distorted. For in Barbados, says the older Warwick, it is

> so much the interest of the planters to be careful of the lives of their slaves, on whose labour their incomes depend, that in general they are not ill-treated;—and if there are some masters whose malignant disposition even avarice cannot controul, there are others whose humanity is not lessened even by the perverse and savage tempers of some of those unhappy beings who are their property. (*WW* 59-60)

In thus making the mature Warwick play down the actual ills of slavery while still declaring against the system on principle, Smith may well have been influenced by her years with her parents-in-laws and her friendship with Richard Smith. She was most definitely influenced by her friend Bryan Edwards, to whose *History* of the West Indies she makes an explicit note in her novel, praising its author's "knowledge of the subject, integrity of heart, and general humanity" (*WW* 66-67, footnote). She also relies on Edwards when making Warwick repeat some of the most common arguments used in proslavery propaganda at the time, as when he claims that the conditions of the enslaved are "in some respects even preferable to that of the English poor" (*WW* 62).

By in this way splitting her first-person narrator in *The Wanderings of Warwick* into a younger and an older self, Smith obviously tries to convey both sides of the infected debate on slavery and the trade. But in giving the more

lenient view on slavery to the more experienced and supposedly wiser Warwick, she in effect seems to end up condoning
the status quo, or, at best, advocating an ameliorist position.
Yet given the short, but quite explicit disclaimers condemning slavery, which are also attributed to the older Warwick,
the final impression that this section of her novel produces is
curiously equivocal.

In *The Story of Henrietta*, published six years after *The
Wanderings of Warwick*, the tone is radically different, however: it is less ambivalent, since slavery is represented in a far
more sordid light, and there seems little hope of resolving
the growing tension between the enslaved and the planters
in a peaceful way. Importantly, though, as little as the West
Indian episode in *The Wanderings of Warwick* does *The Story
of Henrietta* attempt to reproduce events in Jamaica directly
from the viewpoint of the enslaved—not even in the senti-
mentalized manner practiced by some of Smith's contemporary novelists, as for instance Anna Maria Mackenzie
in *Slavery; or, The Times* (1792). It centers exclusively on the
horror and anxiety experienced by the three English narrators when confronted with the atrocities of slavery and of
the revolts provoked by it.

Henrietta's father Mr. Maynard is made an icon of the
cruelty to the enslaved exercised by such planters of "malignant disposition" as we saw the mature Warwick pass over
rather quickly in *The Wanderings of Warwick* (WW 60; see
above). Already when a boy, Henrietta's uncle tells us, his
brother "had been used to exercise the caprices of a very
bad temper on half a dozen African boys and girls" (82), and
these fits of brutishness are said to turn into a permanent
condition when as a grown man he becomes the proprietor
of the estate. Henrietta's mind is, she claims, filled with
"terror and disgust" at the "inhumanity" of the "modes of
revenge" contemplated by her father, should he ever get hold

xxxii   INTRODUCTION

of those slaves who have managed to run away from his plantations; for these modes "are really so horrible only to hear
mentioned, that I am often under the necessity of leaving the
room," she comments (30). Likewise, on arriving in Jamaica,
Denbigh reports hearing of "the cruelty with which [. . .] the
Maroons [. . .] had been pursued, persecuted, and punished
by Mr. Maynard" (54), because they are said to give shelter to
runaway slaves.

   That the Maroons should in turn retaliate on Mr. Maynard
and his likes, and that his slaves should run away, is hardly
to be wondered at in a situation like this. When Smith rep-
resents the Maroons as posing a serious threat to such
Europeans as might fall into their hands, she is clearly out to
show how violence and cruelty always tend to breed more
violence. Denbigh's fate is a case in point. When taken prisoner by the Maroons and their company of escaped slaves,
he fully expects to "receive as little mercy" from them as they
had been shown "by the generality of [his] countrymen" (53).
Although temporarily saved from harm through the intervention of his black servant, who assures his capturers that
Denbigh is "not one of those whom their unfortunate race
have reason to pursue with execrations and with vengeance"
(54), he nonetheless falls victim to their fury in the end, being
stabbed by two of the rebels and left for dead. If this part
of Denbigh's narrative is transparently designed by Smith to
alarm her readers, it is also obvious that her narrator is made
to suffer vicariously for the wrongs committed under slavery, and especially those laid at the door of Henrietta's father.
For the latter is explicitly said to have caused the insurrection to spread by "indulg[ing] his vindictive temper in great
and unjustifiable severities towards the people upon all his
estates," antagonizing even "those who had till then most
faithfully adhered to him" (79).

   The evils bred by the system of slavery also make their

impact on the two other character-narrators, George Maynard and Henrietta, whose anguish and sufferings are equally grim, although different in kind from those of Denbigh. George Maynard is perhaps the character who most poignantly personifies the classic gothic dilemma, in the sense that he finds himself part of a system he abhors, yet unable either to dissociate himself from it or help to abolish it. Although a younger brother, his property in Jamaica is considerable, and when, after the death of his friend, his attention is directed to "the condition of the Africans and their state of slavery in the American colonies" (131), his sudden realization of his own role in their oppression leaves him shocked and ashamed. Yet when he repairs to Jamaica, believing that he has "the means of doing some good to this miserable race" (132), his good intentions come to nothing when confronted with the resistance put up by the plantocracy, whose hostility is adamant to any change that might work to their disadvantage.

The opposition George Maynard meets with is such as would easily bring to mind the horrors threatening heroes and heroines in more traditional gothic stories, such as the risk of imprisonment, and that of mental affliction caused by the stress of the situation. "[M]y endeavours at reformation were not only considered as the idle dreams of a visionary," he says, "but as being dangerous to the welfare of the island"; and when he "persevere[s]" (132) the threats grow more substantial:

> the examples I gave of lenity to and emancipation of the negroes became so much circumstances of fear, that there was, I understood, a resolution taken to confine me as a lunatic; and my brother [. . .] was to be put in possession of my estates. [. . .] The party against me increased every day in numbers and in acrimony. My seat in the council I had long since resigned, and I was accused of fomenting

the discontents among the black people, and of having communicated with the Maroons. In a word, my situation became extremely uneasy to myself, and worse than useless to the unhappy people whose condition it had been my purpose to ameliorate; for greater severities were often exercised on those in whose favour I had interfered, than if I had never pleaded for them the cause of humanity. (132)

Although Smith makes Henrietta's uncle add that "[i]n a government remote from that of the parent state, intrigue does every thing, and equity has as little to do as reason" (132), Smith's description here of the younger Maynard's persecution would indeed seem to have some bearing on the situation in "the parent state" in the wake of the French revolution. For in the conservative climate prevailing in the late 1790s, and with the war with France going on while Smith was writing *Henrietta*, the suspicion of political radicalists in Britain had grown to unprecedented proportions, involving several of Smith's friends and acquaintances. That this is partly the under-text of Smith's description of the witch-hunt put on by the plantocracy appears quite clearly from a remark made earlier in the novella by Henrietta's father, who maliciously comments on Denbigh's supposed radicalism as the news reaches Henrietta that his ship has been captured by a French privateer on its way to Jamaica. "My father [. . .] told me [. . .] that he understood you were sufficiently an adept in Jacobin principles, not to make a voyage to France any calamity to you," she writes to Denbigh, citing Mr. Maynard abusing abolitionists in general and Denbigh in particular: "as to the inhabitants of this island, they can well dispense with the presence of such a wrong-headed young man, who sets up, they tell me, for a reformer. We have more than enough of fellows of that description among us already" (36).

This is not to say, though, that the allegations against the plantocracy that Smith makes Henrietta's uncle voice are only a vehicle for her own criticism of the political climate in Britain at the time; they are certainly, as is obvious from George Maynard's tale as a whole, an expression of Smith's severely felt disillusion with the system from which the (now partly wasted) fortune of the family into which she had married derived. But the backlash for the radicalist movement in Britain may have had some impact on the despondent tone prevailing in the hermit's tale. For while making George Maynard, of all her three narrators, the most committed advocate of radical change in the slavery system, Smith nonetheless has him articulate what might be her own severe misgivings as to the possibilities for the anti-slavery movement of actually achieving success. Hence, finding himself prevented by the plantocracy regime "to give freedom to the people who were considered as part of my estate" (133), Henrietta's uncle decides "to retire wholly from the world, and, as he says, "hide myself from the spectacle of human misery which [. . .] made me abhor the species to which I belonged" (133).

Like her uncle and her fiancé, Henrietta too suffers the consequences of slavery, but in the manner usually reserved for women in gothic romances. For if the rebellion is shown to threaten death and devastation to planters and other white males, another aspect of the violence it unleashes is the danger of sexual assault to which Henrietta is exposed. The threat of rape recurs with double force in Smith's novella as Henrietta first becomes the chosen object of Amponah's amorous affection and then of the Maroon general's marital plans. Amponah, the enslaved servant of Henrietta's father and an acquaintance from England, where he had spent some time in her aunt's family, becomes her only confidant while staying at her father's estate. This explains why she accepts his offer to help her escape when the forced marriage threatened by her father seems imminent, at the same time as an attack on the plantation by the rebelling Maroons is expected. Henrietta's terror at perceiving Amponah's changed manner once they are in the woods culminates as he declares his love for her. "Missy [. . .] I love you. I no slave now; I *my* master and yours. Missy, there no difference now; you be my wife." (142). The fate that seems to await Henrietta could hardly be expressed more clearly; for notwithstanding that Amponah's infatuation may be represented as genuine, his blunt disregard for *her* feelings as he declares himself her husband is only made possible by the rebellion, where roles are reversed and Henrietta is now in his power.

Despite Smith's claim that the story of Amponah is based upon a real event (note, p. 141), the motif of an African slave falling in love with, and abducting, his white mistress is by no means unique in British colonial literature. A similar incident is for instance featured in the Isabinda and Domingo episode in Penelope Aubin's *Charlotta Du Pont* (1723). The attraction that European women were supposed to hold for men from other cultures, apparently only because of their skin color, had in fact become a cliché in popular fiction by Smith's time—so much so that it is immediately re-employed in Henrietta's story. Now the situation is different, however; for when she is saved from Amponah and becomes a prisoner of the Maroons, she is in their power as a representative of the planter class—that is, of the enemies whom the Maroons and their runaway-slave associates are warring against. Documented experiences from the twentieth and twenty-first centuries have shown how rape is consistently used in wars as a means of subjugating and humiliating the opposite side, but the popular fictions of the eighteenth and nineteenth centuries preferred in most cases to romanticize the topic, representing the encounter between non-European warriors and their white prisoners in terms of erotic attraction. Hence, when the Maroon general announces to his people "that he had in the woods rescued a beautiful white woman from a negro, and had brought her to be added to the number of his wives" (143), the sexual aggression implicit in this statement is, just as in the pact proposed by Amponah, dressed in a rhetoric of would-be social decency through the explicit reference to matrimony.

But if there is nothing in the general's actual words to indicate that his plans for Henrietta should be motivated by a wish to punish and humiliate her father, there is a greater awareness of the realities of warfare in Denbigh's narrative, even though he, too, stereotypically assumes that European women hold some kind of special attraction for non-European men. For on hearing that Henrietta has become a captive of the rebels, he plainly relates the fate that might befall her to her father's reputation for cruelty: "She was released from the power of Maynard only to fall into that of savages, always terrible in their passions, and in whom the fierce inclination for European women was now *likely to be exalted by the desire of revenge on a man so detested as the father of my unhappy Henrietta!*" (55; italics added). Fearing "to find her disgraced and undone," he decides to stand by her to the last and "die with her"; for, he says, "I knew she never would survive the horrors I dreaded for her" (55).

Slavery as Metaphor in Women's Gothic

Although the assaults on Henrietta made by Amponah and the Maroon general can thus mainly be blamed on the upheavals of the rebellion, they are not fundamentally different from the forced marriage planned for her by her father, as in each case the heroine is facing severe violation of her person. Clearly, Smith uses the story of Henrietta's tribulations not only to make a case against slavery, but also to draw an excruciating parallel with the exposed situation of women under patriarchy. Outraged when learning of her father's matrimonial plans for her, Henrietta feels only "horror and detestation" (38) at the thought of marrying Mr. Sawkins who, she claims, has "[t]he base spirit of a parasite" (34). Yet her father is inflexible: "[I]t is my intention to have your marriage with the person I have elected for you concluded within a month. [. . .] I never suffer contradiction. Your arguments will be in vain; your opposition fatal to yourself" (33-34). No wonder Henrietta comments on his behavior in terms that explicitly allude to the absolute rule of the former French monarchy: "'Tel est notre plaisir,' was never uttered from the most despotic throne with more inflexible harshness. I was forbidden all reply; and ordered not to remonstrate, but to prepare to obey" (33).

When learning of Henrietta's precarious situation as he arrives in Jamaica, Denbigh fears that "she is condemned by her cruel and brutal father to [. . .] become *a legal prostitute* to a contemptible wretch whom she must loath and detest!" (52; italics added). We have already seen how Smith made George Maynard's friend chime in with Mary Wollstonecraft when lamenting women's limited possibilities in society, and Denbigh's reference here to marriage as "legal prostitution" is another expression reminiscent of Wollstonecraft, who famously used that metaphor in her *Vindication of the Rights of Woman* (ch. 9). That this caustic outlook on marriage also had some bearing on Smith's personal life is obvious, as she would later use the same analogy in a letter to a friend, where she claimed to have been "sold, a legal prostitute" to her husband when she was not yet sixteen (Stanton 625).

Continuing to draw on Wollstonecraft's use of metaphors in the *Vindication*, Smith equates the disempowered position of women with African slavery, making the horrors of the one reflect back on the other, while at the same time

confirming Mr. Maynard as the gothic villain par excellence
in both contexts. While the latter's cruelty to his slaves and
to those willing to help them is consistently described as hei-
nous; and while his sexual exploitation of his female slaves—
women whose right to refuse would have been virtually
nil—is made quite evident from the existence of Henrietta's
half-sisters, even though it is not elaborated in detail; while
he thus is shown to exercise his willful tyranny over the
enslaved in his power as he pleases, it seems only logical that,
when he is about to subject his daughter to the same treatment by marrying her to the execrable Mr. Sawkins, Smith
should make Henrietta refer to the marriage contract drawn
up by her father's lawyers as "the bill of sale" (38). For her
father, she says, being "used to purchase slaves, [. . .] feels
no repugnance in selling his daughter to the most dreadful of all slavery!" (38). In thus conflating the oppression of
women under British law with the bondage suffered by the
enslaved in Britain's Caribbean colonies, Smith does not only
strike a blow for two issues obviously close to her heart at
this time; but by showing how the present is still haunted by
a despotism more befitting a feudal past than the dawning
nineteenth century, she also manages to write a gothic terror
story that continues to thrill readers even today.

Reception

The three volumes of *The Letters of a Solitary Wanderer*
published by Sampson Low were reviewed together in
the spring and summer of 1801. The reception was generally favorable, if not exuberantly so, the reviews varying in
length from a four-line entry in *The Monthly Review* (July
1801: 332), praising the tales as "entertaining and interesting"; to a longer paragraph in *The Monthly Magazine* (July
1801: 606) commending the author for her "general justness

of sentiment and consistency of character"; and a more than six-page long review in *The Critical Review* (May 1801: 35-42).* Commenting on Henrietta's story in the second volume, the *Critical* reviewer avoids any overt reference to its concern with slavery and slave-holding, but finds Smith "perhaps excelled" in "the tale of horror" by John Thelwall's "Adopted Daughter" (38), a novel published roughly at the same time as *Henrietta* and parts of which were set during the 1791 slave revolt in San Domingo.† Yet "the description of the hurricane" finds favor with the reviewer who, quoting a long excerpt from this part of Henrietta's narrative, claims it to be "sublimely terrible" (38-39).

In a letter written in late November 1800, Smith herself thought the volume containing Henrietta's story the best of the volumes so far written,‡ and it was apparently popular enough to stimulate the imagination of other writers as well. For a reviewer for *The Lady's Monthly Museum*, commenting on a short-lived Covent Garden performance called *The Fair Fugitives*, wrote: "The Author of this little Drama is indebted to Mrs. Charlotte Smith's story of Henrietta for part of the plot" (415), an observation confirmed by the rather extensive plot summary of the play included in the review.§ *The Story*

---

* See *British Fiction, 1800-1829*. The only altogether dismissive review was a sour comment in *The Flowers of Literature* (1801-2):452, whose reviewer (somewhat surprisingly with regard to *Henrietta*) found the volumes devoid of Smith's former originality.

† *The Daughter of Adoption*, a four-volume novel published under the pseudonym John Beaufort in 1801. The "horror" in Thelwall's scenes set during the slave revolt may indeed be more explicit than in Smith's novella, which foregrounds instead the terror of anticipation at such horrors as *might* occur.

‡ Letter to the Duchess of Devonshire on 23 November, 1800 (Stanton 361).

§ *The Lady's Monthly Museum* (June 1803): 415. *The Fair Fugitives* was ascribed to Anna Maria Porter in *The European Magazine and London Review* 43 (May 1803): 371.

of Henrietta was also translated separately into French in 1819, even though the French version, *Les Cavernes des Montagnes-Bleues, ou Orgueil et haine*, was considerably enlarged and rewritten.

After this first period of relative success, *The Story of Henrietta* met with the same fate as did many other gothic works of the prolific last years of the eighteenth century, by being largely forgotten for a long time. In recent years, however, it has been attracting increasing attention among readers and scholars interested both in the gothic and in the transatlantic history of slavery, as well as among those wishing to explore the overall literary achievement of Charlotte Smith.

Janina Nordius
Göteborg

October 21, 2010

ABOUT THE EDITOR

Janina Nordius is Associate Professor Emerita of English Literature at Gothenburg University, Sweden. She has published *"I am Myself Alone": Solitude and Transcendence in John Cowper Powys*, articles on various topics including Gothic and colonial fiction, and edited Anna Maria Mackenzie's *Swedish Mysteries* for Valancourt Books.

WORKS CITED AND CONSULTED

Beckford, William. *A Descriptive Account of the Island of Jamaica*. 2 vols. London: T. and J. Egerton, 1790.

Boulukos, George. "The Horror of Hybridity: Enlightenment, Anti-slavery and Racial Disgust in Charlotte Smith's *Story of Henrietta* (1800)." *Slavery and the Cultures of Abolition: Essays Marking the Bicentennial of the British Abolition Act of 1807*. Edited by Brycchan Carey and Peter J. Kitson. Woodbridge: Boydell & Brewer, 2007. 87-109.

British Fiction, 1800-1829: A Database of Production, Circulation & Reception, Cardiff University, accessed at http://www.british-fiction.cf.ac.uk/titleDetails.asp?title=1800A068, on Aug. 30, 2010.

Campbell, Mavis C. *The Maroons of Jamaica 1655-1796*. Trenton, N.J.: Africa World Press, 1990.

Cassidy, F. G. and R. B. Le Page. *Dictionary of Jamaican English*. Cambridge: University Press, 1967.

Davis, David Brion. *The Problem of Slavery in Western Culture*. Ithaca: Cornell University Press, 1966.

Dorset, Catherine Ann . "Charlotte Smith." In Walter Scott, *Biographical Memoirs of Eminent Novelists and Other Distinguished Persons*, vol. 2. *The Miscellaneous Prose Works of Sir Walter Scott*, vol. 4. Edinburgh: Robert Cadell, 1834. 20-70.

Edwards, Bryan. *The History, Civil and Commercial, of the British Colonies in the West Indies*. 2 vols. Dublin: Luke White, 1793.

Edwards, Bryan. *Observations on the Disposition, Character, Manners, and Habits of Life, of the Maroons* . . . . [Prefaced to:] *The Proceedings of the Governor and Assembly of Jamaica, in Regard to the Maroon Negroes*. London: John Stockdale, 1796. iii-lxxxix.

Fletcher, Loraine. *Charlotte Smith: A Critical Biography*. Basingstoke: Palgrave, 2001.

Hays, Mary. "Mrs. Charlotte Smith." In *Public Characters of 1800-1801*. Vol. 3. London: R. Phillips, 1801. 42-64.

Hilbish, Florence May Anna. *Charlotte Smith, Poet and Novelist (1749-1806)*. Philadelphia: University of Pennsylvania, 1941.

Hogle, Jerrold E. "Introduction," *The Cambridge Companion to Gothic Fiction*. Edited by Jerrold E. Hogle. Cambridge: Cambridge University Press, 2002. 1-20.

Labbe, Jacqueline, ed. *Charlotte Smith in British Romanticism*. London: Pickering & Chatto, 2008.

Long, Edward. *The History of Jamaica*. 3 vols. London: T. Lowndes, 1774.

Macdonald, David Lorne, ed. *The Letters of a Solitary Wanderer*. By Charlotte Smith. London: Pickering & Chatto, 2007. Vol. 11 of *The Works of Charlotte Smith*. 14 vols. 2005-2007.

Punter, David and Glennis Byron. *The Gothic*. Malden, Mass.: Blackwell, 2004.

Richardson, Alan. "Romantic Voodoo: Obeah and British Culture, 1797-1807." *Sacred Possessions: Vodou, Santería, Obeah, and the Caribbean*, edited by Margarite Fernández Olmos and Lizabeth Paravisini-Gebert. New Brunswick, N.J.: Rutgers University Press, 1997. 171-194.

Smith, Charlotte. *The Banished Man*. London: T. Cadell. 4 vols. 1794.

Smith, Charlotte. *The Wanderings of Warwick*. London: J. Bell, 1794.

Stanton, Judith Phillips. *The Collected Letters of Charlotte Smith*. Bloomington: Indiana University Press, 2003.

Wollstonecraft, Mary. *A Vindication of the Rights of Woman*. London: J. Johnson, 1792.

Note on the Text

The first edition of *The Story of Henrietta* was published in 1800 by Sampson Low in London, as the second of Smith's first three volumes of *The Letters of a Solitary Wanderer*. A two-volume Dublin edition, comprising the whole text of these first three volumes, followed in 1801, published by Burnet, Wogan, Brown, *et al.* Almost two centuries later, a one-volume facsimile edition of the first three volumes of *The Letters* originally printed by Sampson Low was issued by Woodstock Books, Poole, in 1995; and in 2007 all five volumes that finally came to make up *The Letters* were published by Pickering & Chatto, London, as vol. II of *The Works of Charlotte Smith*. The Valancourt edition includes the complete text of volume two, based on that of the first London edition, published by Sampson Low in 1800.

Sampson Low's edition presents, however, quite a few problems to an editor. One such problem has to do with the family names of the major characters, where Smith initially seems to have intended the name Denbigh for members of Henrietta's family before settling on Maynard, reserving instead the name Denbigh for Henrietta's fiancé. Some copies of the 1800 edition include an errata list at the end of volume two, where most—but not all—of the instances of erroneous naming have been corrected. To facilitate reading, the Valancourt edition substitutes the correct names throughout in the text, indicating the changes in the list of emendations.

Many of the other corrections proposed in Sampson Low's list are, as in the case with the names, apparently authorial, consisting of substitutions of specific words, whereas others refer to more commonplace typographical errors. At least one of these changes seems however clearly problematic:

Smith's changing the age of one of the characters from fifteen to seventeen, when everything else in her text points to him being indeed only fifteen. Yet regardless of such slips, *all* the changes suggested in the 1800 errata list have been implemented in the text of the Valancourt edition, and indicated in the list of emendations by the parenthesized word (*errata*). In case of inconsistencies like the one mentioned above, these have been commented on in the explanatory notes.

Part of Smith's text (probably not more than a few words or a line) was lost in a faulty page break in the 1800 edition, leaving readers only to guess at what is supposed to have happened to Henrietta's father (p. 80 in the Valancourt edition). The location of the gap is indicated in a footnote.

It should also be noted, that in books printed at Smith's time there may be minor textual variations between different copies belonging to the same edition, presumably the result of accidents happening during printing (such as types being lost or erroneously replaced) and corrections made during the same process. In the case of volume two of the *Letters of a Solitary Wanderer*, there are quite a few such variations between copies now made widely available to readers through modern techniques, such as for instance the New York Public Library copy (reproduced by Google Books), the microfilmed Harvard College Library copy (available in the Research Publications microform collection *The Eighteenth Century*), and the Woodstock facsimile edition. The latter, being a modern facsimile, may of course be reproducing the cleanest and most legible page images from several different copies of the 1800 edition, but it still evinces unique deviations from the microfilmed Harvard and the digitalized NYPL copies. To mention just a few examples of the way these three versions of the *Henrietta* text may vary: both the Woodstock facsimile edition and the NYPL copy print the phrase "delights of nature" on their p. 196 correctly, whereas the Harvard copy erroneously gives the first of these words as "deights"; likewise, the Woodstock facsimile and the NYPL copy both refer correctly to "the person of" Henrietta on their p. 166, while the Harvard copy mistakenly has "t he person." This is not to suggest that in terms of printing the Harvard copy should be in any way inferior, or perhaps prior, to the other two; for the NYPL copy loses several letters in the phrase "w t gr a affectation," which the Harvard and the Woodstock texts reproduce correctly as "with great affectation" on their p. 203 (the "with" in the Woodstock being rather faint however); and the Woodstock facsimile loses the first person pronoun in the phrase which the other two print correctly as "had I not seen" on their p. 182. Variations like these, occurring within a single edition, were as mentioned not uncommon at the time; and I have made no attempt here to reconstruct any kind of chronological order between various copies. As the variations I have come across in *The Story of Henrietta* exclusively concern punctuation or minor printer's errors, I have silently chosen the alternative that seemed to me the most correct one, without recording my choices in the list of emendations.

My ambition throughout has been to retain Smith's own spelling, despite some occasional inconsistencies, as well as her at times rather complicated sentence structures. I have, however, corrected such obvious typographical errors as occur in all the copies I have had the chance to look at, and have included these corrections in the list of emendations (well aware that had I had access to still more copies, some of these apparent errors might turn out to be just variations too). In a very few places the mistaken use of the singular instead of the plural, whether due to an authorial or a typographical oversight, has also been corrected and indicated in the list of emendations.

As far as possible, I have also retained the first edition's

punctuation, but obvious printer's errors have been corrected, and the use of quotation marks has been regularized.
The first part of the Wanderer's recital of Denbigh's narrative (pp. 6-19), which in the 1800 edition loses its introductory
quotation marks after the first paragraph, has thus been supplied with double quotation marks at the beginning of each
paragraph, as is already the case in the 1800 text when he later
continues his retelling of Denbigh's tale (50-81). In George
Maynard's inset narrative (81-138), repeated by Denbigh to
the Wanderer, who in turn retells it in his letter to his friend,
each paragraph is in the Valancourt edition introduced by a
double quotation mark followed by a single, the latter being
omitted in the 1800 edition except for a few paragraphs at the
beginning and end of Maynard's tale. The concluding part
of Henrietta's narrative (138-147), repeated by Denbigh to the
Wanderer who then reproduces it verbatim in his letter, has
likewise been supplied with a double and a single introductory quotation mark at the beginning of each paragraph. On
the other hand, the introductory double quotation marks in
the first installment of Henrietta's narrative (19-49) have been
retained as they were in the 1800 edition, since the Wanderer
here reproduces her tale directly, as written down in her
journal, and not mediated by Denbigh. Quotation marks in
dialogue have been adjusted according to the above emendations, and inconsistencies in their use silently corrected.
Running quotation marks in the left margin have been
replaced by the modern initial and concluding mark.

List of emendations

The page number and the corrected reading in the Valancourt edition are listed first, followed by a single square bracket; then follows the supplanted reading of the 1800 text, preceded by the year and the page number in parenthesis of the first edition. Corrections listed among the errata in the 1800 edition have been marked by the word *errata* within parentheses.

4   rather] 1800 (5): rather,
8   estate, he imagined] 1800 (11): estate, imagined
8   had always maintained] 1800 (12): has always maintained
8   Mr. James Maynard] 1800 (13): Mr. James Denbigh (*errata*)
9   milk] 1800 (14): mlik
14   as his] 1800 (25): ashis
22   feel] 1800 (43): fee
23   Mrs. Apthorp] 1800 (45): Mrs. Sibthorp
24   ships?'] 1800 (48): ships?"
26   one of his managers] 1800 (51): one of his manager
26   me as] 1800 (52): meas
27   better] 1800 (54): bet-better
34   directs.'] 1800 (68): directs."
34   his countenance] 1800 (69): his countetnance
36   'as to] 1800 (73): "as to
38   the destiny] 1800 (77): th destiny
40   that held] 1800 (82): h at held
44   with all] 1800 (91): withall
44   limes] 1800 (91): lime
45   property and] 1800 (93): propertyand
52   loath and detest!] 1800 (108): loath and abhor! (*errata*)
60   my poor Ambo,] 1800 (125): my poor Amo,
69   The light came] 1800 (144): The lights came
72   notwithstanding] 1800 (151): notwithstahding
73   Henrietta, however,] 1800 (153): Henriettta, however,
78   each of us] 1800 (165): each us of
83   to be a slave] 1800 (175): to be himself a slave (*errata*)

84   his tyranny] 1800 (177): his tyrannny

84   ample fortune,] 1800 (178): ample fortue,

86   persuade] 1800 (181): persnade (*errata*)

90   to me. I checked]1800 (190): to me, I checked

90   towards] 1800 (191): towarde

96   settled on them] 1800 (204): settled to them (*errata*)

100 infidelity] 1800 (212): fidelity (*errata*)

100 grandmothers] 1800 (213): grandmother

101 opportunity of personally] 1800 (215): opportunity personally

102 wretched."] 1800 (217): wretched.

107 Mrs. George Maynard] 1800 (228): Mrs. George Denbigh (*errata*)

107 towards my son] 1800 (229): towards m son

107 Frank was then seventeen] 1800 (229): Frank was then fifteen
     (*errata*)

108 reluctance, though Mr. Warley] 1800 (229): reluctance; and
     though Mr.Warley (*errata*)

108 Mrs. George Maynard] 1800 (229): Mrs. George Denbigh
     (*errata*)

109 in consequence] 1800 (231): inconsequence (*errata*)

109 I spoke to Mrs. Maynard] 1800 (232): I spoke to Mrs. Denbigh

110 the malice of Mrs. Maynard] 1800 (234): the malice of Mrs.
     Denbigh (*errata*)

111 during which time Mrs. Maynard] 1800 (237): during which
     time Mrs. Denbigh (*errata*)

112 but I could not distinguish] 1800 (238): but I could not perceive
     (*errata*)

115 the room where I was] 1800 (245): the room where I was in
     (*errata*)

118 ignorant myself of the situation] 1800 (251): ignorant myself
     the situation

118 I will not be again] 1800 (253): "I will not be again

119 a village some miles from London] 1800 (255): a village four
     miles from London (*errata*)

128 meritorious] 1800 (274): meritorous

130 consigned him to the earth] 1800 (279): consigned him to he
     earth (*errata*)

131 quiet, yet generous] 1800 (279): quietyet generous (*errata*)

131 to its enjoyment.] 1800 (279-80): to its enjoyment. joyment

132 since I had made use of my reason] 1800 (282): since I had
       made use my reason
135 "I found," resumed Denbigh, "by the vehemence] 1800 (288):
       "I found,' resumed Denbigh, by the vehemence
137 never, never!——"] 1800 (294): never, never!——
138 "You will easily believe,"] 1800 (295): "'You will easily believe",
148 friend] 1800 (316): friends

The Story of Henrietta

LETTERS, &c.

You agree with me, my friend, in lamenting the evils which the superstitious folly of mankind has in so many instances brought upon them. Yet you seem to doubt whether the extraordinary calamities which I have related, as having befallen the family of Falconberg, are to be imputed solely to that cause. You say, Sir Mordaunt's* insanity, and not his prejudices, was the chief source of those calamities. But is there not every reason to believe that his derangement of mind was occasioned by his bigotry, and that the men to whom he gave up the little understanding he ever possessed, found, that by influencing and irritating a disposition naturally selfish, violent, and suspicious, they should have the power to detach him from all those affections which humanize the heart, and obtain such a command over him as would throw his large property into their hands? How well they succeeded my narrative has declared. You are, however, a little disposed, I see, to cavil at the probability of my story. My good friend, is there any thing impossible in it? Unless there be, suspend awhile your desire to criticise its probabilities; and recollect how many strange things both you and I (whose ages together make not half a century) have seen, which had we read of, or been told of them, a few years ago, we should have considered as the visions of a disordered imagination.

Believe, for it is true, that Miss Falconberg still exists, or did

---

* EDITOR'S NOTE: Sir Mordaunt and the Falconbergs mentioned in the two transitional paragraphs introducing Smith's second volume of *Letters of a Solitary Wanderer* are characters appearing in volume one.

very lately exist, in the neighbourhood of Florence; where, for aught I know, I may one day or other be tempted to seek her, and, like a wandering knight of old times, listen to the history of her sorrows, told in her own interesting words. Nay, do not begin to cry psha! and pooh! and do not write to me another long lecture on eccentricity, or hint at a suspicion that I seek a sort of solitary fame, by thinking, or at least acting, as no reasonable man ever thought or acted before. I seek no fame. Of what value would it be to me, since I should certainly never hear of it? Or wherefore should I concern myself about opinions entertained of me by half a score or half an hundred insignificant people, who, five minutes after they have most dogmatically decided on my conduct, will forget my very existence? You have asked me, my friend, if, by my desultory and wandering life, I expect to regain happiness?—Happiness? Alas! can any rational being say that he ever tasted it? I once, indeed, fondly believed it within my grasp; but it is gone, fled for ever!—and now all I attempt is to make the life I must endure as tolerable as possible, and for this purpose I pass wherever novelty or curiosity attract me. An author, who appears to me to have been one of the most illustrious men that any age or nation has produced, says, in one of his letters written towards the end of his life, that—to the end I aim at, "tout est bon, pourvu qu'on attrape le bout de la journée; qu'on soupe et qu'on dorme: le reste est vanité des vanités, mais l'amitié est chose véritable."[1]

My life, whatever it may be to myself, is not however always useless to others; I have more than once met in my wanderings with those whose sorrows I had the power at least to suspend; while, by remarking the various miseries of life, I have learned better to endure my own. I am now therefore going.——"Going?" you will impatiently ask: "whither, and for what?" In truth, it is not always easy for me to answer those questions; but now I rather think, however, it will be northward; and from the north-western coast of England, or from Scotland, you may perhaps hear from me again. I have some business at Liverpool, which I may as well do now as hereafter. It relates to accounts between my late father and a gentleman, the son of an old friend, who was sent from Jamaica for education, and was some time his ward. They have been long ready, and the balance long since paid; but some trifling adjustment yet remains, for which he refers me to his merchant at Liverpool. It is lucky, you will say, that I find any reason for going to one place rather than another. I own I do want motive in general to exert myself at all. How sad is the task of escaping from oneself!

LETTER II.

Liverpool.

I PASS over my journey from my late solitary abode to this busy town, where every object is assembled that I dislike the most, and where I certainly should not have staid three hours, had I not very unexpectedly found here the young man of whom I spoke in my last letter; and still more unexpectedly discovered in him, after a very short conversation, qualities of the heart and the understanding, which I hardly expected had survived some years residence in Jamaica, and which made me wish to know more of him such as he now is; for when we last parted we were both boys. He appeared happy to see the son of a man to whom he considered himself so much obliged. My father had, he said, been to him more than his own; and the gratitude and tenderness with which he spoke of his guardian would alone have attached me to him more than is usual with me: but I found another reason to give up, at least for awhile, what you call, and perhaps with reason, my gloomy eccentricities, when he introduced me to his wife, whom he married in Jamaica about two years since, and on whose account principally he came to England.

I know exactly the look you will put on when you read this part of my letter; but a truce, my friend, with your raillery till you hear why I found Mrs. Denbigh singularly interesting and attractive. It was not her beauty, though she is a remarkably delicate and pretty woman; for I can now behold the most dazzling beauty with indifference. It was not what are called accomplishments, for with those she is not eminently provided; but it was a sort of tenderness of manner, without any of that affectation of peculiar softness which has so often disgusted me; a manner which is rather to be felt than described; and which perhaps, though it created in me a great degree of interest, might not have any effect on another. You may remember, that formerly, in our disquisitions on the characters and manners of women, I have frequently ridiculed the languid indolent style which some of them affect, and the trembling timidity which is so prettily put on by others. My friend's wife has a great deal of both these female faults; but they are, I am now convinced, the effect of some singular circumstances of her life; and, knowing that, her languor is not repulsive, or her timidity disgusting.

Denbigh and I had not been two days together before our former intimacy was renewed. He talked to me now of the affairs of his fortune just as he used to tell me of his school adventures; and, on some points where he found himself in doubts, consulted me on his future proceedings. The most important of these was his design of selling his whole property in the West Indies. "'Tis an hereditary estate," said he, "and has belonged to my family ever since the first settlement of the island;² but though I know, that from the utmost amount of the sale, I shall not make any thing like the income it now brings me; yet I so extremely dislike the

nature of the property, that I should, I think, determine to
part with it, even if my wife's great aversion from residing
there did not weigh so much with me, who cannot live without her; and know that residence alone on a plantation can
make either the master rich, or his people contented."[3]—"I
thought," replied I, "that Mrs. Denbigh had been also a native
of Jamaica, and had merely come to England, as you did, for
education." He answered, "She certainly was born there; but
from a very early age was brought up in Europe, under the
care of an aunt, a remarkably sensible woman, who, having
been left early her own mistress, found independence so
much more desirable than a matrimonial connection with
any of those who offered, that she voluntarily became what
is called an old maid; and taking her niece from school before
her mind was vitiated by the rivalry too common among all
girls, and too much encouraged by the common mode of
education, she undertook to instruct her at home; but her
plan for that purpose did not embrace numberless frivolous
attempts at arts, which are nothing, if not obtained in perfection, but rather in useful acquirements, writing correctly
her own language, understanding and speaking Italian and
French,[4] and forming her taste while the virtues of her heart
were not forgotten. Mrs. Maynard, her aunt, who piqued herself on strength of mind superior to her sex, endeavoured to
communicate the same disdain of feminine weakness to her
niece: but I think that my Henrietta has escaped the hard-
ness of character which such attempts frequently produce;
and, perhaps being sensible a little too much of it in her aunt,
has rather indulged the natural tendency of her mind to the
opposite extreme.

"Henrietta had never seen her father since her childhood:
he was a man whose ideas had received all their colour from
his situation. The only son[5] of a very rich planter, he had never
been in England since he left school at ten years old,[6] and had

conceived such an aversion from a place where he had been on the footing of equality with other boys, that he never desired to revisit Europe. From being a despot on his own estate, he imagined he might exercise unbounded authority over every being that belonged to him. But his sister, as haughty in her way as he was in his, had always maintained her independence; and as she had a very considerable fortune at her own disposal, and was not likely to marry, he thought his daughter would be provided for by suffering her to continue with her aunt. He had a son by a second wife, on whom all his affection was placed, and for whom all his fortune was, he thought, too little. By a variety of other women of every various shade, from the quadroon to the negro[7] of the Gold coast, he had many other children,[8] who were brought up by their mothers on his estates; and who, though not actually slaves, were considered as attached to the soil. The boys as they grew up became overseers or accomptants; and some of the girls were received into the house, where, as it had no regular mistress, (his second wife being long since dead,) they held a sort of middle place between the servants and the children of the house. Mr. James Maynard,[9] the young heir, had been recalled by his impatient father at about seventeen, and was some time unwillingly an inhabitant of Jamaica; but to be confined to any spot, or under even the questioning eye of his father, was what he could not resolve upon. He passed almost all his time with the officers of the English regiments at that time stationed at Jamaica, and engaged deeply in their amusements; where, in the midst of his thoughtless dissipation, he was attacked by the fever[10] which has now for so many years been raging with fatal fury in America, and died before his father even knew that he was ill.

"So fell at once all those splendid visions of continuing and aggrandizing his family, which had for years been the favourite contemplations of the elder Mr. Maynard. His temper, naturally violent and irascible, became after this disappointment so tyrannic and intolerable, that those most accustomed to endure his brutal caprices found it almost impossible to continue with him. Imagine then, my friend, what must have been the situation of my poor Henrietta in the scenes she was involved in. Her aunt, with whom she had travelled for two years through France and Italy, had been at home only seven or eight months, when she became frequently subject to a pulmonary complaint, which she neglected; assuring Henrietta, who saw its progress with great uneasiness, that it would yield only to summer. It was, she said, useless to apply remedies which would be ineffectual; and she projected, as soon as the spring arrived, a long tour northward, to end in a residence of six weeks in Wales, where she persuaded herself goat's milk and pure air would entirely restore her. During the winter she became evidently worse, yet still looked forward to spring as a period which would renew her existence. Spring indeed came, but coldly and reluctantly; perpetual rain, or north-east winds, checked every effort of the approaching sun, and my poor Henrietta lost her aunt, her only friend and protectress: nor was she at all consoled by finding herself, at hardly twenty, mistress of a fortune of upwards of seventeen thousand pounds.

"I had met with her and her aunt at Pezena's,[11] when they were about to return to England; where when I arrived some months after them, I had renewed my acquaintance. Henrietta made at first a very favourable impression on my mind: our fortunes, our condition of life, and our ages, all seemed to unite in making an union between us desirable for both parties; but I had seen among my own friends two such striking examples of the unhappy consequences of early and hasty marriages, that I determined to see more of the fair Henrietta before I put my happiness in any degree in her power. We parted therefore at that time without my having professed any warmer sentiment than friendship: and when our intercourse was renewed in town, her aunt was in such a state of health, that Henrietta would, I found, have been offended, had I then named to her a passion which was now become the liveliest sentiment of my heart. It was, however, impossible to conceal what I yet feared to explain; till one evening, when I called with my usual inquiry, and was admitted, I found Henrietta drowned in tears: sobs choked her utterance, and her bosom heaved with convulsive agonies; while with difficulty she repeated what the physician who attended her aunt had just told her, that he thought it impossible she could survive the week. Her grief was so affecting, her attendance on her dying relation had been so exemplary, that I loved her at that moment more passionately than ever; and I know not how, but I contrived to offer my protection as a husband, as the fondest and most adoring husband, when sorrow for the cruel event which I feared was inevitable, should permit her to look forward to the prospects of her future life. Henrietta was not ignorant of my attachment to her. Her aunt had perceived it with pleasure, and I now reproached myself for the needless reserve I had held. We soon came to a perfect understanding. Mrs. Maynard herself, trembling on the brink of the grave, joined our hands, and blessed us. She bade her beloved Henrietta look on me as her best friend, entrust me with the management of all her pecuniary concerns, and suffer no forms of mere custom to delay her giving me a right to be her friend and protector. Scarce had we performed the last offices to this respectable woman, when Henrietta received letters from her father's agent, informing her of the death of her brother, and his orders that she should immediately come over to Jamaica. To these were added two very short and peremptory letters from her father himself, one addressed to his sister now deceased, the other to his daughter, in both of which he expressed himself like a man who would be obeyed, without any attention to the feelings or inclinations of those whom he thought he had a right to command.

"Henrietta put these unwelcome mandates into my hand, and told me she must prepare to obey them. I instantly perceived that my hopes of immediately calling her mine were considerably diminished by this unexpected change, and dreaded lest her father had views for her which might separate us for ever. I communicated my fears to Henrietta: they were founded on what I had heard of her father's character, of which she seemed more ignorant than I was; for Mrs. Maynard, however she contemned her brother, had always respected the duty which her niece owed him, and had as much as she could concealed from her his vicious character. Henrietta therefore heard me with astonishment when I told her that I foresaw, if she returned to Jamaica, our union would be deferred, if not broken for ever. She contended, that her father could not be so unreasonable; that if, like the generality of fathers, fortune was his object, I was heir to, or already possessed, a property which was more than equal to hers; that in point of family and connections mine was infinitely superior; and that it appeared to her almost impossible for her father to make any objection.

"That such was the flattering opinion of Henrietta was to me a misfortune; for it furnished her with arguments against what I ardently solicited—an immediate marriage. It was in vain I represented to her, that, firmly persuaded as she appeared to be of her father's concurrence, there would be no breach of duty in fulfilling the last wishes of her deceased friend, and marrying before she obeyed her father's summons. She combated all I could say with arguments which I soon found were not her own; and I discovered with undescribable mortification, that she was dictated to by one of those officious people, who, having a very high opinion of their own wisdom, delight in directing the conduct of others, and are never so happy as when they can busy themselves in affairs of which for the most part they can have only an incomplete knowledge. Artful, insinuating, and specious, Mrs. Apthorp, who had been an intimate friend of her aunt's, now used her utmost endeavours to preserve the power which that title and her own art had given her over the mind of Henrietta. She had other views in doing so than merely to gratify her love of meddling and dictating; and she succeeded but too well.

"The nonage[12] of Henrietta, and every other objection, was pleaded in support of the resolution which I found she had taken of returning to Jamaica, and soliciting her father's consent to our marriage. I then insisted upon accompanying her in the same vessel; but I found her equally prepared with reasons against that. Her cunning directress had foreseen that I should endeavour to obtain that proof of her regard, and had armed my poor Henrietta with so great a store of prudish, and as I thought unnecessary objections, that my patience was exhausted; and for the first time since our acquaintance, I remonstrated with some degree of asperity against this mistrust of my honour, and these doubts of my real affection. Henrietta answered only by her tears; but her resolution seemed unshaken: and vexed beyond all endurance at the influence which I found an artful woman had obtained over so good an understanding as Henrietta possessed, I was rash enough to declare to her, that we must either go together, or part never to meet again. I left her in a temper of mind not easy to be described; but repenting, and even detesting myself for the pain I had inflicted, I flew back to apologize, and to implore for pardon. Henrietta, however, was already gone to pour her sorrows into the bosom of her friend, who knew so well how to inflame her naturally gentle temper, that, when I again sought her the next day, she was denied to me; and a few hours afterwards she was carried into Hampshire by her zealous and prudent monitress, whose ascendancy seemed to increase as mine I thought declined. It was not difficult for me to find whither Henrietta was gone; and I followed her: but determined never to enter a house of which Mrs. Apthorp was the mistress, I went to an inn in the village, and, by writing, at length engaged Henrietta to see me. Withdrawn from the immediate presence of her officious directress, (who had persuaded her that she stood in the place of her deceased aunt as a guide to her conduct,) Henrietta wept, and forgave me: but I could obtain my pardon on no other terms than those of relinquishing my resolution to take my passage in the same vessel. As the most impertinent affectation of prudery could not venture to object to my proceeding in another, I immediately went to Portsmouth,[13] and engaged my passage in a sloop,[14] the only vessel in which any tolerable accommodation was left for passengers; for the fleet was full of West Indians, going to visit or return to their property across the Atlantic.

"I then acquainted Henrietta with what I had done, and hastened to London to settle some affairs which my father's death and that of your father had left upon my hands. I hurried them over, and flew back to Portsmouth, where I was indeed permitted to attend my Henrietta into the ship which was to convey her from England: but imagine my surprise and vexation when I found that Mrs. Apthorp, whom I had so much reason to detest was to be her companion and protectress during the voyage! I expressed my astonishment the more forcibly, because the company of this lady had been one of the expedients I had proposed, when Henrietta objected to the impropriety of my accompanying her alone. I was then told, that notwithstanding the very great affection of Mrs. Apthorp for her dear adopted child, her own family, to whom her first duties were due, could not dispense with her presence in England. I now found her in great form, sharing the state-rooms, as they are called, appropriated to Henrietta, in a ship of which her father was principal owner, and directing every thing with the air of a person whose judgment and sagacity were to be generally referred to. The captain, a rude blunt seaman, who had very soon seen more of her than he liked, perceived, what indeed I had not affected to hide, that this woman was utterly hateful to me; and calling me aside, he asked me if I did not see what she was at? 'The devil fly away with her!' said he, 'she's as cunning as his dam.'[15] Why, no wonder the gentlewoman wants to take Miss in tow—Her father is a widower—No bad look-out for the widow herself, who is not over-burdened with money. But more than that, there's a son in the case.'—'A son?' cried I, imagining I at once saw the cause of Henrietta's coldness to me. 'Yes,' replied my informer; 'but Miss has never seen him yet. You must know, that in this madam's jiggeting[16] backwards and forwards, getting things to rights, I've laid my tackle to make out what she was; and I find she's mother to one Apthorp, a lawyer, who had a place under Government in Antigua, and who is now removed to Jamaica to a better thing; I don't know your law terms, not I; but though I've seen this mother what d'ye call 'um but twice, I know she intends nothing more or less than to marry the father herself, and her son to his daughter.' Numberless circumstances now occurred to me, to convince me that the old captain guessed the truth. Yet Henrietta was at once acquitted; for I knew she had never seen the son, or at least not since she was a child: my indignation, however, against the mercenary art of her pretended friend was such as I no longer attempted to disguise.

"You must often, my dear friend, have seen and lamented the occasional weakness of the strongest minds, when either from habit or prejudice they put their understandings into the guidance of others, and are either too indolent or too

timid to dare to think for themselves. Henrietta had infinitely
more natural sense than the woman by whom she suffered
herself to be led; yet, being accustomed to the government
of her aunt, and hearing perpetual changes rung upon the
words prudence, propriety, discretion, and decorum,[17] the
opinion of the world, and the necessary submission of every
body to its decisions, Henrietta had given up every opinion
of her own, and even her affection for me seemed suspended
by her apprehensions of censure. But my indignant impatience now broke through all forms; I openly declared my
conviction that Mrs. Apthorp had designs against her fortune
in favour of this son; and, I believe, gave hints of what would
follow *his* avowing his pretensions—which threw the lady
into very distressing confusion; while Henrietta, taking me to
another part of the ship, endeavoured to soothe and appease
me, by protesting that Mrs. Apthorp had never once named
this son in the way of recommending him to her; that she
was persuaded her views were very different, and that affection for her, disinterested affection, had more weight than
any thing else in the resolution Mrs. Apthorp had taken to go
to Jamaica. Though I was farther than ever from being convinced, I could not bear the tears of Henrietta, who implored
me not to part with her in anger. 'Though propriety forbids
our going in the same ship,' said she, 'we shall yet be on our
way together. I shall learn to distinguish that in which you
are to embark. We may be often near each other; nor, as I
understand, is it impossible for you to come on board this
vessel. Absent or present, I shall consider you as my future
husband. As such I shall, I am sure, have courage to speak
of you to my father, and a very few weeks will unite us to
part from each other no more.' Smiling through her tears,
Henrietta endeavoured to prevail upon me to be as satisfied
as she wished to appear with the flattering prospect she thus
presented to me. But though I could not resolve to distress

her by shewing how little all this pleased me, I left her 'rather in sorrow than in anger,'[18] vainly attempting to argue myself out of a persuasion, that, far from meeting happily as she had described, we should never meet again.

"But," continued my friend, "I have a sort of history of my poor Henrietta's voyage, and subsequent adventures, written by herself, which I will put into your hands. She began it at my desire, while she was on shipboard, to fix in her mind the ideas of such objects as then occurred in a new mode of life. When, after the alarming situations she was afterwards thrown in, she began to recover health and recollection, she added the incidents as they affected her, and she has from time to time corrected the narrative, as the cruel circumstances of those hours of terror returned to her mind.

"But, before you read this, let me fill up the chasm there will otherwise be in the story, by telling you, that when we had been about a fortnight at sea, (during which we had such very bad weather that I never could go on board the Argonaut,[19] a merchant ship in which was Henrietta,) one of the frigates which were our convoy made a signal for separation; and with the vessels under his care, whalers for the South Sea,[20] and victuallers[21] for St. Helena,[22] he left us. We some days afterwards made the Madeiras[23]; where, going on shore at Fonchiale,[24] I once more saw my Henrietta, and once more implored her to change a resolution, which I had a strange prevention[25] would be fatal to one of us. I saw that she too had her fears, and that the tedium and sickness which are usually felt in such a voyage had greatly enfeebled her spirits. Yet the change seemed not to be favourable to me. It rather served to put her more than ever into the power of Mrs. Apthorp; who hardly allowed me, during our short stay on shore, an opportunity of conversing alone with Henrietta even for five minutes. Yet I thought it evident that the restraint to which she thus submitted was uneasy to her, though she had not the courage to throw it off; and I will own, that, irritated beyond all patient endurance, I returned on board more than half resolved to break an engagement, however dear to my heart, which, if it were completed, would, I feared, unite me to a woman of a feeble mind, whose affection for me it would too probably be in the power of any artful busy meddler to weaken or estrange. Yet scarce had I suffered myself to dwell a moment on this idea, before that of Henrietta, lovely in the unsuspecting innocence of youth, such as I had first seen her; her simplicity, her beauty, her early talents, of which she was totally unconscious; her mild temper and sensible heart, all assembled to dissolve it: and again I fondly flattered myself, that when we should meet in Jamaica, her sense of duty being satisfied, she would be restored to me such as she once was—and that even her errors, while they gave me pain, were the effect of virtue.

"My eyes were incessantly in search of the ship in which she was. If for some hours I lost sight of it, my impatience to regain it made me importune the master, and bribe the sailors, who however were willing enough to gratify me. But though that in which I had taken my passage was a lighter vessel than the Argonaut, she was old and foul,[26] scantily manned, and a very indifferent sailer,[27] so that we were often very far from the convoy: and one morning, five days from our leaving Madeira, we found ourselves, after a stormy night, in which the dead-lights[28] had been put up, absolutely alone; being but just able from the mast-head to discern the top-sails of our companions many leagues[29] to the westward. It was in vain that the captain and crew appeared to exert themselves to fetch up the way they had lost. Even the distant view of the sails, with which I had for some time consoled myself, was now lost; a wide, wide horizon was before me, but the objects I sought were vanished into air. To add to my anxiety, it fell a dead calm,[30] and our vessel lay like a log on the water. A storm would have been a thousand times more welcome, for then my mind would have been occupied. Now I felt as if I desired to disengage my soul from its earthly bondage, that I might flit through the air unobstructed, and watch over Henrietta, whom I had but a few days before thought of as one who could never constitute my felicity, and whom it would be wise to endeavour to forget: so strange and capricious an animal is man!

"I will not attempt to describe my impatience, or the torments in which I passed some hours. A favourable wind then sprang up, which bore us directly on our course; and though I had very little hope of overtaking the fleet, I now flattered myself that I should not be many days after Henrietta at Port Royal.[31] I redoubled my entreaties to the men—as if they could do any thing more than they had already done. But, unfortunately for us all, they had soon another motive for exertion. On the fourth day after we had been thus deserted, there was a cry of 'two sail to leeward!'[32] I ran eagerly to know if they were any of our fleet. The captain assured me, that they were not, but, he apprehended, enemies;[33] and in a very short time we were convinced that they were large French privateers.[34] Our attempts to escape were vain, and resistance would have been a mere waste of life. Instead therefore of landing in Jamaica a few hours or days after Henrietta, I found myself a prisoner, and was carried by my captors into Rochfort.[35]

"Imagine, my friend, what I suffered when I reflected on the distance that was now between us, and the time that must elapse before I could rejoin Henrietta, at this moment dearer to me than ever. I figured to myself her anxiety for me, and the reproaches she would make herself for having refused to admit me on board the same ship; while on the other hand the triumph of Mrs. Apthorp, perhaps the success of the plans which I could not doubt her having formed, tormented me incessantly. As money was the sole object of my captors, and no advantage could be gained by my detention, I agreed with them for my release; and after having been about six weeks a prisoner, I was suffered to depart. But I had a great part of France to cross before I could reach a port from whence cartels[36] passed to England, and it was six weeks longer before I arrived in London. The necessity of repairing the losses I had sustained detained me only a few days. I hastened to Falmouth, to embark in a Government packet;[37] but there I was kept near a month by winds so violent and contrary, that it was impossible to put to sea. Our passage was afterwards unusually tedious, so that I arrived not in Jamaica till almost six months after I lost sight of Henrietta. Her own narrative, which is addressed to me, shall tell you the rest. To you I make no scruple of confiding those simple effusions of tenderness with which it is intermixed:"

On board the Argonaut, at Sea,
quitting the Madeira Islands.

"I HAVE lost sight of you, Denbigh; and once more the land where we last met recedes, and we enter again on the wide world of waters. I obey you in committing to paper my sensations and my remarks, though the first are all melancholy, and the latter will perhaps be puerile. You were displeased with me, my friend; I saw uneasiness and resentment beneath the forced kindness of your last adieu, and the recollection of that moment is embittered by it. Yet how often has it been inculcated, how often have you enforced the maxim, that when we feel we have done right we should be at peace with ourselves! And surely, when you will allow yourself to reflect coolly on my situation, you will acknowledge that I have acted with propriety. Surely, Denbigh, this is the only subject on which we could differ. May we never differ again!—Oh! if you knew how anxiously I look out for the vessel which bears you, and which I am even in search of with a glass,[38] and know from the observations you taught me to make, you would not think that the refusal you complain of arose from indifference.

"Ah! had not prudence, and deference for the customs and opinions of the world, determined that it must be otherwise, to say nothing of the absolute necessity of my not appearing to act in so important a matter decidedly without the concurrence of my father, how happy would it have made me to have had your conversation to animate the tediousness of the voyage! and how doubly delightful would every appearance of nature be, which I could remark with you, or which you would point out to me!

"Last night, after we weighed anchor, and were leaving the Bay of Fonchiale, I sat upon deck with my female companions. They were talking of I know not what parties and people with whom they are acquainted, and by their vivacity seemed, from the recollection of what had passed in these societies, to receive great pleasure; but did their conversation convey any to me? Alas! no. On the contrary, I withdrew from them as far as I could; and, as it became dark, I watched the lights of the different ships. But I could not distinguish yours—when all were colourless upon the water, and none particularly marked but the convoying frigate. Yet I loved to imagine that you were engaged, as I was, in observing the beauty of the moon and stars, brighter and differently coloured, surely, than they appear in England. I loved to fancy that you were admiring, as I was, the long stream of ineffable brilliance, with which the moon illuminated the slowly undulating waves—while I saw successively several ships cross this radiant line, their sails catching the moonbeams for awhile, and then gradually and majestically falling

into shadow. I had never observed the night sea so beautiful;
and again how earnestly did I wish you with me, and how
sad sunk my heart when I thought of the half-stifled coldness
with which you said 'Farewell, Henrietta!' as you descended
the ship's side into the boat which was to take you to your
own! 'Farewell, Henrietta!' Ah, Denbigh! it was the tone with
which you spoke that has so affected me. Indeed my dear
friend! it was unkind. Yet you did not intend, perhaps, to give
me pain. Oh! no, you could not intend it; nor could you guess
that I should pass a wretched restless night, repeating continually to myself 'Farewell, Henrietta!'

"It was utterly impossible for me to sleep. The heat, added
to the anxiety of my mind, compelled me to quit my uneasy
bed. I went out into the gallery, and beheld a spectacle so
glorious, as might, to a well-regulated mind, suspend all the
petty cares of this world. The sun arose in all his undescribable glory. A thousand transient hues, such as I had never
remarked before, wavered on the sea, now glowing with rose
colour fading into pale orange; then amber, blue, and purple,
like the fleeting shades of the most brilliant opal, varied the
softly swelling waves, till towards the west they became of a
deep green, the sky above yet tinged with dark clouds that
hang on 'the rear of night.'[39]

"I perceived, in proportion as the sun became higher, that
clearness of the atmosphere which I remembered you had
told me was to be seen in these high latitudes;[40] I saw too in
greater numbers, what I had before observed, the flying fish,
pursued by the dolphins or other fish of prey, emerging from
the waves on their wing-like fins, and flickering along the surface of the water; from whence they were sometimes driven
by the appearance of a sea-bird, from whose attack they sheltered themselves again in their native element. Their silver
scales and tremulous cobweb wings glancing[41] with a singular
kind of short flight over the blue waves, and the rapidity with

which their aërial enemies darted upon them, while I saw
every where the many-coloured dolphins[42] throwing themselves half out of the water in the eagerness of their pursuit, interested me for some time, or rather gave me cause
for reflection. I tried to remember where I had read a comparison between some unfortunate persecuted characters in
human life, and those poor harassed inhabitants of the sea,
who seem to have gained but little by their faculty of flying.[43]
As the land receded, however, the birds were less frequent.
The heat soon became intense; and I received some remonstrances from my careful companion on the impropriety of
exposing myself to the sun, and the reflection of the sea. Yet,
believe me, Denbigh, I would not retire for the morning,
till I had, with the assistance of poor Juana,* who is more
adept than I am, descried the Emily;[44] though surely she does
not sail so well as most others of the fleet, for she is always
pointed out to me farther off than almost any of them.

"Well, my good friend, have I not begun to obey you?
Alas! in the monotonous life we lead on board ship, how little
is there to write about. After a day sufficiently calm, yet with
wind enough to bear us on our course, we have nothing to
do but to wish that the following day may be equally favourable. Oh! how weary am I already of the sea!—Yet do I long
to be on shore? I can hardly answer in the affirmative, though
I go to the arms of a parent.

"I fear that so long an absence as mine, for it is eleven years
since I was sent from the paternal roof, may have estranged
my father from me. Certainly he never expressed the least
wish to see me till after the death of my brother. I have wept
at the coldness which I thought was visible in the few letters
he wrote either to me or my aunt. I feel such an awe of him,
that I tremble when I think of the first interview; and sometimes, to appease the dread which perpetually assails me, I

---

* A black female servant. [Smith's note.]

endeavour to form some idea of the manner, the person, and the character of my father, and for that purpose to engage Captain More[45] to describe him to me; but I observe that all he says is constrained, and he seems to answer not as he thinks, but as it is necessary for him to do to the daughter of a man who has it in his power so materially to befriend him. He speaks of the luxury of the table at my father's house; of the number of slaves kept solely for domestic purposes; of the quantity of wine consumed at his table, and of his consequence in the island. But why do I hear nothing of his benevolence; of his private friends; of his kindness to his people, and of his being beloved as well as feared? Ah! if he should be harsh to me—if he should not love me—if he should have other views for me——But wherefore should I thus torment myself? Mrs. Apthorp very justly, though very severely, reproves me for it. She says, I am too apt to anticipate evil; and that, after all, a young woman should have no will of her own. But you love her, Denbigh, so little already, that I will not make you love her less by repeating axioms to which I know you will not agree; though indeed she is a very excellent woman, and one whom you would have liked in any other character than that of my adviser. Ah! Denbigh, does it never occur to you, that when I put myself thus under the guidance of another, it is a proof that I am conscious of my own weakness, and of an inability to govern myself."

"I again begin to write, though I have nothing, alas! to say but a wretched repetition of what I have so often written already—yet with one aggravating circumstance—I have looked in vain these last three days for the Emily. I have employed Juana to look, and to engage two of the sea-boys in the same inquiry; but they have every day repeated that they do not see her. I never felt till now the misery of suspense. The wind is fair, and carries on the ship with a rapidity which will bring us they say into port in three weeks, if it continues. Would it were over, since it must be, this meeting so dreaded at once and desired! But if I were sure, Denbigh, that the Emily will arrive at the same time, I should, methinks, look forward to that period with more confidence than I now do. Alas! my friend, another day is passed, and still Juana answers my inquiries with 'No, Missy, not see hims yet.'"[46]

"These last days have been passed in a most comfortless way. One of the children of Mrs. Willis, a fellow-passenger, has been ill; and the poor mother, half distracted, has found some relief in my sharing with her the fatigue of attending on the poor little patient, who is now, I trust, out of danger. But how greatly are the anxieties of their friends, and the sufferings of the sick increased by being on ship-board! Mrs. Willis, as nobody in this vessel pretends to act in the capacity of doctor or surgeon, attempted to procure assistance from the ship of war; but the captain made so many difficulties, and appeared so little sensible of the painful solicitudes of a parent, that three days were wasted, and at last the surgeon came on board. He is intelligent and obliging; and it was at least a satisfaction to Mrs. Willis to find that all she has done is right, and that the little girl is out of danger. Yet to me this visit has been productive of new alarm. I ventured tremblingly to inquire whether any of the ships of the convoy were missing, and had the inconceivable mortification of hearing, that there was one, if not two, which had not been seen for many days. I then hazarded another question: 'Do you know, Sir, the names of these ships?' I believe the young man discovered from my manner the particular interest I took in his answer; for he smiled, and assured me, he was very sorry that he was unable to answer my question, but that he was wholly unacquainted with the names of any of the ships; nor should he probably have known that any of the number were missing, had he not heard captain Ramsay[47] exclaiming vehemently against the commanders of the merchantmen, who he declared were often in league with the enemy, and left the convoy on purpose to be taken.

"Alas, my dear Denbigh! this has not served to elevate my spirits. Should the man who commands your ship be one of this description! . . . . . I sometimes reproach myself for our separation, and am weak enough to yield to those strange forebodings of evil, which for want of a more appropriate word we call presentiments. If we are separated to meet no more!—Oh! no. I dare not trust myself with an idea so utterly insupportable."

———

"I have been many days incapable of writing. The Emily is certainly not with the convoy, and for what purpose should I commit my thoughts to paper, since he whom alone they are likely to interest will not see them? A thousand conjectures torment me. I put Mrs. Apthorp out of humour by my questions, and weary every body else, who 'answer neglectingly they know not what.'[48] And why, indeed, should I expect that my solicitude will interest them?—Alas! Denbigh, I begin to feel all the wretchedness of being an insulated being, even for this little space. Mrs. Apthorp loves me—I am sure she does; but she cannot comprehend my feelings, and seems to disapprove of my indulging them. I endeavour therefore to conceal them. The island of Jamaica is now visible from the mast-head. To-morrow evening they say we shall cast anchor.—To-morrow evening!—And you, Denbigh, will not be there to support me. Yet do I not go to a father?—have I not a friend with me, whose affection for me is almost maternal? If I were satisfied of your safety, I would endeavour to tranquillize my spirits, and to meet my father as I ought to do;—but this cruel uncertainty is insupportable."

"The poor Henrietta is at last at what she must call her home; and in pursuance of her promise will endeavour to relate her sensations and describe her situation. But while I attempt it my spirits sink; for who knows if ever you will read what I write? You, who do not appear, of whom nothing is known, and of whom I dare not now venture to inquire!— But they told me before I left Kingston,[49] that it was probable the ship in which you were, together with another missing ship, was taken by the enemy. My friend, I have always been told, that the consciousness of having acted right would in every event of life bestow a certain degree of happiness and tranquillity. I thought I had acted right when I resisted your wish of accompanying me in the same vessel. Yet I am unhappy, indeed I am very unhappy; and I have not now one friend to whom I can venture to say so, or from whom I can receive the pity and consolation I so greatly need.

"My father did not meet me at the port as I expected; he sent one of his managers or agents[50] to receive and conduct me to this place. Overcome with all the disagreeable circumstances of our landing, almost fainting with heat, anxiety, and fatigue, I was not sorry that a meeting to me so awful was postponed. Yet it appeared unkind; and I felt that I never wanted more the presence of a friend. Mrs. Apthorp prepared to accompany me, as she had always promised; and as her son, who was the principal object of her voyage, was not yet arrived, I had no hesitation in accepting this farther proof of her friendship: but Mr. Grabb the manager, who was to be my escort, having learned what was her intention, very gravely approached me as we were nearly ready to set out, and told me, without much circumlocution or apology, that he had his employer's directions not to suffer any person whatsoever to go with me. I was grieved and astonished at such an order, and represented to the man, that my father could never mean to exclude a female friend so respectable as Mrs. Apthorp, who had so kindly protected me during the voyage. Mr. Grabb replied, that he had nothing to say to all that, but his orders were so positive, that he dared not and would not disobey them. Mrs. Apthorp, extremely morti-fied, then desisted, and prepared to depart for the house of a relation, where she now said she intended to stay till her son came; who, from something she unguardedly dropped, was, I found, wholly unacquainted with her arrival, and was first to learn it from letters she was now to write to him. Our separation was immediate, and melancholy enough to me. I got into the post-chaise[51] which my father had sent for me, attended by Juana, who, however pleased to revisit her native land,[52] thought I could perceive with sentiments very far from pleasure of her former master. Escorted by so strange a look-ing man as Mr. Grabb, who rode very magisterially by the side of the chaise, as if to guard me, my poor heart became heavier than ever, and I anticipated with increased terror the meeting which I ought to have considered with pleasure.

"The journey was tedious, and the heat almost intoler-able. This distance is about thirty miles, and though my father's horses were excellent, and his whole equipage well appointed, the road was rugged, and the heat extreme, so that it was the evening of the second day before we arrived at Horton's, an house my father built about eleven years ago, on one of his largest estates near the sea.[53] In despite of the agitation of my spirits, I could not help admiring the beauty of the country I had passed through; and the house to which I now, at night-fall, approached was better than any I had seen on the way. A great number of slaves crowded round the carriage when it stopped. Some seemed eagerly watching an opportunity of being noticed by their young lady, others greeted their old friend or relation Juana. I was shocked at the harshness with which the man who attended me drove them away; and his countenance, as he helped me from the carriage, expressed so disagreeable a mixture of arrogance and submission, that I involuntary recoiled from him, and felt a sort of relief in seeing Amponah, my father's black servant, who attended my brother to England, and was almost a twelvemonth in my aunt's family. He now seemed rather an old acquaintance whom I was rejoiced to see, than an abject slave, such as by the manager's behaviour towards him he appeared to be considered; and I followed him, trembling, when he led the way to my father's apartment.

"I was soon in the presence of this parent, from whom I have been so long estranged; but I became so ill from the variety of emotions assailing me, that I merely saw him, endeavoured to kneel to him and kiss his hand, and then sank down insensible before him and some other persons (I knew not then who they were) that were about him. When I recovered my recollection, which was in a few moments, I saw strange female faces of many shades around me. My father was not there, and the dreaded interview was to be again attempted. It is so difficult, my friend, in some cases, for a child to speak of a parent consistently at once with truth and duty, that I must be allowed to be entirely silent in regard to my father; unless I should be compelled to speak of him, in consequence of the power he possesses over me, and on the manner of his using which, it depends, whether I shall be happy, or the most miserable of human beings.

"Oh, Denbigh! that you were here, that this fearful point might be brought to an issue! But you are afar off. You cannot even advise. 'Farewell, Henrietta!' were the last words I ever heard you utter—The tone in which they were uttered vibrates on my ear; I repeat it to myself; it appears like an eternal adieu!

"I have had nothing to add to my narrative for some days, at least nothing that I like to write on, or that you would like to read; and for the persons who surround me, I would I could escape ever naming them! Do you know, Denbigh, that there are three young women here, living in the house, *of colour*, as they are called, who are, I understand, my sisters by the half blood! They are the daughters of my father by his black and mulatto slaves; and the awkwardness I felt when I was first under the necessity of addressing myself to them, seemed very wonderful to the people here, who see nothing extraordinary or uncommon in such an arrangement as my father has made in his family. They speak an odd sort of dialect, more resembling that of the negroes than the English spoken in England;[54] and their odd manners, their love of finery, and curiosity about my clothes and ornaments, together with their total insensibility to their own situation, is, I own, very distressing to me. The youngest of them, who is a quadroon—a mestize[55]—I know not what—is nearly as fair as I am; but she has the small eye, the prominent brow, and something particular in the form of the cheek, which is, I have understood, usual with the creoles[56] even who have not any of the negro blood in their veins. As I am a native of this island, perhaps I have the same cast of countenance without being conscious of it, and I will be woman enough to acknowledge that the supposition is not flattering.

"This little girl, however, (for she is but twelve years old) I have attempted to instruct, when I could enough command my spirits to attend to any thing: but she is so ignorant, so much the creature either of origin or of habit, that I cannot make her comprehend the simplest instruction, and our lesson generally ends in her begging of me some ribbon, feather, or other trifling ornament, which I give her on her promising to attend more another time:—a promise which she never remembers. Alas! Denbigh, my days pass most

unpleasantly here: besides the continual uneasiness which I
suffer from the uncertainty I am in about you, which would
no where allow me a moment's repose, I am most comfortless in having no one to whom I can speak unreservedly, no
one who understands me. My father is often absent. Why am
I compelled to say, that his absence relieves me from a part of
my sufferings?—He is engaged, deeply engaged, in quelling
those unhappy people whom they call Maroons,[57] who have
done him, I understand, considerable injury, and have now
among them many of his runaway negroes; against whom,
if they are taken, he meditates, I find, modes of revenge,
which are really so horrible only to hear mentioned, that I
am often under the necessity of leaving the room. Yet dare
I not express the terror and disgust with which such inhumanity fills my mind; for, whatever I say, whatever I do, is
related to my father, who reproves me with so much harshness, that I cannot help sinking before him into tears and
despondence, such as guilt alone ought to subject me to. But
from mere unwillingness to name it, I delay to tell you—(tell
you? Alas! will you ever read this?)—the heaviest and most
menacing of all the evils which either surround or threaten
me. We deceived ourselves, my dear friend! while we hoped
and believed that my father could have no objection to you;
when we took it for granted, because reason seemed to
authorise our doing so, that there could be no obstacle to
our union. There is an obstacle my trembling hand refuses to
write, an unconquerable impediment, of which we dreamed
not:—My father's strange resolution to *raise* a dependent to
the rank of his son-in-law; to make the fortune of a man in
humble life wholly dependent on, and owing every thing to
him. Such a man, willing to be wholly his creature, and to
owe his fortune to him, had my father found when he so
peremptorily directed my ill-fated voyage. And hence it was,
that, having had some intelligence, I know not from what

quarter, of the attachment you honoured me with, as well as of Mrs. Apthorp's designs in favour of her son, he sent orders that no one should be suffered to accompany me hither.

"For many days, however, after my arrival, I was kept ignorant of this. But the person for whose slave my father designs me[58] was introduced to me as a friend of his, for whom he had a particular esteem. I hardly looked at the man. Naturally careless and indolent, you have often told me I am too indifferent about the people I meet with in the common intercourse of life, and make no remarks on character. I own I see so little worth remarking, and people seem to me to be so little distinguished one from the other in this money-get-ting country, that, were I to see half the land-holders of the island assembled, I should probably be unable to remark in one of them any discriminating feature. I therefore saw this man, whose name is Sawkins, without noticing him when he was present, and, the moment he was absent, forgot I had ever seen him at all.

"Not only so, but when two or three days afterwards he came again, and smiled and smirked, and looked I thought marvelously impertinent, his name had so entirely escaped me, that, when I left the room in disgust, I inquired of Amponah, one of the few servants in the house to whom I can speak, who that person was. The poor fellow appeared to be surprised at my question, and answered, 'Master not tell you, Miss?' I said I should not have inquired, but that I had forgotten his name. 'Ah, Miss, Miss!' replied Amponah, 'dat man is one day n'other to be our master.'—'Your master, Amponah?'—'Yes: master give him you, Miss, and all this great rich estates, and pens[59] and all.'

"This was the first intimation I had ever received of my father's intention, and it seemed now to be so utterly improb-able, that I fancied Amponah must be mistaken. I smiled therefore as I told him so. The poor fellow sighed deeply, and, shaking his head, replied, 'What I say is trute;[60] that man is him master means to make marry you, Miss.'—'But, Amponah, what is he?'—'What is he, Miss? Oh! he nephew to a vidow[61] lady master like, and go see sometime t'other side de Island. Ah, Miss! we know well enough who he is; he is poor man, bad man, cruel man; but *we* must not speak. Yet,' added Amponah, in a tone and manner altogether unlike his usual way of speaking, 'yet, for *such* man to be *your* husband, Miss!'—I was, I hardly know why, terrified at the honest indignation of this faithful servant. There must, surely, be something singularly obnoxious in the character of this man, that the very idea of his becoming the master of these people could thus move one of them. I was unwilling, however, to continue the conversation, but went to my own apartment, my heart more agitated than it has ever yet been, my whole frame trembling, and my thoughts confusedly recurring to what I had heard. I seemed unable to breathe, and was compelled to lie down for half an hour to recover and argue myself into a state of more rational composure.

"I was willing to flatter myself that Amponah was mistaken. 'What motive can there be?' said I, 'what end can my father propose in marrying me to a person who seems, if he is not rich, to possess no one recommendation? It is, I must believe, it is impossible!'

"So I argued, and by such means I endeavoured to quiet the cruel alarm that Amponah's information had given me. But the longer I reflected, the more probable it seemed, because I recollected many circumstances which had escaped me in my father's conversation and manner. As there are various species of pride, there are various ways of indulging it. Some men are delighted by allying themselves to rank or to riches. My father's pride has, it seems, taken a contrary direction, and is to be gratified only by raising an inferior to affluence and consideration, who shall be wholly the creature of his power, and owe every thing to his favour. How he may to this end sacrifice his daughter, and ruin her peace for ever, appears to be no part of his consideration. Always accustomed to command, and to look on those about him rather as machines who were to move only at his nod, than as beings who had wills and inclinations of their own, a man of equal or even of affluent or independent fortune would not on these terms become a part of his family. His choice therefore is necessarily directed to such an animal as this dependent; for Mr. Sawkins is, I understand, the nephew of a low woman, who came from England some years ago as housekeeper to a planter, and, being rather well-looking at that time, became so great a favourite with her master, that at his death he left her a large *pen* near Kingston, and a con-siderable sum of money, with which she has since purchased a plantation and slaves, of which her nephew is the manager. And it is to such an alliance, Denbigh, that my father sacri-fices his daughter. I talk, however, as if this detested alliance would ever take place. It never shall; never, though I perish in attempting to avoid it. . . . . .

"Another week is passed, and my father's intentions have been formally announced to me; I might rather have said, peremptorily declared. 'Tel est notre plaisir,'[62] was never uttered from the most despotic throne with more inflex-ible harshness. I was forbidden all reply; and ordered not to remonstrate, but to prepare to obey. I was told that Mr. Sawkins was then in the house, and that I must receive him as the man chosen for me by him who knew how to make him-self obeyed. 'I know,' said my father, 'I know that you have presumed to have other views for yourself. I know that artful people, calling themselves your friends, have had their views also on *my* fortune. To put an end at once and for ever to all such projects, it is my intention to have your marriage with the person I have elected for you concluded within a month.'

He perceived that I had collected courage to speak, and stopped me, by abruptly saying, in an angry tone, 'Look'ye, Henrietta, I never suffer contradiction. Your arguments will be vain; your opposition fatal to yourself. I expect to hear, in the course of the day, that you have acquitted yourself in regard to your behaviour to my friend, as common sense and duty, or, if those have no influence, as my positive *command* directs.' So saying, my father left the room; and Mr. Sawkins, with a cringeing bow, made his appearance. I had hardly a moment's time to recover my recollection, and to repeat.[63] Yes, Denbigh, in that moment, I solemnly repeated a vow to Heaven, that never should my hand be given in marriage but to you. Having thus called upon all that is held sacred to witness my unalterable resolution, I felt my courage renewed, and turned to meet the unwelcome candidate for my father's estate, who seemed to be very little at his ease. The base spirit of a parasite was visible on his countenance,[64] yet still there lurked under it a sort of malignant expression, which, while I positively, and I own with very little attention to politeness, rejected his suit, acquired insensibly the ascendant, and I shuddered while I remarked it. I cannot, Denbigh, repeat the particulars of our conversation; which I shortened as much as possible, and left him with a declaration couched in the strongest terms I could find, that my father might take away my life, but never should compel me to plight[65] at the altar my faith to a man of whom I knew little, and towards whom that little had only served to excite my dislike, nay, even my contempt. I then left the room, and hastened to my own, where I locked myself in; breathless and half dead, trembling at the resolution I had executed, yet feeling the immediate and dreadful necessity there would be for farther exertion. Oh, Denbigh! how did your unhappy Henrietta now regret the want of a mother, to whose affectionate bosom she might have flown for protection and consolation! With what anguish did she dwell on those days for ever gone, when this loss was supplied by the best of women and of friends; and when she was bade to consider you as the guardian of her youth, and the friend of her future life! Terrible was the contrast as she now looked around her: a father possessing unlimited power, and surrounded by slaves; in a remote house, of an island, many parts of which are liable to the attacks of savages driven to desperation, and thirsting for the blood of any who resembled even in colour their hereditary oppressors:—so that, to escape from the evil I dreaded by flight, which had at first struck me as possible, now seemed to be only exchanging one mode of hideous and intolerable sufferings for another.

"Such was, Denbigh—alas! such is the situation of your unhappy friend. It is vainly, very vainly, I have attempted to collect that fortitude which you so often, as if you had foreseen how much I was to need it, have tried to teach me; and with which in the first misfortune I had ever known, you never ceased trying to arm me. You then, I remember, used to lead me into the air, to turn my mind to the contemplation of the beauties of nature, and to point out to me a thousand proofs of the benignity of that Being in whose hands I was; and who would not, you told me, afflict me beyond my strength. I wept, and my tears were not tears of despair. They relieved my bursting bosom, and I breathed more at liberty. Now, I try the same means to obtain only the power of weeping. I go out into the open corridor, and gaze on the magnificence of heaven, spangled as it is with myriads of stars, brighter than I ever saw in Europe. The palmetos[66] and mountain cabbage,[67] of which there is a high wood adjoining to the house, bend their graceful heads, and wave their feathery leaves in the soft land wind which blows here at night. All is still and calm; even the slaves who have toiled through the day, now rest in tranquillity; but I am wretched, my eyes

are turned towards heaven, filled with burning tears of hopeless anguish. It seems hardly in the power of Heaven itself
to help me. And you, Denbigh!——It is now, I understand,
certain that the ship you were in was taken by a French privateer. My father, my cruel father! who has acquired more
information than I ever gave him, or was ever asked to give,
told me so yesterday with an ill-natured smile, adding, that
he understood you were sufficiently an adept in Jacobin principles, not to make a voyage to France any calamity to you:
'and,' continued he, 'as to the inhabitants of this island, they
can well dispense with the presence of such a wrong-headed
young man, who sets up, they tell me, for a reformer.[68] We
have more than enough of fellows of that description among
us already. I heartily hope Mr. Denbigh will stay at Paris.'

"You have often told me—Ah! how continually do I recur
to those dear lessons, of which, when they were given, I
surely knew not the value!—You have often told me, that a
woman should acquire fixed principles, and upon them act
with decision; and that there is nothing else that can prevent
that wavering imbecility which makes us the sport of every
accident, and often ridiculous as well as wretched.[69] I tried to
do so—I acted on those principles of duty towards my father,
and of reverence for the opinion of the world, which every
body around me had taught me; and, contrary, oh! how contrary to my own wishes! refused to accede to your proposal
of accompanying me in the same ship. The consequences are
to me so dreadful, that I know not how I shall ever venture to
decide again that I am acting right. Perhaps, disgusted by my
want of confidence, by my prudish mistrust in you, and trust
in another, you have determined, Denbigh, to forget me.
Needless indeed is this aggravation of my miseries; for, even
if you have not thrown off the unfortunate Henrietta, an over-
ruling and unconquerable destiny seems to have determined
that we shall meet no more! Death, my dear friend, will end

my distresses; for I feel it to be impossible that I should live to
be the wife—(how can I write the words?)—of Mr. Sawkins!
You are good and generous; you will not pity me the less
for having brought all this upon myself. I remember often
to have heard, when a circle of *friends* were talking over the
misfortunes of some poor sufferer, those who affected compassion answered by others of a less gentle disposition, with
'How can one pity a person who has brought their misfortune on themselves?' Ah! surely, where self-reproach is added
to misery, it embitters every pang. Yet I acted from prudence,
from principle, from an unwillingness, at my time of life, to
set at defiance the opinion of the world, which I was assured
must be absolutely against my leaving England accompanied
by you. I recollect too, Denbigh, your frequently ridiculing
those who have what you justly called the myopia of the
mind, who seeing only immediate and minute objects, suffer
such as are really of importance to escape them. I feel that
I have been a myops[70] in the present instance; and fearing
the unreasonable censure of half a dozen old women, who
would perhaps have forgotten me as soon as I should them, I
have incurred the heaviest calamity that could possibly over-
take me."

"Gracious God! what will become of me! I have just heard
that I am to be removed to another estate my father possesses in the northern part of the island. It is now the very
midst of the autumnal rains; and such rain, such cataracts
rather, and torrents of water, that no one thinks of travelling till it is over; but, from the information I have received,
I doubt whether I shall be allowed to remain here even till
these periodical tornados cease. My father, I am assured by
the faithful Amponah, the only servant in whom I have any

confidence, is determined to proceed without farther consulting me; and lawyers have been some days in the house drawing up the bill of sale, for what else can I call it? He has been used to purchase slaves, and feels no repugnance in selling his daughter to the most dreadful of all slavery! The more I reflect on the destiny he proposes for me, the more impossible I find it to reduce my mind to submission. No, Denbigh, I can die—but to live the wife of a man I despise and abhor, I feel not to be in my power. Would I could believe that an alteration in my appearance would change the intentions of the purchaser whom my father has chosen! for then I should rejoice at these pallid looks, and this emaciated form; which now I only consider as symptoms of decline, that though not rapid enough to save me from the tyranny so immediately meditated, will yet perhaps so enervate me as to prevent my escape; for to escape I will attempt if I am able, though every distress that human nature shrinks from most should be inevitable.

"I have been compelled to submit to three or four interviews with Mr. Sawkins. I cannot dwell upon them; they serve only to increase my horror and detestation. I must take some resolution. What can I do? I address myself in vain to Heaven; Heaven is deaf to my prayers. I call upon you, my best, my only friend! You are afar off; you cannot hear me.

"This last night, which has impressed every one else with terror, has to me given a few hours during which a gloomy hope suspended the bitterness of my despair. After a most oppressively hot day, the sun sunk in blood-coloured light, and huge clouds of a dark leaden hue, spotted with reddish purple, collected in the horizon. A sort of tremulous shivering ran among the leaves which no wind agitated, and the echo of the waves of the sea was heard like the regular firing of distant artillery. The negroes apprehended an earthquake, and their fears were presently communicated to the women,

who form what I must I believe call my father's seraglio in
this house. The vulgar of all nations seem to have a particular pleasure in exaggerating danger, and frightening each
other; and these ladies of every shade appeared to be trying
who should most express apprehension. The little girl who
had interested me more than the rest threw herself into my
arms, and wept bitterly; for she had heard a great deal about
hurricanes, and was persuaded her last hour was come. I
endeavoured to re-assure her, and prevail upon her to go to
her mother; for I thought there might be some place more
safe than the rest, which these people might know, and wish
to take shelter in; and I desired to be alone, determined to
take no precaution for my own safety; and as the storm now
came on with a fury of which I had before no idea, I felt
a gloomy satisfaction in the hope that my cruel solicitude
might be ended for ever. The peals of thunder bursting, as
it seemed, immediately over the house, and shaking it to its
very centre, mingled with the roaring of the wind, the crash
of trees which were swept away before it, the howling of the
negroes, and the cries of the women, who, as the tempest
raved with renewed violence, uttered shrieks and yells more
terrific than can be imagined; the vivid flashes of lightning,
which seemed to penetrate every part of the building, and
ran in blue rays along the floor; the flames of some of the
negro houses, of which the palm thatch had been fired by
the lightning; and, above all, a hollow and undescribable sub-
terraneous noise, muttering so as to be heard notwithstanding the warring elements without, all combined to make
me believe some fatal accident must happen: I say believe;
because I did *not* apprehend it. Maria, the little girl, perceiving she could not persuade me to fear, or to quit the part of
the house where I was, and which was thought, I know not
why, to be the least safe, had gone to her mother, and I was
quite alone in the apartments I usually inhabit. No candle

would remain burning, and I was involved in darkness; save only when the sudden glare of the lightning momentarily illuminated every object. Yet so much greater is my dread of living in the power of a man I abhor, than of dying by the act of that God on whom innocence may rely, that I felt myself ready to exclaim with Zanga, 'I like this rocking of the battlements;' [71] and I do not know that I have for many weeks felt less wretched. In about an hour and a half the hurricane seemed to have been re-incited instead of exhausted, till all at once there was a pause; a silence more terrific while it lasted than the fiercest rage of the storm. I thought I remembered to have heard, that such a dismal stillness preceded an earthquake, and I almost believed that I felt the ground opening beneath my feet. I listened, breathless; and then fear for the first time during this dreadful night took possession of me. I was without light; but I fancied I heard somebody breathe short and quick close to me. I spoke. 'Is it you, Maria?' said I, imagining it might be the little girl. I had no answer; yet the person, whoever it was, seemed to be nearer to me, and to draw breath with still greater difficulty. I rose, and put my hands forward. They encountered a human creature, who trembled excessively as he seized one of them. I struggled to disengage my hand, and in a voice expressive of terror, insisted on knowing who it was that held me. 'Be not frightened, dear lady, it is me.' I knew with astonishment the voice of Amponah.

"The great distance which is in this country kept inviolable between the black people and their master's family, and the degraded light in which they are considered, made me shudder and recoil from a liberty even the occasion did not seem to warrant. Amponah, who trembled so much that he could hardly speak, said, he was too much afraid of what might happen to be able to leave me alone, and he came to conjure me to go where the rest of the family were assembled,

in the most secure part of the house. This, however, I positively refused, unless it was my father's orders. My father, he
told me, had gone away the day before with Mr. Sawkins to
St. Jago de la Vega.[72] This accounted for my not having seen
him during the danger, at which I had before been surprised.
Not to prolong a conference with Amponah, who told me
the tempest would begin again more violently than ever, I
ordered him to go for lights, and assured him I had no apprehension, and desired no one to have fears for me. He obeyed
me, though it seemed to be with reluctance; but, before he
could return, the raging elements had renewed their con-
flict, and I thought it even worse than before. I again ordered
Amponah to leave me. He would have remonstrated, and
really seemed, poor fellow! to be quite bewildered and lost
through the extreme fear that possessed him; and as he put
the candles down on a low table near me, there was an expression so wild and fearful on his dark countenance, that I felt
it alarm me even more than the whirlwind and thunder that
were roaring without. I could not help imagining, from his
manner, that he knew of some danger awaiting me, greater
than that I shared in common with others, of suffering from
the tempest.

"He left me, however, in silence; for I was afraid to question him. I shut my doors as securely as possible; having first
satisfied myself, that no other of the black people had crept
into the rooms, from the same motives as had influenced
poor Amponah; and I listened, I think, with more indifference than before to 'the pelting of the pitiless storm.'[73] It
ceased not, however, till after day-break; and then the female
negroes and mulattoes, who belonged to me, crowded into
my room, each with some story more terrible than the preceding, of what she had feared or suffered. The devastation
on the trees, the cane grounds, and garden, was indeed visible enough. One poor negro had been killed by the fall

of a beam in one of the boiling-houses,[74] which had been unroofed and half carried away; others had been bruised and wounded, and the manager was busy in repairing the mischief till a late hour; while I exerted myself all I could to assist the nurses who attended the women, some of whom had just lain in, and had been exposed with their infants to the rage of the hurricane, by having the roofs or other parts of their little cabins carried away by the wind.

"Nothing so much blunts the sense of misery as the activity of humanity. I returned from my visits to these poor and apparently grateful people, at once so satisfied and so much fatigued, that I slept many hours, and forgot for awhile all I have to apprehend for myself."

————

"Alas! Denbigh, the tranquillity with the boast of which I finished my last sentence, was of no long duration. This morning the order arrived from my father, that I should immediately remove, with the attendants he named, to the estate on the northern part of the island; which is, I am assured, a much more lonely situation than this. It is almost among the mountains, and no other cultivated land is within many miles. Surely, I can no where be more completely in his power than here. I have discovered this moment the reason of his removing me: a note has been clandestinely delivered to me by Amponah, from Mrs. Apthorp. She is at the house of a relation four miles from hence; and, alarmed for my safety, as every one, indeed, has been for that of his neighbour, sent this inquiry, which Amponah has ventured to give me notwithstanding the strict injunctions, with menaces of punishment for disobedience, which my father repeated to his whole household, and left orders with Mr. Grabb to enforce.

"I have answered her: for even the semblance of friend-ship is soothing to one who lives, as I have lately done, cut off from all human intercourse, and persecuted even to death by him who ought to be my protector, my friend, my father! Yet I own, that since I have been convinced she had designs of her own in those proceedings, which I thought arose solely from disinterested kindness, I do not feel that affection for her which I did."

————

"Scarce, my dearest friend! was I allowed to finish the last sentence, before I was informed that the people and car-riage appointed to conduct me hither were ready. I had no choice; my remonstrances, my entreaties for time were not even listened to. I will not describe my journey, in which I was attended only by a mulatto woman; for Juana was not allowed to accompany me, and as her children were slaves on the estate I have left, I would not have pressed for her atten-dance hither, even had it been likely that it would have been granted. I was miserable, even more so than I had ever been yet. Ah! surely, if ever you should read these pages, many of them hardly legible, others blotted with my tears, you will be even weary of my miseries, and my real distresses may have the effect of those generally popular novels I remember to have read in England, of which I heard people complain, that they contained such a series of impossible calamity, as to blunt at once compassion and curiosity. I write on, however, notwithstanding this painful idea, which perpetually intrudes upon me. I write without knowing, and hardly daring to hope, that my narrative will be read by him for whom it is intended.

"I expected to have found my father, his elected son-in-law, and a friend of his, a clergyman (Heavens! *are* there in the church such men as *he* is represented to be?), waiting my

arrival; and—no, Denbigh, I dare not tell you the projects
with which my mind was occupied, nor what I might perhaps have been driven to, had they been so assembled with a
view to this detested sale, which my father means to make of
his unhappy child! I felt as if a weight, under which it would
have been impossible for me to have supported myself, was
suddenly taken from my mind, when I found that this party
not only was not there, but that they had yet sent no notice
of the time when they intended it. General orders of preparation had, however, been received; but that the dreadful alternative to which I might be exposed was not so immediately
to crush me, I was thankful. I slept with some tranquillity
the evening after my arrival; and yesterday, as the weather,
particularly on this side the island, is comparatively cool, I
had command enough over myself to detach my mind, for
a little while, from the sad subject of my apprehensions, and
examine the singular scenery with which I am surrounded.

"And it is, indeed, scenery so new and magnificent, that
I must be quite crushed by my miseries, if I could behold
it without admiration. The house, a very indifferent one, is
about three quarters of a mile from the sea, of which there is
from the front a noble view. To the southward run out green
promontories, covered with mountain palms[75] and plantains,[76] with all the singular appendages of Indian[77] landscape.
Around the house here, contrary to the other part of the
island, for land seems as of no more value than in Europe, is
an inclosure like a small English park; and here are many beautiful trees and shrubs: the tree jasmine, the pomegranate and
the mango; together with groups of oranges, lemons, limes,
and shaddocks,[78] that perfume the air with almost oppressive odours. Behind the house, and beyond this half natural
shrubbery, rise the mountains, which gradually increase in
height to the distance of fifteen or twenty miles, where they
seem to tower to the clouds,[79] and of which many parts of

them have, as I am told, never been visited by Europeans. It is there, amid the forests of mahogany[80] and ceiba,[81] the Indian fig,[82] and other immense trees whose names I do not know, and amidst the deep gullies with which those towering ridges are intersected from the immense volumes of water that fall during the rainy season, that the Maroons, those people who have lately excited so much alarm,[83] live sequestered from oppression, and are often able to issue from their sylvan fortresses, and retaliate on their oppressors. Their community is frequently increased by fugitive negroes, and is lately become so formidable, that means have been devised wholly to extirpate and destroy them; which is, perhaps, very politic, but I can hardly think it just.

"As very great apprehensions had been felt on the other side the island, on account of the depredations[84] of these people, and as I am afraid, by all I can learn, that my father is among those who, from the rigour of his proceedings, is very likely to be particularly obnoxious to them, I cannot help feeling some surprise at his choosing his present residence, where it seems to me that his property and his family are much more exposed to any injuries they are capable of doing. The nights are now more calm and mild, and the climate not much unlike the south of France; at least I love to recall that country, where I was happy, and where we first met. I sat last night under a sort of corridor that goes round the house.[85] There was a solemnity in the scene, and in the sounds, that I felt but cannot describe. To the north, a heavy swelling sea broke monotonously, though violently, on the rough shore; the rocks and caverns re-echoed to the thunder of the waves. In the measured pauses of this burst of water were now and then heard, among the woods that clothe the mountains, noises which, I was informed, are the signals used by the Maroons and runaway negroes to collect their numbers or hold their councils. Sometimes it was a few dull notes struck in a particular manner on their gombay[86] or drum, answered by the same number of strokes from another quarter. At another time, it was the sullen sound of a great shell;[87] which is, they say, used every where by the savages as a war signal; and this was answered by hollow human voices from different parts—Some I supposed to be very near the house, so near, that at any other time, I own, I should not have thought of such neighbours with indifference. But it is not for me, who momentarily expect the arrival of my father and his friend, to dread any other earthly calamity that can befall me.

"Had I not these very serious miseries to overwhelm my mind, I should feel more relief than I do from the absence of many petty inconveniences which the season and the climate occasion. The muskitos, against which none of the contrivances we have are entirely a security, are now no longer troublesome; nor do the cock roaches, knockers,[88] and other odious insects, now torment me as they did on the other side of the island. I have so little fear of the Maroons, who I am persuaded would not injure me, for I have never injured them, that I ventured out yesterday evening beyond the inclosure surrounding the house. I never saw any thing so beautiful as the woods, which are for some extent up the hills quite clear of bushes or thorns, and overshadow, not turf indeed, such as we sometimes see in England, but long and luxurious grass; among which creep the little lizards, green as animated emeralds, and not only perfectly harmless, but, as it is affirmed, friendly to the human race; and a sort of ground dove,[89] still more interesting—while innumerable other doves and plovers find food and shelter among the trees above. I should, perhaps, have wandered much farther than prudence would have permitted, had day sunk gradually into night as it does in other latitudes; but here it becomes dark at once: and as I was hastening back, yet dreading to enter the

house, where I feared I might hear my father was arrived,
I was surprised by perceiving sudden flashes of vivid light
darting about among the trees. As, however, they gave me
no idea of any human contrivance, I was not alarmed; and
it immediately occurred to me that they were fire-flies,[90] and
I remembered your having described some you saw in Italy.
They are not common here, but among the mountainous and
woody parts of the island; and I find the negroes have some
strange superstitious notions about them, as, indeed, they
have some wild and absurd impression or other in regard to
every object that surrounds them. It is weak and ridiculous,
I know, and you, my friend, will severely reprove me for it,
if I should ever be so fortunate as to know that these letters
reach you. But I will not disguise my folly: there are times
when the hideous phantasies of these poor uninformed savages affect my spirits with a sort of dread, which all my conviction of their fallacy does not enable me to subdue. Little
Maria used to talk to me of their Obeahs,[91] persons who
persuade others, and perhaps believe themselves, that they
possess supernatural powers, acquired by I know not what
operations, resembling, as far as I could learn, those of the
witches in Macbeth round the magic cauldron.[92] I afterwards
fancied that the two or three the little girl pointed out to me
had something particularly horrid in their appearance; yet,
as they are liable to severe punishment[93] if their being Obi
men or women is known, they carefully conceal any outward
appearance of their profession. But the mulattoes, and the
unfortunate children belonging to them and white parents,
who are brought up amidst all the vices and superstitions
of the negroes, are too apt to imbibe both the one and the
other; and what attempts have been made to give them other
ideas, seem to me only to have made in their minds a sort
of 'darkness visible.'[94] These Obi men and women are, as I
have been informed, more numerous here than in the other

plantations: and I shudder involuntarily when I fancy, from the mysterious looks and odd gestures of some of them, that they are deeply initiated in these wild rites of superstition.

"Amponah was among the people who were appointed to attend me hither, and it is from him that I receive almost all the information I am able to obtain from any quarter. The poor fellow, from his residence in England and his attendance on my brother, has acquired more knowledge than the generality of the people of his colour; and all the attachment he felt for my brother, near whose person he was brought up, is very naturally transferred to me. As to my father, he has conceived such an extreme terror of him, owing, I believe, to some severities that have been inflicted on him for trifling faults, that I have seen him turn pale and tremble when he has been speaking of him; and while he has been telling me what he has discovered, or heard from others of people, of the intentions that have been formed as to the conclusion of my marriage, his agitation has been so extreme, that he suddenly became inarticulate, the big drops trembled on his forehead, and his breath became so short, that he could not continue speaking, but was compelled to leave the room to recover himself. Alas, Denbigh! to what a situation is your unhappy friend reduced, when her only counsellor is a poor negro slave! and when she has no friendly bosom on which she can rely for more rational advice, or to whom she dares to confide the information he ventures his life to procure for her!

"I here break off. I lock my papers and your letters, Denbigh, into a very small cabinet, made for me, of the fine woods of this country, by a brother of Amponah's; and I determine to send it to Mrs. Apthorp, Amponah having assured me he will find means to convey it safely, with a few words, the last perhaps after these that I shall ever write; for Amponah has discovered, that to-morrow evening my father, his friend, and a man who is called a clergyman, are to be here. Mr. Grabb, who is a relation, it seems, and protected by Sawkins, is already come, though he keeps himself out of my sight; and preparations are silently making for the wicked, the inhuman sacrifice!

"No, Denbigh! no. It will never, it shall never be. The wretched creatures of whom I have spoken, that pass here for having the power to look into futurity, in vain declare that a marriage and great festival will soon happen here. A funeral will be the festival, if there is any; for I can die. Misery so overwhelming as that which threatens me will destroy me. I hear again the gombay in the woods; I hear the strange yells as of savage triumph, and I shudder to think that there is no alternative. I must either endeavour to fly—yet whither, and to whom?—at the hazard of falling into these people's hands, or I must await the fate designed for me by my cruel, my unnatural parent! Oh, my dear, dear friend! how would your generous heart feel for your unhappy Henrietta, could her present calamitous condition be known to you! Should this reach you—(it cannot reach you till long after my destiny is decided, probably not till long after this poor form is perishing in the grave)—forgive me, Denbigh! my errors (and severely have they been punished) were rather of my head than of my heart; the effects of prejudice rather than perverseness. Denbigh! when some happier, some more deserving woman is in possession of that place in your affections which I was unworthy to fill, do not speak of me with the indifference I deserve; but recollect with compassion the poor Henrietta, whose last wish will be for your felicity. My tears—yet it is not always that I can weep—my tears blind me; and scarcely can my trembling hand make legible this last adieu."

LETTER III.

THE narrative of the poor persecuted Henrietta was here interrupted; and on my applying to my friend Denbigh for the sequel, he thus related it, filling up the chasm till she again resumed the pen:[95]

"You see," said he, "the date of this last letter.[96] I arrived at Jamaica three days earlier than that date; and without any inquiry after my other friends, I hastened only to inform myself of Henrietta: but the accounts I received bewildered for awhile, and then nearly distracted me. By some persons I was assured she had been married some time; by others, that she had been sent no one knew whither, by her father, for having positively refused to accept the husband he had chosen for her. Kingston was, however, remote from any of Mr. Maynard's houses; and though the colonies in general are as much or more infested with talebearers and gossips than the provincial towns of England, it happened at that time, that public events materially affecting them, the increasing alarm from the insurgent Maroons, and an epidemical complaint of the most alarming nature,[97] had co-operated to call off the attention of individuals from every thing but the preservation of their property and their families. And though Mr. Maynard was, on account of his fortune, one of the Assembly,[98] he was very little beloved, and his daughter not at all known; and of what had befallen either the one or the other it was impossible to obtain correct intelligence where I was. I lost not a moment, therefore, in hastening to his principal residence on the other side of the island, that to which Henrietta had been first carried.[99] Arrived there, I inquired of the first negro I met for Mr. Maynard. The poor fellow appeared to be afraid of answering me; and upon my

entreating him to speak out, and assuring him I had business
of the greatest consequence with his master, he pointed, with
evident symptoms of apprehension, to the house of the overseer,[100] at the end of a row of palmetos, many of which had
been blown down by a hurricane that had happened, he told
me, in that part of the island three weeks before. 'None of
the family suffered?' said I eagerly. 'Only two tree negro kill,'
replied the man. 'But Miss Maynard, your master's daughter,
where is she?' The negro shook his head: 'No say, massa. One
my ship-mate[101] flog for make question—for tell tings.' This
mystery was insupportable. The manager[102] to whom I was
then compelled to apply was only a sort of second or third
under the chief deputy, who was, I found, absent. This man
seemed the most sullen brute I had ever talked to; he either
could not or would not give me any satisfaction whatsoever.
I presently became impatient, and insisted upon his telling
me where I could speak to his master; which he refused to
do unless I would tell him my business. There was something so ferociously mysterious in his manner, that my alarm
increased, and I tried to conquer my indignation, while I
said, 'You will surely tell me, Sir, whether Mr. Maynard is
at home?'—'I cannot tell you, Sir, what I do not know.'—
'Is he here, on this estate?'—'No.'—'At which of his estates
is he?'—'I cannot tell.'—'Where is his daughter?'—'I know
nothing about his daughter.'—'Good God, Sir! you can tell
me whether she is married or single?'—'She was to have been
married as last Thursday; but I do not know that she was.'—
'Where, Sir,' continued I in increased agitation, 'was the ceremony to have taken place?'—'At Mr. Maynard's northern
plantation.'—'And did it not take place?'—'I—I—really, Sir,
these questions from a stranger are somewhat extraordinary.
I do not know, Sir, that you have any right to ask them; but,
be that as it may, I have no authority to answer them. Your
servant, Sir; I wish you a good day.' The worthy manager

then retired to his *sangarie*,[103] and, turning away in inexpress-
ible mortification, I was about to inquire of some of the
negroes; but a servant from the manager's house followed
me, and at a signal he made every person disappeared; and
none, I was persuaded, would have answered my question,
had I found an opportunity to put it. Half frantic, I stopped
merely to argue with my impetuous passions on the necessity of patience and resolution; resolution, without which
it seemed to be impossible for me to know, or, knowing, to
endure, the extent of the misery to which I might be condemned. Henrietta married under circumstances of compul-
sion; or, Henrietta forgetting me, and throwing me from her
affection for ever, were almost equally terrible to my imagination: yet, so truly did I love her, that it was less terrible to
believe her faithless to me, than the sad victim of her father's
inhuman tyranny. If, said I as soon as I could reflect, if she has
broken for ever all those ties which united us, I shall, it is true,
be wretched. But time will enable me to look with calmness
on the conduct of a woman, who, if she could so act, could
never deserve the tenderness I have felt for her. If, on the
contrary, she is condemned by her cruel and brutal father to
throw herself into the arms of a man she abhors, to become
a legal prostitute[104] to a contemptible wretch whom she must
loath and detest!—The very idea is so hideous to my imagination, that it would be impossible for me ever to suffer the
reality; and I should undoubtedly sacrifice to my vengeance
the monsters that had dared to use the established forms of
life in violation of every principle of moral or human rights.
Alas! all these meditations, far from forwarding any project
for the relief of my poor Henrietta, served only to render
me incapable of assisting her. I felt my brain inflamed by
the violence of my emotions. I became giddy and confused;
yet, determined not to ask, what would probably have been
refused, a moment's repose at the house or among the people

of Maynard, I rode forward not knowing where or why. The hottest season was now at hand: the ardour of a tropical sun, darting on my throbbing temples, was, though I was myself almost insensible of it, not long to be endured with impunity. Even the poor faithful black servant, who followed me on horseback, was nearly overcome; when, arriving at that part of the country where the blue mountains begin to be very steep, and are cut with wide and deep gullies, my horse, quite exhausted with fatigue, (for I had heeded his corporeal feelings no more than my own) fell with me in a very rocky and stony road, and I know not what became of me for many hours.

"This happened in the country which was actually the seat of the Maroon insurrection.[105] I knew very little of it. I had inquired after nothing, I had thought of nothing, but Henrietta! My sensations therefore, if personal safety had been the object of my solicitude, would not have been very comfortable, when, awaking from insensibility, I found myself surrounded by men of colour, whom I immediately knew, as well by their appearance as by the place where they were, to be Maroons and runaway negroes, and from whom it was likely I should receive as little mercy as had been by the generality of my countrymen shewn to them. They appeared, however, to be administering remedies to the hurts I had received by my fall; and Ambo, my servant, perceiving that I was sensible, uttered an exclamation of joy, and, kneeling by me, wept like a child. I understood, that when he saw me fall, and found I was severely hurt, he ran into the woods, whence he imagined he perceived the smoke of negro-houses, and had soon fallen in with a party of armed Maroons and blacks,[106] to whom, without attending to their hostile appearance, he had briefly related my misfortune, and entreated their succour. These men were lying in wait for a small detachment of militia, who, they had been told,

were to pass that way; and it was only his agitation for my
safety, and the extreme simplicity of my servant, that convinced them I was not, what they had at first supposed, one
of the officers of that militia. They followed my servant to
the place where he had left me, and I was now their prisoner; yet a prisoner towards whom they were disposed to
shew every sort of kindness, on the report of my servant,
whose honest solicitude for me convinced them I was not
one of those whom their unfortunate race have reason to
pursue with execrations and with vengeance. I soon recovered recollection enough to endeavour to avail myself of
their favourable disposition towards me. I represented to him
who seemed to have the greatest authority among them, that
more than my life depended on my being suffered instantly
to depart; and when he asked an explanation, I briefly related
whither I was going. Appealing to all of nature that oppression had left in the hearts of these wild people, I told them
of the force which I had reason to dread would be put on
the inclinations of the woman I loved, and to whom I had
been betrothed in England. I observed, that when I named
Mr. Maynard, and said that I was going to his northern estate
in hopes of preventing this accursed marriage, they looked
significantly at each other; and at length one of them, who
appeared to be more ferocious and less considerate than the
rest, told me, that to hasten whither I was going was utterly
useless, because it was now some days since that plantation
had been destroyed, in retaliation for the cruelty with which
their people (the Maroons) had been pursued, persecuted,
and punished by Mr. Maynard. I felt my blood run cold to
my heart at this information, and hardly had strength and
courage to ask, what became of the persons who were in the
house, when it was, as I understood, set on fire? The same
man answered, that the women and slaves were carried up
the mountain—Maynard himself was not there—They had

been misinformed as to the time of his arrival to celebrate
the marriage of his daughter, on the very day of which they
intended to have struck the blow; but having gone too far
to retreat before they were aware of their mistake, they had
executed their plan as far as it related to the destruction of
his property, and the captivity of his family, reserving their
vengeance against him personally till they could completely
gratify it.

"While the man continued to speak, I was become half
frantic from the crowd of terrific ideas that rushed on my
mind relative to Henrietta. She was released from the power
of Maynard only to fall into that of savages, always terrible
in their passions, and in whom the fierce inclination for
European women was now likely to be exalted by the desire
of revenge on a man so detested as the father of my unhappy
Henrietta! I cannot—no, my friend! I will not attempt to
tell you what were at that moment my feelings. Yet, dread-
fully acute as they were, I knew it was absolutely necessary
for me to disguise them. Henrietta might yet live; and however wretched it was likely we should both be, I could not
determine to abandon her, though I were sure to find her
disgraced and undone. I could die with her—(for I knew she
never would survive the horrors I dreaded for her)—I could
die with her, if to live for her were denied. Once certain,
therefore, and I soon was but too certain, that Henrietta was
carried to the fastnesses[107] among the mountainous forests,
where the Maroons held impregnable stations, I no longer
sought my liberty. I endeavoured only, by means of Ambo,
to prevail on my captors to allow me to go with them; and
they were assured that I would remain as a hostage, while
Ambo should be dispatched to bring them an ample ransom,
and that I would, in the mean time, submit to the restraint of
following their party whithersoever they went.

"Captain Degomai, the commander, to whom it was left

to decide on my destiny, took some time to consider of my proposal, and at length told me, that he could not entirely assent to it. The offer of a considerable ransom had its weight: yet how could he trust to the faith of Ambo, who seemed so attached to me, and who, instead of returning, might bring the enemy to their strong holds, and utterly undo them? That proposal, therefore, he must reject; but he would take both myself and my servant up the country to the woods, and consult with his chief; while, on my tranquilly submitting to my imprisonment, and not attempting to make myself master of any of their secrets, it must finally depend whether I should be treated like an enemy or a friend. I found all remonstrance would be in vain; but delay in any way was death to me. It happened, however, an alarm was given at that moment, that a large body of regular forces and militia, assembled by the gentlemen nearest to the estates that had lately suffered, was rapidly advancing with artillery towards their principal fortress; and a scout came from their main body with this intelligence, and orders from their Maroon general to hasten thither with all possible speed. This appeared to be a very unfavourable moment for me; and under some circumstances it would have probably happened that I should have been stabbed, or shot at once, to prevent all inquiry or the hazard of my escape; but Ambo, who had found means to make himself much beloved among them, had, by this time, discovered his near relation, a brother by the same father, who was a sort of second in command; and, I believe, that circumstance saved my life. I was, however, marched up the country as a prisoner; while the agony of my mind, dwelling continually on the fate of Henrietta, so far rendered me unconscious of personal suffering, that I neither felt the fatigue of such a march, or the pain from my bruises. I hardly heeded what was said; I hardly felt my own situation, and remembered I was a captive only because it prevented my throwing myself at all hazards into any place where it was likely my dear unhappy girl might be found.

"I was conscious that my life hung but by a thread; the slightest suspicion was sufficient to destroy me; and more than one of the party, whose prisoner I was, regarded me, as I could plainly perceive, with distrust. Occupied, however, by one object, my own danger became indifferent to me; and I appeared to be so totally insensible to every thing, which, if I had any invidious designs, would have attracted my attention, that during our march my captors gradually became less careful of confining me amongst them. On the second evening, while they still lingered around the woody region of a mountain, for reasons which I did not comprehend, and dared not inquire into, the whole party sat down at night-fall under a high chain of rocks, which formed a natural and almost insurmountable barrier to the higher grounds, unless to those who knew the winding and rugged paths which led among them. The men produced two small casks of rum; and while some went to fill their calabashes at a spring, which gushed through the cliff, glittering in the moon-beam as it fell, others made a fire, and prepared the pork and kid, which they had brought, with yams and bananas. I shall never forget the group as they appeared beneath the bright light of the moon then at full. The strange dresses, where Indian nakedness[108] was oddly intermingled with military ornaments; their dark faces, and that peculiar look of ferocity which the eye of the negro rolling in its deep socket[109] gives to the whole race of Africans, and which was, in one instance, rendered more so by the plumed helmet of an English soldier, whom the black had killed and stripped; in another by a sort of turban, from which waved the scarlet feathers of the mackaw;[110] and in a third by part of an old uniform, and a laced hat.[111] I stood leaning against an excavated rock behind them, listening with increased anguish to their conversation, as the spirits and good cheer began to make them noisy and unreserved. I had, from a boy, understood a little of their wild jargon, and now fancied they spoke of their women, and of white women whom their chief had made captives in their late excursion among the plantations to the north. I looked at Ambo, to whom I dared not speak apart, for any conversation between us was, I found, offensive; but I was sure, from the countenance and gestures of Ambo, that he understood their discourse better than I did, and that it related to Henrietta. This terrible certainty, since every hope that it might not be so seemed now to be at an end, quite subdued my fortitude, and I sunk almost senseless on the ground. Poor Ambo obtained for me a glass of their rum, and was kneeling to administer it to his apparently dying master, when a sudden shout in the woods below suspended at once the savage mirth of the Maroons; they listened, but it was not repeated: yet every man flew to arms. A scout immediately sprang forth to discover whence proceeded a noise which they knew was not made by friends. Hardly, however, were these precautions taken when a volley of shot was fired amongst us. It killed two, and wounded five; among whom was my poor Ambo, as I afterwards found. No description can do justice to the hideous yells which now resounded among the rocks and woods. The assailants and the assailed mingled their cries, which were returned and deepened by the hollow caverns. Another volley from the still concealed foe silenced for ever some of the most clamorous; and the rest being driven to despair, their natural and acquired fierceness of character urged them to such revenge as was yet in their power; and the man whom I had considered as a sort of second in command, and in whom I had observed symptoms of peculiar malignity, rushed with another towards me, and, each seizing an arm, hurried me away into the thickest covert of the wood near them, exerting such strength and agility as I could not perhaps have effectually resisted at any time; but enfeebled as I was, yet animated by the hope that I might rescue Henrietta, if I could speak to the armed party who had made the assault, I struggled with my utmost power to disengage myself; when the place we were in being choked with trees and pieces of rock, it was impossible for the men to compel me to go on; and to consult at once their safety and their vengeance, one of the negroes drew a dirk he wore, and stabbed me twice. The first blow penetrated my arm, the second my side; and imagining he had killed me, or not daring to stay to complete his work, he and his companion fled, and left me weltering in my blood. I was not, however, insensible, and had sufficient presence of mind to endeavour to stop the blood which gushed from the wound in my side, while I listened attentively in hopes of hearing the hostile party, who would be friendly to *me*, approach; but after a tumult of some moments, and some conversation in which I supposed it was discussed whether they should pursue the fugitives, their voices as they descended among the woods were more faintly heard, and then gradually died away. The only poor hope I had seemed to perish when I no longer distinguished the voices of the English soldiers. I collected, however, all my strength, and endeavoured to get up and follow them: but though I was upon my feet, and able to stand supported by a tree, yet in a moment my eyes grew dim, my head giddy, I concluded my death immediate, and, faintly uttering the name of Henrietta, ceased to think or to breathe. I lay some hours in that state; for when I recovered myself it was the dawn of day. My wounds had ceased to pour forth the blood in which I found myself lying; but I was deadly sick, and for some time unable to recall distinctly what had happened. With consciousness returned my intolerable anguish; and I figured to myself my wretched Henrietta under sufferings which maddened my brain. I knew not what I did; yet I crawled with extreme difficulty to the scene of the preceding night's attack, and with horror beheld the distorted countenances of several Blacks and Maroons who had been killed; while among them I distinguished, with the greatest regret, the face of my poor Ambo, who had perished for his attachment to me. Sinking to the earth, I believed myself about to follow him, when, in the woody cliffs above, I heard the sound of those savage instruments by which the Maroons call to battle, and I doubted not but that they were coming down in force to meet the party who had attacked them. If I was perceived, it was probable that my existence would end amidst the most excruciating tortures: and wretched as I was, the instinctive love of life, or rather dread of such a death, urged me to attempt my escape. I crept, therefore, again into the descending woods, in a direction opposite to that whither I had been forced by the Maroons. My progress was slow; for I was so weak, that I was compelled to drag myself along by holding the trees on either hand. Yet even thus heavily advancing fatigued me so much, that I felt my wounds beginning to bleed afresh; and that I should again faint, if I could not staunch the bleeding. I gathered some leaves, and, folding one on another, applied them to my wounds, which I thought I perceived would not be mortal, if the loss of blood they occasioned did not exhaust me. On these high regions there are few cocoa or other fruit-bearing trees; but I found some of the fruit called sweet sop,[112] which for a while extremely refreshed me. I continued to creep on, being sometimes under the necessity of resting for many minutes; and in these intervals I anxiously listened to the noises which would give me any information of the motions of those whom I now considered as my murderers; and from whom, if they tracked me, I imagined it to be impossible to escape. But it was high noon, and the continual

buzzing of the muskitoes and other insects made it impossible for me to distinguish any distant sounds, while their stings
greatly increased my torment; and the heat, notwithstanding
I was among high grounds, was so oppressive, that it was
almost impossible for me to proceed. Yet to obtain any repose
was equally impossible; and despair of being able to save my
unhappy Henrietta added so severely to my personal sufferings, that I hardly retained my senses, the cruel agony I
endured being such as I could not long sustain and live. An
insatiable and tormenting thirst added to my bodily pain, and
the fruits I found were insufficient to allay it. I listened for the
sound of water, and at last thought I heard it murmur in the
gulley below. But in my situation, an attempt to follow a
descent of near a hundred yards, which, but for the trees and
shrubs, would have appeared almost perpendicular, was by
no means easy. These gulleys I knew to be the peculiar lurk-
ing-places of fugitive negroes, who had fled from their masters without having yet had courage or opportunity to join
the insurgent Maroons; and I might perhaps meet with some
who might quickly put an end to my faint and almost involuntary struggles to preserve a worthless or miserable
existence.

"Once more, however, exerting myself to the utmost
of my power, rather from instinct than reason, I began to
attempt descending this fearful chasm. The bolls[113] and
branches of the trees sustained me, while the roots, starting
in many places from the rock, gave me a footing which the
rock itself often denied. I believe I was almost three hours
laboriously reaching the bottom of this chasm. I did, however,
reach it, and threw myself more than half dead on the high
and luxuriant grass, or rather reeds, which bordered a small
rapid stream, whose spring was far on the cliffs above. When
I had recovered my breath and recollection, I eagerly turned
to the water; and with my hands, for I had no hat or anything

else by which to convey it, I endeavoured to appease the consuming thirst which devoured me; and never did the pure element administer its refreshment to lips more parched, or weakness more oppressive than what I suffered. Quite overcome by excessive exertion and loss of blood, which always disposes to sleep, forgetfulness stole over me. The dark recess where I lay seemed never to have been trodden by human feet, and monkeys, parroquets,[114] and doves appeared to be the undisturbed proprietors of the soil. But had there been vestiges of more hostile inhabitants, I was no longer capable of calculating my danger, and the body refused to support any longer the overwhelming agonies of the mind. Had I been told that I could sleep for many hours (for now I really slept) without once remembering that Henrietta was lost to me for ever, and was in all probability suffering indignities which were infinitely worse than death, I should have spurned at the supposition as a calumny most derogatory to every feeling of affection or honour. Yet there is a period of suffering when the most active mind sinks into torpor, and the vital principle alone keeps up the languid pulsation of the heart. Even this degree of life I should not have retained, had I not been in the very strength of youthful manhood, and possessed a sound and unbroken constitution.

"In the partial insensibility I had thus fallen into, fancy was at length busy; and after some hours I imagined that a person stood by me, spoke to me in a friendly voice, touched my face and hands, and bade me try to rise. The vision was confused, and soon disappeared. Yet a second time it came, and a second time faded into air. Again I imagined this compassionate voice murmured in my ears: and that a man of my own colour and country stood near me, chafing my temples and hands. I opened my eyes, and perceived a human figure, but a very unusual one; and still believing myself in a dream, I looked round me, saw the objects I had seen before

I slept, and recovered a sort of confused consciousness of all that had happened, and of the place where I was. The figure, seeing that I was sensible, then sat down by me, and inquired who I was, and by what chance I came in that condition into such a place? I tried, but in vain, to answer his questions coherently. He perceived how unable I was to satisfy his curiosity; and asked me, if with assistance I could rise from the ground? I found it very difficult, as well because of my weakness as the soreness of my limbs. At length, however, I found myself able to move, leaning on my friendly conductor; and after walking, or rather creeping, along among brushwood and mangroves,[115] on the edge of the rivulet, which were sometimes so thickly interwoven, that it was to me a most laborious task to get through them, we arrived at a narrow path up the precipice, which might be almost called a ladder of rocks. I climbed, or rather was dragged up with considerable difficulty by my conductor, till suddenly I saw one of those caves so frequent in these mountains,[116] and usually the abode of those giant bats[117] which are found in the tropical regions, or of wild pigeons; and often of wretched negroes, who hazard the want of food, or live by nightly plunder, to escape from punishment or oppression. The place I now saw, however, was in some degree accommodated to the residence of a being of another description; and when I looked around it, and beheld its inhabitant, the fable which had most delighted my youth occurred to me, and I imagined myself in the inward apartment of Robinson Crusoe.[118] My new friend was an Englishman, between fifty and sixty: his complexion was that of one who had lived much in hot climates, and his features bore the traces of some deep affliction. It was easy to perceive by his manner, and the tones of his voice, that his education had been that of a gentleman. His dress was not much unlike the costume of some religious orders, except that his robe was of the blue cotton, woven and dyed

by the negroes, and his grey hair was covered by a large hat
of woven straw or reeds, not unlike those worn by peasants
in some parts of Italy. He seemed unconscious of the singu-
larity of his appearance, and how much surprised I must be
to see such a person in such a place: but, attentive only to my
wants, he hastened to dress my wounds, which he performed
with the skill of a surgeon; then furnished me with a slight
repast of cassada[119] bread, yams, and chocolate, not allowing
me to take any thing spiritous. He gave me some of his own
linen, which was extremely refreshing; and forbidding me to
speak more than to tell him my name, and that in crossing
the country I had fallen into the power of the Maroons, he
led me to an enclosure hung with matting within the rock,
where there was a mattress on the floor, and some cotton
bedding, on which bidding me repose myself he left me.
Repose, however, it was impossible to obtain. I looked round
me by the light of a small lamp fed with palm oil, and could
hardly persuade myself that all that had passed was not a
dream, from which I was not yet awakened. I raised myself
on the arm of which I had still the use, and listened, trying
to ascertain if I was really in possession of my senses. I found
myself now able distinctly to carry my mind to the progress
of my sufferings; and then the cruel recollection of Henrietta,
lost for ever, came with all its former force, and I ceased to
think of myself, or to recollect that I personally suffered.
It immediately occurred to me, that my new friend might
know something of the late transactions of the Maroons; for
it seemed difficult to conceive how a European could live, as
he appeared to do, in the very midst of their recesses, without being, if not their associate, at least one who knew how
to conciliate them—or to inhabit such an abode would have
been impracticable. Again I listened; but besides that it was
now night, the intervention of the rock prevented my hearing any thing without but a dull indistinct murmur of the

land-wind among the high trees rising above it.

"My spirits became more and more active, and I believed myself capable of rising, seeking my incomprehensible host, and relating to him the cause of my wanderings, and the great source of my disquiet; when, having crept to the sort of door, composed of reeds, joined something in the manner of the fences with which we enclose our melon-grounds in England, I thought I heard two persons in the outer cave conversing; and though they spoke in a very low tone, I fancied one of them was a woman. On a sudden they seemed to be alarmed at some noise, and I held my breath lest it should have been my approach that put an end to their conference. One of them I could hear glided away; for I now found the reeds were in some places broken, and in others might easily have been removed by the hand; but it was too dark for me to discover who the other person was whom I had for a moment heard conversing with the hermit of the cave, for so I called him, not knowing indeed to what description of being he could be said to belong.

"My movements were not so silent but that my host heard me. He appeared, on opening the door, to be astonished to find me able to move, and gently remonstrated with me on my imprudence. I answered him, by saying, that I was ashamed of having suffered personal considerations to detain me a trespasser on his humanity, while a dearer interest, the welfare of one for whose preservation my life would be readily relinquished, was probably in a situation which I could not think of without being driven to phrensy.[120] While I spoke, my agitation became so great, that my new friend, believing I should fall led me to a seat on one side of a table, while he sat down opposite, and in a firm yet soothing voice bade me remember, that to suffer was the lot of man, and that superiority of mind was shown only by suffering well. There was a lamp on the table between us; his hat was off, and I now saw a countenance where the hand of misery had deepened the traces marked by the lapse of almost sixty years. Yet it was one of those faces on which the eye loves to dwell, while it gives confidence to the heart. There was, however, a peculiar though transient wildness in his eyes, while he thus spoke: 'I have been,' said he, 'so wretched a wanderer in this world, that, quitting it as far as was in my power, I no longer consider myself as one of its inhabitants. Yet here, even here, amid the mountainous forests of a tropical island, does the voice of misery reach me. Hither am I pursued by the sight of sufferings and of sorrows which man brings on man!'

"He paused, and seemed to await a reply—I was in no condition to give one.

"'Misery,' continued he, 'is, indeed, the certain concomitant of slavery. It follows with undeviating step the tyrant who imposes, and the slave who endures the fetters. Are you of this country, Sir? or are you one of the military sent from England?'

"A brief yet incoherent account of what and who I was followed. I added the short story of my separation from Henrietta, and the hopes of saving her from a detested marriage, with which, not knowing much of the situation of the country, and totally careless of any consequences to myself by travelling through it, I had hurried away from one of Mr. Maynard's houses to the other. The friendly recluse heard me with surprise, which was, I thought, accompanied by an expression of countenance very different from that of concern. He seemed to be considering of his answer, when the conchs[121] and gomgoms[122] of the Maroons suddenly broke the silence of the night, and appeared to be very near the habitation of my protector. He changed countenance; but immediately recovering himself, he put out the lamp, and said in a low voice: 'These people, though in a state of warfare against

Europeans, are not inimical to me. They are used to see me, and know that I take no part against them; but it will not be safe for you to be seen. Retire, therefore, to your mattress, remain quite still, that, should any of them enter this place as they sometimes do, I may appear to be as usual—alone.' I hesitated not to do as he bade me; yet I own I was very far from being at my ease, when I heard three or four hoarse voices salute my host in a language of which I understood nothing but two or three words, and those hostile, borrowed from the negro English of the colonies.[123] My friend answered them in the same jargon in a mild and manly tone; and offered them, as I imagined, some kind of spirits, which they accepted. Some of them laughed immoderately, shouted, and clapped their hands, appearing to describe some recent success, and sounding to my ears like expressions of barbarous triumph. Perhaps they were relating their having possessed themselves of the daughter of Maynard, after having ravaged his estate. I found this apprehension so terrible, that I could not long have remained tranquil; I think, had no consideration for my kind protector interposed, I should have rushed out to have met death, rather than sustain the horrors of my imagination in regard to Henrietta. But it fortunately happened that their arrangements for the night did not allow them to stay long; they apparently went away, and silence followed their wild clamour, save that drums, as of other parties about to assemble at some place of general rendezvous, were remotely heard about the mountains. Within the strange abode that sheltered me, all soon became profoundly quiet, so much so, that I began to doubt whether the inhabitant of the cave had not himself been compelled to accompany them, or, thinking he might mitigate their ferocity, had voluntarily been of their party. My sensations were in the mean time the most uneasy and insupportable. Nature was absolutely exhausted by fatigue and loss of blood, yet it was impossible for me to take the repose even of a moment. Again I listened, and then, impatient of the uncertainty and suspense, again ventured to creep on my hands and knees to the door; and by attentively laying my ear to the vacancies in the reeds, I thought myself sure that the master of the habitation was no longer in that part of it where we had conversed; he was then, perhaps, retired to some other part where he slept (for I had observed another passage worked in the rock, and secured by another door of reeds or canes); yet it seemed inconsistent with his humane and manly bearing that he should leave me, after such an alarm, to pass a sleepless night in uneasy conjectures. The longer this uncertainty continued, the more I became persuaded that for some reason or other my friend had found it expedient to leave his hermitage with his late unwelcome visitors; and in that conviction I ventured softly to open the door which he had shut upon me. There was no other light than what the brightness of the night afforded, through a sort of circular opening above the door; but in these regions, and at this season, the innumerable stars, and a sky without a cloud or a vapour, afford such clear vision, that I had no difficulty in immediately assuring myself my new found friend was not there. It was certain then that he was either gone with the Maroons, or had retired to sleep; and it was very material to me to know to which of these circumstances his absence was owing. I ventured, therefore, to try whether the door which I saw at the end of the cavern would yield to my efforts. The fastening was a simple latch lifted by a string, such as is frequent in cottages in remote parts of England. This door, which I shut after me, did not, as I expected, lead immediately to another excavation of the rock, but opened to a narrow passage, just wide enough for one person to thread it at a time. I passed *a pas de loup*[124] along it for about thirty yards. It then seemed to narrow; but I was now in total darkness, and the hand alone of that arm I could use was my guide. I came at length to what appeared to be rock, and to bar my further progress. I was, after some moments of unsuccessful examination, about to return, when on one side, within a cavity, I felt that there were reeds such as the outer doors were composed of. This then probably led to the place I was searching for. I found a string such as opened the other doors, and, pulling it, entered a larger apartment than I had yet seen. The light came from the roof, which was glazed like sky-lights in England; but the creeping plants and the high trees above it a little obscured the window. I could notwithstanding discern that on one side of the room lay on a mattress a human figure. I took it for granted it was my friend, who, overcome with fatigue, had retired without thinking it necessary to assure me of safety, which, on the departure of the Maroons, he might not suppose I should doubt. Almost ashamed therefore of having doubted, and unwilling to intrude upon his repose, I was about to withdraw as silently as I had entered, when I stepped on something I knew not what, and I was afraid I might make a noise if I entangled myself among it. I stooped therefore to remove it, and to my astonishment found in my hand the small satin slipper of a woman!

"Almost involuntarily I looked on the figure I had till then taken for my sleeping friend. The moon was now high enough to afford more light than had been lent by the stars that preceded her; and earnestly fixing my eyes on the face of the person extended before me, it seemed—(gracious Heaven! was I not still in a dream?)—it seemed to be the face of Henrietta—of my own long-loved, lost Henrietta!

"I uttered an exclamation of astonishment, and the uneasy slumber of her I saw fled instantly. Those eyes whose every look was imprinted on my heart were unclosed with an expression of dread and amazement. They beheld, as Henrietta supposed, a stranger, even whose colour, as I bent

my head over her, she could not by that light distinguish. She
uttered a faint shriek; and terror so immediately possessed
her, that she became incapable of hearing what I, kneeling
on the ground beside her, attempted to utter. I knew it was
Henrietta; but I was in too great confusion of mind to be
able to ask, had she been in a condition to reply, how she
came there, or what had befallen her. I will not attempt,
therefore, to describe the sensations of that moment, or the
incoherency of our first attempts to relate to each other the
history of a period I trembled to inquire into, and believed
Henrietta would never live to relate; for, no sooner was she
assured it was Denbigh who spoke to her, than she appeared
to be so overwhelmed by a variety of afflicting emotions, as
to lose the power, if not of utterance, of clearly expressing
her thoughts; and she continued to press my hand, and in a
low and tremulous voice to implore me to forgive her. This
scene was interrupted by a noise sullenly echoing along the
narrow passage that led to the outward cavern. I felt a degree
of fear which throughout my life I had never been sensible of
before. The Maroons, with whom I now supposed my host
was an associate, were, I concluded, returned, and Henrietta
was to be their victim. Of my own life, which would have
been undoubtedly the first sacrifice, I thought not: nor do I
claim any applause on that account, either for fortitude or
courage. Absorbed in one idea, the danger of the creature
dearest to me on earth, my own preservation, though it has
been called the first law of nature, was not even recollected;
and whoever has fondly loved an amiable object by whom
he was beloved, will easily understand how little every other
consideration influenced me. Having rapidly conceived the
idea that the persons I dreaded were without, and that by
opposing them I might afford Henrietta the means of escape,
or at least die without witnessing her second captivity and
disgrace, I ran, more than half frantic, through the narrow

pass, and, unarmed and weakened as I was by my recent wounds, rushed into the outward excavation, where I saw its inhabitant alone, having apparently just lit his lamp; and with a countenance of astonishment, he inquired where I had been, and why I was thus disordered?

"Amazed and ashamed, for his questions immediately restored to me some power of reflection, I said some incoherent words—I hardly know what. 'I understand you,' said he: 'impatient at my absence, you have sought me, and, in doing so, have met another. Is it not so?'

"'It is,' I replied; 'and that other—'

"'Is Henrietta,' interrupted he; 'is that Henrietta whom you love, and have so ardently sought. I knew it from the moment you related to me your name and your situation.'

"I gasped for breath: the violent agitation of my spirits prevented my speaking. I dared not ask, 'How came Henrietta here?—What has she suffered?—In whose power is she now?'

"My host, however, entered at once into my meaning. 'Be more calm,' said he; 'I know all the terrors that possess you; for I also have loved, and have been wretched, more I trust than you ever will be. You have unexpectedly found her whom you sought; but in a moment she may be torn from you for ever!——You must know, from what has just passed, that this place is not secure. Do not, therefore, let us waste the time in wondering or lamenting. Even while we speak, danger may be impending which would overwhelm us all.' He spoke this in a low and slow manner, listened at intervals, and extinguished his lamp. 'Speak very low,' said he, 'or rather retire for the moment without speaking. I will go to Henrietta, and appease the fear she must be in.' He arose, and left me in darkness, while those doubts and suspicions returned which I had been a moment before ashamed of having felt. I dared not, however, move; for not my life only, but that of a being infinitely dearer to me seemed to be in the hands of him, into whose power chance had so unaccountably thrown us both. What could he be? By what strange chance or choice did he live in such a place, where he must either be in perpetual apprehension from the revolted Negroes and insurgent Maroons, or in league with them? Surely, notwithstanding the mild candour of his appearance and his apparent humanity, this mysterious being must be a criminal, who shelters himself from justice by means of the hostile savages among whom he dwells! Henrietta! her name seemed familiar to him—He acknowledged that her story was known to him—He could have heard it only from herself—She must then have been some time with him!—I relate these questions with more precision than I at that time made them. They passed confusedly through my mind, and I now determined to interrupt the conference which the stranger was holding with Henrietta—now trembled at my own rashness, and said, I *may* destroy her by it; but if she is already lost to me, I cannot retrieve my own destiny. It is so impossible to convey to another the sensations which at that moment agitated my heart, that I will not attempt it. They were vague, tumultuous, confused, and painful beyond any that I had hitherto experienced.

"Breathless, undecided how to act, and almost doubting my senses, I listened, and, trembling, approached the entrance to the inward cavern. I fancied I heard the sobs and deep sighs of Henrietta. It was enough; all my attempts at prudence and patience were forgotten; and once more I penetrated the recess, and saw, for there was now a light, the supposed hermit kneeling beside the mistress of my heart, apparently expostulating with her. She sat on her mattress weeping, and, as it seemed, expostulating also. The noise I made, however, on entering, made them both look towards the door. The stranger continued to hold one hand, while Henrietta, extending the other towards me, faintly uttered my name. Perhaps no human being was ever shaken by a more extraordinary variety of violent emotions than at that moment assailed me. Henrietta, however, appeared to be agitated by other passions than those with which I was distracted. Eagerness to clear up a circumstance which she saw I misunderstood, fear of the consequences of my head-long impetuosity, and doubts of her own power of explana-tion, combined to deprive her of the little strength she had left. Perhaps some recollection of the coolness there was on my part when we last parted, might add to her uneasi-ness and embarrassment. 'Denbigh!' said she in a faint voice, 'Denbigh! I beseech you to hear me, to hear this our good friend, who has been in the hands of Providence the means of saving me from the most terrible evils. Denbigh, my best, my first friend! help me to thank him. I am poor, even in thanks!' By this time the hermit had arisen, and said 'Henrietta! if Mr. Denbigh will command himself and hear reason, I shall be able to explain to his satisfaction all that now appears extraordinary. If he will *not*—but I do not sup-pose it'——I own, that almost for the first time in my life I was over-awed by a consciousness of superior reason and rec-titude. My breath was oppressed; my head became confused, from the contrariety of emotions that assailed me.

"My benevolent friend, into whose bosom I doubted whether I ought not to have plunged a poniard, took advan-tage of my indecision. 'It is no time,' said he, 'now for explanation: your life, and, what I have no doubt is dearer to you, the life and honour of Henrietta, saved once almost by miracle, depend on our instant resolution. I dare not let either of you remain here two hours longer. Let it not be said, that a delicate woman can, in a case of necessity, exert the virtues of fortitude and patience, to which you, Denbigh, are unequal: but I persuade myself that you will, each for the sake of the other, forget every thing but the necessity of

prompt resolution and execution.'—'What must I do?' cried
Henrietta, making an effort to rise: 'what is there I will not
try to do, when you my benefactor direct me?'

'"We must hasten from hence,' said the recluse, 'instantly.
I have now for three days baffled the suspicions which I think
I plainly perceive are entertained by the Maroons and their
adherents, as to my having an inmate here. It was to obviate
those suspicions that I to-night accompanied them nearly to
the foot of the mountains. They are gone on an expedition
in which it is highly probable they may be successful. It is
equally probable that, intoxicated with spirits, and rendered
careless of every consideration by success, they may return,
and, even if their doubts are not renewed, demand of me
refreshment and repose. I can neither evade nor deny their
request, and a discovery must inevitably ensue.'

'"Let us go,' cried Henrietta, exerting as it seemed all her
strength. 'Let us not, I implore you, lose a moment.' She arose
and approached me. 'Denbigh!' said she, 'is it really Denbigh
I see, or a phantom sent to mock my misery? Will you then
abandon me?'—'Never,' answered I, 'though I believe myself
every way the most wretched of human beings!'—'Is this a
time,' exclaimed our host with some degree of indignation,
'to indulge lamentation, or torment oneself with conjectures?
While you hesitate, Sir, we are lost! I say we; because my own
safety is hazarded by the share I have had in rescuing this dear
unhappy girl from the most hideous evils. Yet I name not that
as a motive to hasten you, for I set not my life at the value of
a straw. I seem again to be thrown among my species, only
to be convinced anew of their worthlessness.'—'Well, Sir,'
interrupted I, 'what am I to do? I no more wish to waste time
in needless words than you do.' Henrietta was now wrapped
in a sort of capot,[125] and prepared to go. Our host put away
every vestige of any one having been with him in his hermitage; lit a candle in a dark lantern;[126] and having insisted on

our swallowing each a glass of rum, he took Henrietta's arm within his, and, bidding her be of good courage, desired me to follow him, and we left the hermitage.

"Instead of taking the most obvious of the narrow paths that led from it, he struck into one hardly perceptible, which went almost perpendicularly down the woody declivity, where the trunks of pimento[127] and mahogany trees were not so thick as their boughs were shadowy and extensive. We walked in profound silence, each occasionally assisting Henrietta, who could only slowly make her way along so steep and rugged a path; I was near our conductor, and plainly perceived that he was extremely agitated, and could hardly conceal his apprehension; when Henrietta suddenly uttered a faint shriek, and clung to us both with every mark of extreme terror. It was the scintillation of the fire-flies that alarmed her, as they now glittered and were now lost among the trees; and though she had seen them before, they seemed to her terrified imagination to be the lights of her pursuers. Our march was fatiguing and tedious. I saw Henrietta ready to sink; and though we between us rather carried than led her, I doubted whether it would be possible for her to proceed. Sometimes we were compelled to let her rest for some moments, each of us supporting her; and each appeared to avoid speaking to the other, yet to be equally interested in her safety, and to attend with equal solicitude to her faintly whispered answers to our anxious inquiries. In one of these pauses we heard the Gombay sullenly and slow in single measured strokes, and apparently not very far off. The moment was terrible; our conductor tremblingly urged us to hasten on, and fear again conquered the sense of fatigue in my unfortunate Henrietta.

"I would have inquired whither our mysterious guide was conducting us? but as I had no power to change whatever resolution he had taken, I might have done harm, where to do good was beyond my power. Again we resumed our march; the way became rather easier; and our friend endeavoured to raise the failing courage of poor Henrietta, by assuring her the greatest difficulty was conquered, and that we were not far from a place of safety.

"Day, however, broke in all its splendour, just as we quitted the thickest shade of the trees, and emerged into a valley, lovely as fabled paradise. Shadocks, limes, and wild oranges,[128] perfumed the air, and the yellow star-like blossoms of the graceful tamarind[129] enriched the summits of its long flexible boughs. Wretchedness like mine has no eye for beauty. I saw the Eden around me illuminated by the bright rays of morning only with dread, lest the rapid stream that hurried through this recess, and the wild fruits with which it abounded, should have tempted those to frequent it whom it must be death to us to meet.

"But our conductor seemed not to feel the same apprehensions. 'It is now,' said he, 'that my fears abate; the people we have reason to dread are probably retired to their fastnesses in the caverns of the forest, and I trust we shall escape them. While we were yet among the woods I extremely apprehended meeting either parties of them, or single stragglers silently creeping along these obscure paths to reach their principal rendezvous in the mountains. Come then, my friends, within a mile is a place of security.' Henrietta thus encouraged renewed her exertions, and after walking another hour we approached a small neat house, situated in the midst of a cotton plantation. Our conductor bade us wait a moment without; he returned almost immediately, and introduced us to a middle-aged decent-looking woman, who seemed by her manner to be a dependent on our strange acquaintance. He recommended Henrietta to her immediate care; she was indeed so overcome by fatigue and fear, that she could not much longer have supported herself. She consented therefore, at our joint entreaties, to withdraw. When she was gone, my yet nameless companion, whom I could hardly now consider otherwise than my friend, said, 'The gentlewoman of this house is the widow of one of my overseers. She has some obligations to me; she is grateful; and if the few negroes about her are faithful, or, if they are otherwise, but can be kept in ignorance of Henrietta being in the house, her perils, and I trust yours, will be at an end.'

"This speech, by making me suppose the stranger was himself a planter of the island, redoubled my astonishment at all I had observed. He guessed at my thoughts: 'I see,' said he, 'that I excite your curiosity; this is not a place nor a time to gratify it. It is necessary for me to return as expeditiously as I can to my hermitage: for you, repose, and some attention to your wounds, are, I am persuaded, still more necessary. But you will not, I imagine, thank me for my care, if a proposal to separate you from Henrietta be annexed to it.'

"I interrupted him. 'No, Sir, I will not quit the spot where she is, let the consequence be what it may. All the wretchedness we have suffered has been owing to our separation. Disgraced, undone, as perhaps she is, I will now stay near her till——My fate at least will soon be decided, after hers is known.' The recluse then left me with an air of compassion; he said he would give directions for my accommodation, and that I should see him again in a few days.

"The good woman of the house soon came to me herself, and brought with her a surgeon who usually attended her people. He applied remedies to my wounds, which were by this time in a very uneasy state, though I had for the last few hours been quite unconscious of them. He recommended quiet; and I suffered myself to be led to a small upper room, where I consented to attempt taking some repose, on the assurance that Henrietta was much recovered, and, being convinced of her present safety and of mine, that she had fallen into a profound sleep. I now understood that it would be adviseable to conceal my being in the house from every one but an old mulatto woman, on whom my hostess could depend, and who was to bring me food. I endeavoured then to calm my over wearied spirits; but it was impossible. Every circumstance, from my first encounter with the Maroons to my present situation, appeared like the dream of a fevered imagination. If fatigue overcame the tumult of my spirits, the respite was only momentary. I started from this transient forgetfulness, and my bewildered senses awake only to scenes of horror, represented Henrietta in new perils, and I was flying to rescue her or perish in the attempt. Not, however, to play the egotist, and dwell too long on my own feelings and sufferings, I hasten to the fortunate period when my friend and protector re-appeared. I had been persuaded not to see Henrietta, but not till I was satisfied of her safety by a note written in her own hand, in which she conjured me to follow implicitly the directions of our host of the hermitage; 'who has,' said she, 'been under Providence the means of saving your Henrietta from the most deplorable evils, and who is still I am convinced occupied in securing our safety.'

"Henrietta did not then tell me that her fears of her father returned the moment others of a yet more hideous description subsided. From both the one and the other, however, she was in a great degree relieved by the appearance of a strong military escort from St. Jago de la Vega; the commanding officer of which presented to each of us a few words written by our excellent friend, in which he informed us he had sent a carriage for our conveyance to the protection of the Governor, and such a force as would preclude the hazards that might otherwise have made our journey unsafe or uneasy. Once more I mistrusted my senses when I found myself seated by the side of Henrietta. Yet in her altered countenance and tremulous tones there was but too

much evidence of the reality of her sufferings; and the cruel
fears of the past that had so distracted me, now recurred in
despite of my reason; nor, whatever effort I made, was I able
to conceal from the object of them, the variety of apprehensions that tormented me. But when Henrietta understood
me she could only say, 'Denbigh! I have suffered a great deal;
more perhaps, yes, surely more, than even my folly and my
mistrust of you deserved. But if I live, it will be to prove to
you the sincerity of my repentance: and Denbigh surely will
not suppose she could wish to live, if the person of his poor
Henrietta was become an object of abhorrence to him. Nor
would she have survived even till now the disgrace which
might have befallen her.' Relieved by this declaration, and
shocked to have given rise to such oppressive and distressing feelings as I saw agitated the bosom of my beloved girl,
I commanded myself during the rest of our journey, and we
arrived in safety at the seat of government. Henrietta was
received into the house of a gentleman, to whose wife our
mysterious friend had recommended her; and one of my
own former acquaintance waited our arrival, to conduct me
to apartments he had prepared for me in his own house.

"My eagerness for information could now no longer be
restrained. I found that one of Mr. Maynard's plantations had
been destroyed by the Maroons, (to whom he was particularly
obnoxious,) joined by some of his own runaway-negroes;
that, urged to more than his usual extravagance of passion by
this outrage, he had indulged his vindictive temper in great
and unjustifiable severities towards the people upon all his
estates; severities which served only to irritate the minds even
of those who had till then most faithfully adhered to him. At
length the insurrection suddenly spread to the northern plantation, whither Mr. Maynard was returning to celebrate the
compulsatory marriage of his daughter. He heard what had
happened, some miles before he approached it, and hastened

to a small encampment of British troops which had been stationed at the foot of the mountains, waiting a reinforcement before they made a general attack on the strong holds of the enemy. Having prevailed on the commanding officer of this detachment to accompany him with his soldiers, they approached the plantation, where a scene of devastation and horror awaited them. The Maroons, who had not yet retired, met them undauntedly, and repulsed them with considerable loss. Mr. May[nard . . . .]* His intended son-in-law waiting no longer fled back with the intelligence. The military, after considerable loss, returned to their camp; and of the fate of Henrietta as nothing was known certainly, the most terrible conjectures were formed; and she had been reckoned among the most lamented victims of this disastrous warfare, till intelligence had been received of her being at the widow's house, and an escort demanded to conduct her from thence in safety.

"I found that he who informed me of these particulars knew no more. He was neither acquainted with the circumstances of Henrietta's danger, nor by whose means she had escaped it. And when I reflected that she must have been two or three days in the power of the enraged and unrestrained savages, from whom the mountain recluse had, I knew not how, rescued her, my horrible apprehensions returned, and it was with difficulty I concealed from the friend with whom I was conversing, the thoughts that shook me with dread.

"The following day, however, I received a note from my mysterious friend, desiring to see me at a place he named not far from the town. 'I cannot,' said he in this short letter, 'mingle in society without so much pain, that I know you will not hesitate to meet me here, unless the state of your health should make it inconvenient to you.' I was too desirous of seeing him to suffer any personal considerations to

---

* EDITOR'S NOTE: Due to a page break error in the 1800 edition, part of Smith's text has been lost here.

prevent me. I found the recluse in a small habitation near a pen, where the people appeared to treat him with great respect. His aspect was calm and benign: I imagined that his looks were those of compassion, and that he was considering how to palliate the blow I should receive when the whole of poor Henrietta's disastrous story should be known to me. Determined to attempt bearing my miseries like a man, I stifled the anguish of my heart, and endeavoured to oppose with all my fortitude the effect of the certainty of evils worse even than death. I observed a profound silence. My singular acquaintance thus began:

"'I have perceived, ever since your interview with Henrietta, (which I wished, had it been possible, to avert, till I could have prepared you for it,) that you have considered me as a strange and equivocal being, whose intentions in regard to you both were suspicious. She knows nothing more of me than that I am her friend, and have fortunately proved her deliverer from a situation of extreme peril. Had she been merely what I, when I first saw her, believed, an unhappy young woman, I should not with less zeal have endeavoured to serve and protect her; but judge, Mr. Denbigh, of the additional pleasure I felt, when I found I had from such distresses as had environed Henrietta rescued my niece, and almost the only relation I have in the world.'

"I expressed astonishment and satisfaction. My friend thus proceeded:

"'My history is strange. To the young, to the unexperienced, it will appear almost incredible. I will briefly relate it; because, though I have subdued the first and most acute feelings that once accompanied retrospection, I am not yet enough master of myself to enter without pain into the history of my hopes, my disappointments, and the errors that were the consequence of having too much indulged the one, and of being too easily depressed by the other.

""'Though I was a younger brother, I inherited a fortune
that many elder brothers might have coveted. I was, like
other children of fortune from the colonies, sent to England
for what is called education, at so early an age that I recollect little of my childhood; except that, from my having
two young negroes to wait on my caprices, and to enact my
horses, my dogs, or any thing else I required, to indulge my
indolence, and submit to my ill-humour, I really imagined
myself to be a creature of a superior order, whom it was the
business of all other creatures to venerate and to obey. My
reception at the merchant's to whom I was (with my elder
brother, sundry hogsheads[130] of sugar, bags of cotton, and
planks of mahogany) consigned, was such as made me suspect I was not a person of such immense importance in the
great city of London, as I had fancied myself on the plantations of my father in Jamaica. I was equipped with English
habiliments; a sum which I thought a very pitiful one put
into my pocket, and forthwith dispatched with my brother,
under the care of one of my guardian's clerks, to Harrow
School.[131] As I could hardly read English, it was utterly impossible I could learn the rudiments of Latin;[132] as I could not
write my own name, it was still more impossible that I could
execute the tasks, simple as they were, that were assigned to
me. But as my father was a rich Jamaica planter, there was no
doubt of my bills being paid, however extravagant; and my
deficiencies were therefore overlooked, while I was thrust
on from form to form; sometimes flogged, and sometimes
paying other boys to do my task, and save me from flogging.
Out of school, my life was far enough from being pleasant.
My elder brother, who was heir to a fortune thrice as large
as that which in right of my mother (whose name I was to
take,[133]) was, on coming of age, to belong to me, had been
used to exercise the caprices of a very bad temper on half a
dozen African boys and girls. He now found no one willing

to submit to any whim which he chose to entertain: but, if he was impertinent he was *ridiculed*, and if he was insolent he was *beat*. Nay, so far was he from being able to command, that he was compelled to obey; and, from being a tyrant, found himself reduced to be a slave: for, by dint of thumps and blows from boys so much bigger than himself that resistance would have been in vain, he, who had from his earliest recollection been so triumphantly master of every one about him, was now under the hard necessity of becoming shag, fag, skip,[134] or whatever the boys in the higher forms chose to insist upon. This, however bad it was for him, was a great deal worse for me; for, in proportion as his chagrin increased, so did his desire to revenge himself upon somebody else; and unhappily no other person was disposed to bear it, and certainly not one was compelled to bear it, but me. On me therefore fell the weight of his displeasure; and as he was a great deal bigger, and three years older than I was, I assure you my personal sufferings were not inconsiderable. At length my frequent black eyes, bruises which prevented my writing or even going into school, and violent bleeding at the nose, excited inquiry; and as I had no inclination to disguise the truth, and other boys were willing enough to tell it, for they all detested my brother, I was at the recommendation of the master removed to another school; but to this circumstance (for we are the creatures of accident) I perhaps owe that abhorrence of tyranny and injustice which I have invariably felt through the rest of my life.

"'My condition was ameliorated by my removal, and no longer fearing for my *life*, I began to find that I had a *soul*; at least that I had feelings and affections worthy of aspiring to rank above the ferocious animals to whom I had hitherto been subjected. I was a tall lad of almost eighteen, and had been about four years at a private school, when orders came from my father to send me to Cambridge. Thither therefore

I went, extremely to my own satisfaction, yet but little to my classical improvement; for the disadvantages under which I had begun to learn, always adhered to me in some degree, and impeded my progress. My brother was at Oxford; but that we might never meet, and our enmity or rather his tyranny be renewed, I did not go at the vacation to my guardian's, but was received at his desire by a sister of his, a widow of moderate fortune, who, besides a son, who was one of my friends at Cambridge, had three daughters. The arrangement was natural enough, circumstanced as I was, but on their parts it was not altogether without design.

"'The three young ladies were all pretty. The youngest, who was not above fifteen, I thought eminently beautiful. Simple, and soft in her manners, very fair, very blooming; well made, though not tall; with fine flaxen hair waving luxuriantly over her face; beautiful teeth, and lips of coral: these were charms more than enough to fascinate such a boy as I was, who had my head full of romance, and a heart which found itself disposed to love any human creature who would invite its confidence and return its affection. As my pecuniary value was well understood, I met with no discouragement; but after my affections were not only supposed to be irrevocably, but really were madly fixed on Miss Fanny, I was told by her mama, that our acquaintance must be suspended till my father was written to, and his consent obtained to our union. I was not of an age or of a disposition to hear reason, had reason been presented to me. I knew that on my majority,[135] to which I wanted hardly three years, I should be independent, and possess an ample fortune, and already I determined to be free. It was not difficult for me to obtain present money, as my prospects of fortune were generally known. I had no great difficulty in prevailing on my lovely Fanny to elope with me. We were married at Gretna Green,[136] and returned to her mother, where I had not much doubt of the pardon that awaited us.

"'The year of our union was undoubtedly the happiest of my life. I had a son born within that time, whom I considered with a degree of infantine fondness; and before the intelligence of my marriage could reach Jamaica, my father died: so that I not only escaped any remonstrance, but found myself entitled to a very considerable addition to my fortune. We resided at one of the pleasantest villages in the neighbourhood of London. Fanny, though persuaded by her mother that she was unable from her extreme youth and delicacy to suckle her infant,[137] was yet a most tender and attentive mother, and passed almost all her time in the nursery, where her cares and pleasures were increased by the birth of a daughter. My felicity was too perfect to last.

"'One of my wife's sisters was about this time married to a very opulent merchant in the city. Successful commerce had long since set him above the necessity of residing near the spot where it was carried on, and his bride became the mistress of a most splendid house in one of the fashionable streets near St. James's.[138] The mother, a very vain and weak woman, whose moderate circumstances had hitherto restrained her expences, now indulged herself in every kind of dissipation, and encouraged it in her daughters. It was not therefore surprising that the infection reached my wife, who was yet hardly eighteen, and that before such examples the soberer habits of domestic life gave way. She was often invited to stay several nights together in town, either with her mother or her sister, that she might enjoy the amusements of London, which till now she had hardly ever been present at: they had therefore all the fascination of novelty; and Fanny soon discovered, that the village where we resided, and where her greatest satisfaction had hitherto been found in her children and her garden, was terribly inconvenient, dull, and even vulgar, since no persons of fashion ever lived so near London. Her mother supported her in her attempts to persuade me to quit it, and to take a very elegant house, which happened at that period to be vacant near St. James's. They represented to me, that with my fortune the world would reflect upon me if I did not live as other people did in a certain style: and the elder lady, forgetting how lately she had rejoiced at so well disposing of a young woman whose beauty was her only portion, told me, with some asperity, that *her* daughter was not to be considered as one who was to be a mere domestic animal; that she was calculated to shine in the *genteelest* circles; and it was a matter of surprise to all my friends, but still more to hers, that I had never appeared to feel the pride which must surely be mine, when so fine a creature as my Fanny could be exhibited as my wife.

"'When first this style of talking was adopted, it was in hints and innuendoes. The good lady my mother-in-law rather talked at me than to me; and the rest of the family conveyed their sentiments still more in the *mezza voce*.[139] By degrees, however, as I appeared determined not to understand them, they spoke plainer, and returned so unremittingly to the charge, that my patience, if not my resolution, began to be shaken. Yet I could have resisted all these importunities had I not seen the cruel effect the pernicious doctrines they enforced had on my wife; that cheerfulness and even infantine gaiety which used to charm me, especially when I saw her playfulness and spirit dedicated to the health and amusement of my children, was now quite lost, and instead of it I was repulsed by silence, sullenness, and tears. Accustomed to domestic life at a period when most young men yield to the wildest excesses, I felt the whole system of rational happiness sinking for ever. I saw my lovely little ones neglected, and their mother estranged from them and from me. I might certainly have continued to live where I did, and have compelled my wife to remain with me; but I could not recall that genuine and unadulterated taste for the duties of a wife and a mother, which had so barbarously been destroyed by those who ought to have honoured and cherished it. I feared I must thenceforth be miserable myself: but I could not determine to see my Fanny avowedly so, when she had been taught to think, however falsely, that it was in my power to make her happy. There was besides a hope that, satiated with what she now supposed pleasures, and finding the empty adulation of a crowd but a poor substitute for the consciousness of doing right, for the delights of maternal love, and the affection of a husband who adored her, she would soon return disgusted by the fallacy of her new pursuit, and be restored to herself and to me.

"'I consented therefore, alas! with what foreboding reluctance, to the plan so assiduously recommended. My family removed to a splendid house in one of the most fashionable streets in the most fashionable part of London. My servants were more numerous, more superbly clad, and more expensively supported and paid. I had three carriages, instead of a coach and garden chair,[140] in which I used to drive my wife about in the green and pleasant lanes around our former residence; and my house, most magnificently furnished, under the immediate direction of my mother-in-law, was soon so constantly filled with company, that I was no longer at home in it; and had it not been that I had insisted on having one of the best bed-chambers converted into a nursery, and reserved one of the back parlours for a library, I should not have had a room in it where I could have found even the shadow of the pleasure and the repose I had lost. My wife was never at home unless on those days when she saw company, or had dining parties, at which I was expected to sit at the bottom of the table, to entertain men with whom I had no feelings or sentiments in common. Officers of the guards, with an infinity of vanity and vice, but a "plentiful lack of wit;"[141] fine feathered and helmeted heroes of the cavalry, (in which department of the army my wife had a brother,) who, out of the mere routine of their profession, had fewer ideas than I had ever believed any of God's creatures could be furnished with; and men of yet another description, members of parliament, who had obtained seats,[142] every body wondered how, for purposes that nobody could be ignorant of—their associates, whose whole fortunes consisted in their birth, their fashionable manners, and their skill at play. A considerable number of very beautiful women were of these assemblies. Fanny had very early discovered that her face and form might fearlessly challenge every comparison, and she appeared to delight in collecting around her those who, when she was not present, were looked upon as the first in beauty and elegance.

"'I now never met her but fatigued with the vigils of the preceding night, or in haste lest she should miss some delightful party on that which was approaching. Our meals, our chamber, were no longer in common. Her mother, her sisters, or her brother, who was so good, uninvited by me, whenever he was in London, to make my house his home, were, one or other of them, always with her, even at those hours that the most dissipated give to domestic society. I attempted to check all this by persuasion. I was not listened to. I represented how inadequate my fortune, affluent as it was, must prove to such a scale of expence as our present establishment was extended to. I was reproached with parsimony. I besought the mother of this young and thoughtless victim of vanity to consider to what she was dooming her innocent grandchildren; but she was so weak, that my remonstrances produced anger and resentment instead of conviction and reform. The wild career of folly was continued, till the arrival of summer exchanged the scene on which it was acted; and the still patient and enduring husband was only the first of her suite, with whom "the beautiful Mrs. Maynard" appeared at a summer resort, where health is the pretence for collecting numbers who continue with very little variation the same life they have led in London during the winter.

"'It may appear strange that a man of my then age, for you recollect how young I married, since which scarce four years had passed, should not have been drawn into the vortex, while he tried to snatch from it his murdered happiness. But so cruelly had the fatal change in my wife's temper and manners lacerated my heart, that I felt a degree of abhorrence toward every one who had contributed to it; and though I sometimes constrained myself to appear at my table with calmness, my resolution carried me no farther; while I have more than once accidentally caught from the men with whom that table was surrounded, half and bye words[143] uttered to each other, which I doubted not were terms of ridicule. I was represented as morose, covetous, jealous, and weak; and I perceived that, more and more estranged from her duty and from me, my wife considered me rather as her jailor than her husband. My sister, the same whom you knew, and to whom Henrietta owes her education, at that time returned from the Continent, where her health and her inclination often induced her to reside for two or three years. She was a woman of sense and spirit, and could not imagine how it was that I possessed so little of either, as to submit to the discreditable if not dishonourable conduct of a woman, who was she thought bound to shew me both gratitude and affection. She undertook to talk to her; but the effect of her remonstrance was as I foresaw it would be. My wife heard her with impatience, and answered her with asperity. The consequence was, that my sister renounced me and my house for ever; and I was thus deprived of the only friend I had left, to whom I could speak of the misery of my heart. Had I not still loved my unhappy Fanny, and had not my children been most dear to me, I could have thrown her off for ever, though I believed her personal fidelity was yet without a stain. But whenever I thought of separating the mother from the children, though she seemed to have forgotten she was their mother, I trembled lest I should be destroying for ever the fabric of happiness with which I had so delighted my eyes and flattered my imagination, and which I fondly hoped was yet to be repaired. For a little while longer, therefore, I resisted the sharp reproaches and exhortations of my sister; who, though she no longer saw, often wrote to me. I checked the natural impetuosity of my temper, which, however patient it may hitherto have appeared to you, is by no means unlike that disposition usually and with justice attributed to West Indians;[144] and I tried once more what effect the friendly yet forcible remonstrance of the father and the husband would have on a heart which, beating in so lovely a bosom, I could not, I would not, yet believe was become callous to the sacred claims of nature towards my infants, and of tenderness and gratitude towards their father.

"'It is useless now to conjecture whether the repetition of this experiment would have succeeded; for just at that time an event took place which considerably changed the ground on which it was made. The husband of that sister of my wife's, since whose apparently affluent marriage my scheme of felicity had been destroyed, suddenly became insolvent. The superstructure of his dazzling fortune, raised on a frail and faithless foundation, sunk at once. To avoid prolixity,[145] suffice it to say, that his schemes, which perhaps only himself understood, were calculated either to raise him to princely prosperity, or plunge him into the lowest abyss of ruin; while his giddy thoughtless wife, who never dreamed that she was sporting over a smooth and glittering surface, which a breath might dissolve beneath her, was so suddenly struck with the cruel reverse, that she fell into a state of mind more deplorable than even phrensy itself. Within a few days her husband was in prison;[146] and her children, whom she had sent at a very early age to school, that she might avoid the trouble of taking care of them at home, were conducted by the respective masters and governesses back to a house of which the Sheriff's officers[147] were now in possession; and which all the servants had forsaken, each taking the first thing of value they could appropriate, as the only chance they had of obtaining any remuneration for their services. In this terrible exigence[148] it was to me that the unhappy family turned their eyes for succour. My wife, in all the anguish of repentance, humbled herself at my feet. Her mother who had lately been supported in affluence very much above her former condition of life by her now undone son-in-law, sunk, like other feeble minds, under this shock to her vanity and ambition; while the unhappy man himself conjured me from his prison to shelter his unhappy children, and to visit though he could not ask me to relieve him.

"'Even the bitterest enemy supplicating for mercy can disarm a generous mind of every desire of vengeance. The unfortunate people who thus threw themselves on my compassion, I had long been accustomed to consider as those who had occasioned all my unhappiness; but I now saw them rendered wretched themselves by the conduct that had occasioned my wretchedness; they had been even more their own enemies than mine. I silently forgave their errors, and actively engaged in the business of relieving their misfortunes. Notwithstanding the expences which my wife's late conduct had brought upon me, my fortune had rather increased than diminished; for, though I had for some years lived beyond my income, the money thus sunk had been very lately more than replaced by the legacy of a brother of my mother, who, dying in this island, where he had conceived an unconquerable aversion from my elder brother, left me not only an estate as large as that I before possessed, but a considerable sum of money in the English funds,[149] with plate, jewels, and other personals[150] to a great amount. I thought therefore I could, without injury to my two children, engage in an undertaking which I believed would not only be in itself meritorious, but, by restoring me to the affection of my still adored Fanny, be the means of giving me back the happiness I had lost. I need not enter into the particulars of my proceedings for this purpose. In about two months Mr. Halwyn was released from his confinement. A composition was made with his creditors. He was permitted, as I was become his guarantee, to pursue those branches of commerce in which he had ventured too far, but which might now by perseverance repay the hazard and even the loss he had incurred. I inherited from my uncle an house and well-conditioned estate in Dorsetshire. Thither I now proposed to retire with my family, as well as *that* I had taken under my protection. There was ample room for both, and the mother and sister of my wife, the latter of whom was now in a state that might be called a slow convalescence from melancholy madness, the husband of that sister, and her children, were assembled. Though this increase of my establishment destroyed all my hopes of domestic tranquillity which I had fondly flattered myself I should regain, if my wife could resolve to live for me and her children, and once more taste the simple delights of nature, I submitted without a murmur to postpone a plan of life still dear to my imagination, believing it was only postponed; and that when the affairs of her brother-in-law were settled, which my purse and my time were incessantly occupied to complete—his family being re-established in *their* home, my friendship towards them would so operate on my wife, that I should have nothing to wish in my own.

"'There was a great number of gentlemen's families in the neighbourhood, particularly of West Indians, who of course thought such an accession to their society should

be assiduously cultivated; but my wife, who now appeared
to have no pleasure but mine, left it wholly to me either to
encourage or decline their advances. I candidly told them, my
purpose was to live very much retired, but yet not wholly to
avoid an intercourse of occasional civility. Mrs. Halwyn was
the only one of the family who, when these parties assembled
at my house, never appeared. Mortified pride is oftener than is
generally believed the source of mental derangement; and as
no human being had ever been more ostentatiously elevated
with her situation during the short course of her prosperity,
so none had ever felt more poignantly the reverse in fortune.
Her vain and weak mind could not bear the superiority of
that man who had rescued her and her family from destruction; and I believe, in the morbid malignity of her spirit, she
hated me more for my kindness than she would have done
had I left them all to their destiny. Confined, however, to her
own apartments, I seldom saw her; her husband too was now
very frequently absent on his affairs, of which I received from
time to time the most flattering accounts; and as to the old
lady my mother-in-law, she had in a great degree regained
her spirits. She was once more considered as a person of consequence; her advice was asked, her opinions attended to,
and she not unfrequently enjoyed the delights of a rubber or
a pool[151] with some other dowagers[152] of the neighbourhood,
and the rector of the parish. My whole household therefore
were apparently content through the winter months, which
I had feared would prove rather a severe trial to those who
had so lately lived among the most dissipated scenes of the
metropolis. My wife, if not gay, was tranquil, and the gratitude she seemed to feel for what I had done for her family,
had I hoped and believed awakened all her former affection.
A calamity, however, of another description than those I had
hitherto suffered under overtook me. My lovely little girl,
now in her seventh year, became ill of a fever. She recovered

from the acute disease, but fell into a decline. I hurried with her and her mother to the West of England; and from thence to those parts of Wales, celebrated for the restoration of consumptive patients;[153] but my anxiety, my endeavours, my sleepless nights and days of stifled agony—all were vain. My little angel expired in my arms; and detesting my existence after a misfortune which I believed it impossible to survive, I felt as if whoever did not lament her as I did injured me. Her mother was affected, but I thought not affected enough by an incident which destroyed the most flattering object of those visions of future delight which I had still indulged. Mrs. Maynard did certainly, however, appear deeply dejected; and when we returned together to my Dorsetshire house, her mother, who had remained there, pretended to dread the consequences of her sorrow, reproached me for encouraging it; and hesitated not to say, that, instead of suffering her to dwell on this useless regret, and destroy herself for the loss of *such a child* (that I remembered was her expression), I ought to promote her going into company, and use every means that my fortune put in my power to recover the spirits and preserve the beauty of my wife; a subject on which the old lady always dwelt with particular complacency. I affected not to understand, though I could not be ignorant what this meant. It was to pave the way for a proposal of going to Bath,[154] for which the autumnal season was now approaching. I determined to be miserable at home; and the good lady, who could not yet dispense with, though she could forget my services, was obliged to submit.

"'Just at this point of time Mr. Halwyn returned in great spirits from a long residence in London and other places where his business lay. He had recovered, he told us, very capital sums of money, which he had considered as desperate.[155] His assignees were convinced that, by their giving him a little more time, he should not only be able to pay to all his creditors the utmost of their demands, but be restored to an high degree of affluence. I was glad of his good fortune, but my heart still suffering the pain of paternal regret, was incapable of any pleasure, and I listened (though attentively) coldly to the minute account he seemed fond of giving me of the various means by which his affairs were to be retrieved. His other auditors were less torpid, and the elderly lady in particular was never weary of hearing the praises of his brother—a young man whom he had taken into a share of his business in the height of his prosperous fortune, and who, on the first apprehension of its decline, had gone to America, to Lisbon, Barcelona, and afterwards to France, in hopes of saving the house by collecting many of its debts before its distresses were known. The activity and spirit, the knowledge and perseverance of this young adventurer were the theme of Mr. Halwyn's panegyric; yet from time to time he artfully introduced his obligations to me, without whose generous assistance, he said, all his brother's exertions and his own would have been fruitless. This young man was soon to go again to the Continent, to put the finishing hand to arrangements so fortunately begun. I found it was expected of me to invite him down on a visit to his brother, by whose account any one would have imagined that he equalled at least "the admirable Crichton."[156] I was ill disposed for any additional society; but, unwilling to appear unaccommodating and morose, and not to do every thing where I had done so much, the invitation was given, and my accomplished visitor arrived.

"'His person was undoubtedly a very fine one; his manners such as evinced how much an active mind may acquire by visiting different countries. The elder brother, with great affectation of knowledge and taste, was, it was easy to see, a mere mercantile speculator; but Mr. Frederic Halwyn had so much of the man of fashion, that it was hard to conceive he

had been brought up amid the dull routine of a compting-
house. He seemed to be deeply impressed with a sense of
the obligations his brother owed to me; while to the ladies of
the family, his politeness, the easy gaiety of his conversation,
could not fail to recommend him. He was occasionally with
us for about six weeks. At the end of that time I consented
to accompany him and his brother to London for the purpose of farther settling the affairs of the latter, who was now
able to repay some part of the advance I had made for him;
and, that I might complete the good work I had begun, I met
the parties who expected my receipt for this money, (about
four thousand pounds,) prepared with a deed by which I presented this sum to the wife and children of my creditor,[157]
on condition of its being settled on them; and I gave him at
the same time a full discharge for the rest. I will not repeat
the acknowledgements made by Mr. Halwyn, nor the praises
I received from the persons interested who were present. It
was not to obtain those eulogiums I had acted. I observed
something singular, however, in the manner of Frederic
Halwyn; who, contrary to his usual manner, was confused
and disconcerted, and hastened from the place of meeting
before the business was entirely finished, on pretence of an
engagement with a military friend, who was on the point of
embarking for India. I had some affairs relative to my Jamaica
property to settle, which kept me three days in town. I then
set out for Dorsetshire, and was sensible of the only satisfaction I had felt since I lost my daughter, when I anticipated the
pleasure my wife would feel in hearing what I had done for
her sister and her sister's children. I had made the journey on
horseback, attended by one servant. It was late in the evening
when I approached my house, which was situated on high
ground, and I looked for the lights, which, as it was now the
month of July, were almost always to be seen from the bow
window of a music room, where my Fanny usually passed

the evenings; but no light appeared either there or from any other part of the house. As my return was expected, though I had not named the exact day, I was rather surprised that my wife should be out, which, however, I concluded, was the case, and I knew it was not always easy for her to resist the importunity of her mother when she was bent on a rubber. It was no small part of the satisfaction in which I indulged myself, to think, that in consequence of the arrangements to which I had so largely contributed, I should become master of my own house, which I never felt myself to be while this lady made it her residence. I was now at the gate which opened into the court-yard of my house. A man was standing there who I soon saw was an old coachman, who had lived with me ever since I married. I spoke eagerly to him: "Well, Hugh, how is your mistress? how is every body at home?" The man opened the gate in silence. I repeated my question: "Is your lady well?—is she at home?"—"My lady— Sir—" said he, "is—I—thought, Sir—My lady—" I was struck with astonishment and terror, and throwing myself off my horse, I demanded impatiently what was the matter, and where was my wife? "My mistress, Sir, is gone from home, has been gone these two days."—"Gone!" exclaimed I; "how gone? what is it you mean?"

""My dear master," said the poor fellow, "I waited here to see you before you went into the house. My lady has left it, not meaning, I fear, to return."—"Not return?—And her mother—is she with her?"—"The old lady went yesterday, Sir, saying she could not bear to see your honour after what had happened."

"'I found myself become giddy, and leaning on my servant, endeavoured to recover recollection and fortitude: but the one destroyed the other. "My son!" cried I, "my boy! where is he?"—"Within, Sir, with his tutor," was the answer. "And my wife is gone, you say, not to return! I do not understand what it means!—Gone! for what purpose?—with whom gone?"

""Ah, Sir!" said the honest man, "it is not for servants to give their opinion on such matters. It is not for us to see more than our betters like we should; but indeed there is hardly one of us who did not guess at the same person as being he who has enticed my lady. It is no sudden thing I fear, though to be sure nobody dared to think of such a notion."

""What is it you mean, Hugh? Tell me plainly and at once."

""Why, then, Sir, it is that Mr. Frederic Halwyn my lady has gone off with. Come, dear Sir, let me lead you into the house. God forgive us, that any body alive could be so ungrateful! Sir—Sir—recover yourself—Let me call the tutor, and my young master. The sight of him will be a comfort to you."

""Stir not on your life," cried I, "to call any one. Go round, and open the door of the library, next the garden. Bring me candles thither, and let me not see any other servant. As for my poor boy!——"

"'My voice failed me; and the worthy-hearted fellow, trembling, entreated me to let him stay to help me into the house; but I fiercely bade him obey me; and hastened, with hurried steps, and in a state of mind I cannot now think of without terror, to my library, where I threw myself into a chair breathless and almost senseless. Hugh followed me with a candle, and two letters which he put on the table in silence. I thought I heard the voice of my son. I started up, bade the man leave me, and locked the door.

"'Who can describe chaos, or analyse the mingled emotions of a soul agonized like mine? My mind seemed to have been at once brutalized. It was not blood, but vitriol and fire that I thought circulated in my veins. I could at that moment have committed any act of desperation, on myself, on my innocent child, or even the first being that came in my way; but no weapon was at hand, for Hugh, in his honest zeal, had thrown my sword (which hung near the chimney) out of the window before I entered the room; and the pistols over the fire-place were not charged. I know not whether, if I had been in my dressing-room, the razor or the knife with which I cut my nails, would not have served for the instruments of vengeance against myself.

"'I groaned aloud; I shrieked; I threw myself on the floor, and beat my head against it, till the blood gushed from my nose, and, half stunned, I lay breathless, and with diminished sensation. There was a noise without: it was like persons whispering. I arose, with a confused idea that I ought to sacrifice the first person who dared to intrude upon me. A voice which I knew to be that of Mr. Warley, my boy's tutor, then entreated me to open the door. All this while I had grasped in my convulsed hands the two letters; one of which I knew was from my wife, and one from her mother. "Sir," said the voice which now addressed me, "let me beg of you to open the door. It is your son, who, by me, implores you."—"My son!" cried I, "my son!—I have no son!—Leave me all of you, or what I shall do may be dreadful. Mr. Warley, take care of your own safety." The whispering was then renewed for a moment, while I placed myself near the door, determined to revenge the intrusion on the first person who dared to enter. But the lock was suddenly forced; and my steward, assisted by Mr. Warley and all my men servants, made me almost instantly their prisoner. What followed was all raving and phrensy. I was, in truth, in a condition of mind that made the coercion now used absolutely necessary, to prevent my doing some injury to others or myself. A medical friend, for whom I had a great esteem, directed these proceedings, and his was the first voice to which I could be prevailed upon to listen. Yet his arguments I should have rejected with abhorrence and contempt, had they been like those which are generally used by the consolers of the unhappy. He preached none of that cold-blooded optimism, to which the hypocrites who recommend it to others know their own hearts refuse to accede. On the contrary, he allowed that my misfortune was the greatest and most insupportable that a manly spirit could be called upon to endure. Yet he bade me look at the calamities under which every one groaned more or less; not to console myself by comparing my case with that of others, but that I might learn to submit to the common lot of humanity, in which evil does most undoubtedly predominate, from the cradle to the grave. "Half the miseries we endure," said he, "we owe to our wild schemes of happiness, our romantic ideas of perfection. You married the woman whose infidelity and ingratitude now deprive you of your reason, at a time of life when, if you had thought any other qualification but those of person necessary, you were no judge whether they existed or no. Eminent beauty in yet early youth; with mild manners and apparent good nature, at a time when she was the idol of a mother who never contradicted her; a few trifling acquirements which neither improved her heart nor her understanding; all this you saw she possessed: and certainly few men of your age would have thought of inquiring for more. I believe, my friend, it is a melancholy truth, that women have no character at all; and what is called their education gives none: it only helps to obliterate any distinguishing traits of original disposition which here and there may rise by chance into higher styles of character. We set out with saying that women *must do* so and so, and *think* so and so, as their grandmothers and mothers thought before them. If any of them venture even to look as if they had any will of their own, or supposed themselves capable of reasoning, how immediately are they marked as something monstrous, absurd, and out of the course of nature! while the most

insipid moppet[158] that ever looked in a glass is preferred to
one of those reasoning damsels, especially by empty and
superficial young men; who, such as the majority of them
are, two-thirds of the younger women, desire only to please.
What then are we to expect from women, who, flattered into
angels in their youth, forget that age will come; and sickness,
perhaps, even sooner than time blast the perfections on
which all their vanity is founded? With this incense, my
friend, your unhappy wife had been fed, till it became impossible for her to live without it. Your tenderness and affection
were not enough for her, when you ceased to tell her she was
more than human. As long as she was suffered, as during
your gay life in London, to hear it from five hundred fools
every year, she was in some degree content; but, reduced by
a residence in the country to dwindle into a mere mortal
woman, a mother and a wife, she hungered and thirsted for
the delectable and high-seasoned admiration, by which alone
she had contrived to keep herself in good humour with herself; and the first man she saw whose taste and elegance qualified him in her opinion to gratify her vanity, easily taught
her to forget her honour, her husband, and her children.[159]
And will *you*, my friend, give up your reason, and abandon
your child and your friends for *such* a woman? Shake off this
unmanly, this degrading weakness. Shew her that you can
live without her; and do not, I beseech you, forget your
duties, because she never understood hers. As to the wretch
who has repaid your unexampled friendship with the black-
est ingratitude, I am convinced he will give you no opportunity of personally punishing him. The lady, you see, says, in
her letter, that as neither of them can ever behold you more,
they have taken such means of concealment as will make it
impossible for you ever to meet them. Tear her then from
your heart for ever. The struggle will be dreadful, but surely
infinitely preferable to the long lingering misery of

contending with insulted affection; of being considered as
the poor-spirited dupe of such a woman." I listened to the
arguments of my friend with the attention his understanding
as well as his regard for me deserved. I learned to blush for
the weakness I had shewn, and resumed, at least apparently,
a degree of tranquillity; but my heart was irrecoverably
wounded. My temper was changed; I had no longer pleasure
in any of my former pursuits. I shunned society, and shut
myself for whole weeks, and even months, among my books.
Even the education of my poor boy, which I used to superin-
tend myself, and which had once been my first gratification,
I now had no courage to attend to. "For what," said I, "am I
teaching him the elegancies of literature and the refinements
of art? To quicken his sensibility, to inflame his passions, to
set high his taste for perfection, all perhaps to prepare for him
the sad certainty of suffering such as mine; all, that he may
be more completely and systematically wretched."
Sometimes, though I doted on my son, I was unable to stay
with him, and wandered about from place to place where I
was not known, or hid myself among the crowds of London,
as the place where I might with the least interruption indulge
the anguish which time itself seemed incapable of healing.
Meanwhile, however, I took the means my lawyers prescribed
to me, to obtain a divorce.[160] The first steps towards it were
attended with considerable difficulties, for the unhappy
woman and her paramour were abroad; where, after eighteen or twenty months, he had left her, promising however
to return, and had gone to America, on one of those commercial speculations in which he was still engaged. Mrs.
Frederic Halwyn, for she had taken the name of her seducer,
had then, (as those my lawyers employed to inquire, informed
us) struggled for some time with the inconveniences of
narrow circumstances, and a doubtful character in a foreign
country, still expecting the return of her lover, till necessity

compelled her to throw herself on the compassion of her mother, who very reluctantly received her, though to the folly of that weak and worthless woman the errors of her daughter may justly be imputed. The lawyers now proceeded to obtain a divorce for me, which, as it met with no opposition, was decided about two years and a half after our first separation; and as I had taken Fanny without any fortune, she was reduced to a very destitute state, and became wholly dependent on her mother and her sister. This I never intended; and as soon as the necessary forms could be gone through, I presented to Miss Frances Berrington, for she was now to bear her maiden name, a thousand pounds for her immediate occasions, and a settlement of four hundred a year during her life. She wrote to thank me; but I would not open her letter: she implored me to see her only for five minutes, in presence of any persons I would name; but worlds would not have bribed me at that time to have heard the sound of her syren voice,[161] or to have looked once at that countenance so long the book of fate to me; and fearful lest she should attempt to procure an interview by stratagem, I set out with my son and his tutor on a journey to Scotland, not with any hope of forgetting my wretchedness, yet determined for his sake, who was now in his eleventh year, to endure it more like a man than I had hitherto done.

"'On him, for he was all I had left in the world, my attention became more and more fixed. I studied incessantly how to secure for his future life that happiness which was for ever to be denied to my own. His person had even more beauty than is to be wished for in a boy: he was the exact image of his mother, and his temper was likely I feared to resemble hers. He had the same indecision, the same facility of being governed by any one who should acquire an ascendancy over him, and, I feared, would have all her faults of personal vanity; and with such a fortune as he would possess, I dreaded

the consequences of this disposition. After a long debate I
could not determine to send him to a public school; yet I
began to see that the wandering and unsettled life I led, was,
notwithstanding his tutor was a very attentive and proper
person, inimical to that persevering application to which I
knew such a disposition ought to be habituated. Just as these
difficulties pressed the most forcibly on my mind, I was at
Buxton;¹⁶² where, on my way from the north, I stopped to
pass a fortnight. There I became acquainted with a family
of the name of Hamilton. It consisted of a father and three
daughters,¹⁶³ of which the eldest was about seven-and-twenty,
the next younger by many years, and the third yet a child. Mr.
Hamilton, who was one of the many branches of the noble
family of that name,¹⁶⁴ was a scholar, and had seen a great deal
of the world, having resided many years abroad in a public
capacity. His conversation was particularly agreeable to me;
for, though he had acquired rather too much of the formality
that is attached to the diplomatic character, his knowledge
was extensive, and his mind well cultivated, while I could not
but admire the manner in which he lived with his family, and
their affection for him. The eldest, who was an accomplished
woman, possessed all his confidence, and he often told me,
that her judgment was always his guide in cases where he
doubted his own. Her understanding did indeed appear to be
of a superior rank, and her management of her father's family,
as well as her attention to the education of her younger sisters, though it was done without parade, seemed so much
what it ought to be, that no one who observed it could fail
to be prejudiced in her favour. Her person was not strikingly
handsome; but it was far from being disagreeable. Her face
was rather agreeable than beautiful; but her large dark eyes
gave it a character of intelligence, which accorded with the
understanding she seemed to possess. Ever to love again as I
had loved was impossible; but I insensibly found reasons for

prolonging my stay at Buxton, and began to consider Miss
Hamilton as one who might again attach me to a home, and
be the best coadjutor I could find in the education of my son.
I studied her carefully, and, I thought, with impartial eyes. All
to whom I spoke of her were unanimous in her praise, and
the fondness she expressed for my boy would have made a
less elegant woman agreeable in my eyes. My story, and the
deep anguish which still preyed on my heart when I thought
(and I could not cease to think) of his mother, were well
known to Mr. Hamilton, and I knew his daughter had heard
it from him. But she seemed to feel for me a degree of pity
which soothed my imagination. I liked her more and more;
and at length, after an acquaintance of about two months, I
offered myself, and was accepted. Two months more inter-
vened before the settlements[165] and other necessary preparations were ready, and during all that time I found, in the
apparent temper, manners, and conduct of Miss Hamilton,
every reason to be satisfied with the choice I had made. Since
the fatal day when the cruel flight of my unhappy Fanny had
rendered my house in Dorsetshire odious to me, I never had
acquired the courage to make it my abode, and now it was
not without a very painful effort that I determined to carry
thither her successor. But, conscious of my own weakness,
and to remove as much as was possible objects that might
nourish it, I had many alterations made in the house, and
entirely new furnished it, as if in compliment to its future
mistress. Thither it was her wish to go in the spring which
succeeded our marriage; and I re-visited with another than
Fanny a place where her image more than at any other residence was perpetually present to me, while the very great
and increasing resemblance her son bore to her, gave me, in
despite of reason, sensations of such mingled pleasure and
anguish as I should vainly attempt to describe.

"'I had, however, a great esteem and even affection for

my now wife. She acquitted herself of every duty she had undertaken, with an exactitude which left me nothing in reason to wish. Yet I was, after eighteen or twenty months had elapsed, insensibly fatigued by a sort of minute attention to economy, which I thought often took up time that might have been much more rationally and indeed usefully employed. Instead of cultivating talents for literature and conversation, which I had fancied were of the first rate, she sat whole mornings with a pen in her hand reckoning the pence and even halfpence that had been expended during the week; and in the household affairs, as well as in all that related to her personal expences and those of my son, there was a superfluous and teasing attention to trifles, that I sometimes found excessively tiresome—and I knew it was wholly unnecessary. Immediately on her arrival at the Dorsetshire House all the old servants had been discharged, without even excepting my faithful Hugh, who (he being now an old man,) I pensioned as well as one or two others, and they still lived in the villages near us, of which they were natives. My wife soon took occasion to forbid their ever coming to the house; and when I ventured gently to remonstrate, she told me, that after the disorders that had occurred in my family while these people lived with me, she was astonished how I could wish to encourage them about me; but, as she should conduct my house in a very different manner she hoped, in *every respect*, from that in which it was then managed, I must permit her to insist on keeping all such persons at a distance. Yet it was from these people that, by means of her favourite maid, she contrived to gather anecdotes of the past, which she treasured up in her mind; and sometimes when her good humour, which I soon found was not invincible, forsook her, she brought them forward in the way of contrasting her conduct with that of her predecessor, with a degree of malignity which affected me more than I wished to let appear; for I hoped that domestic tranquillity might yet be mine, though I felt myself every day more and more hopeless of happiness.

"'The attention of my wife to my beloved boy had never, after her marriage, been what I had flattered myself it would be. I knew how much a woman of sense and spirit can contribute to forming the mind and manners of a young man; but if I hinted at my wishes that she would admit him to be with her whenever his tutor or his exercise left him unoccupied, she resented it by intimating that I had married her only to make her a governess, and that no company was so irksome as that of a great rude boy, who ought to be at school. My poor Francis, however, was not rude; his temper was too mild, too facile, and his turn rather for books and drawing than for the volatility and noisy thoughtlessness of his age. But Mrs. George Maynard was greatly changed in her opinion of him since her marriage; and this estrangement became more visible, when, in the third year of our marriage, she bore a daughter. From that period she seemed to consider my son as an usurper, who would have too great a share of the fortune she wished wholly to monopolize for this and other children she supposed it likely she should have; and, artful as she was, she found it impossible to disguise her real sentiments. My home, whether in London or the country, now became every hour more and more uneasy to me. My son, who was the object dearest to my heart, would soon I foresaw be driven, with his tutor, who was an excellent man, to some less unpleasant residence: yet I could not bear to part with him; and partly by authority and partly by making it her own interest, I prevented for another twelvemonth the increase towards my son of conduct that was become intolerable to me. Frank[166] was then seventeen,[167] very tall of his age; yet the beauty of his face, and the slenderness of his form, prevented him from assuming a manly appearance; but his spirit was high, candid, and generous, and his attachment to me, his tender solicitude to prevent[168] my every wish, and his total exemption from all vice, made him so inexpressibly dear to me, that, though he was qualified for the University, and it had been my intention to send him thither, I could not but with extreme reluctance, though Mr. Warley was to accompany him, determine for the first time to separate myself from him.

"'It was this increasing attachment to merit which malice itself could not deny, and the expence which Mrs. George Maynard foresaw would attend sending him to Oxford, that embittered her spirit against us both. I concealed it from Frank as much as I could, and for that purpose went out more than I had ever been accustomed to do, and took him with me. This, however, only made matters worse on my return, and I was reproached with having not even natural affection for my daughter, now above two years old. The mildest and most forbearing temper cannot endure beyond a certain point; and it most unfortunately happened, that at this period I returned with Frank and his tutor from an excursion of a fortnight, and found my wife in a very ill humour. Her little girl had taken the measles in my absence; and though her life was in no danger, a humour had fallen into her eyes, which her mother thought was likely for ever to disfigure her. I expressed, what I really felt, sincere concern at this circumstance; when, instead of such an answer as might have been expected, my wife bade me not affect what she knew I did not feel. "My child," said she sharply, "never possessed your affections; it is beauty only that engages your heart, although it has brought upon you nothing but shame and disgrace!" My son, astonished at the manner in which this was spoken, and seeing how greatly I was shocked, mildly entreated her to explain herself; when she had the unfeminine inhumanity to tell him to seek it in the disgraceful history of his mother, now a common prostitute in the streets of London!

"'From my poor boy the real circumstances that related to his mother had been carefully concealed. He imagined that she had left me in consequence of some slight disagreement relative to the affair of her sister's husband, and that, having been seized with a fever in London, she had there died before our reconciliation, which had occasioned the deep melancholy I had in the succeeding years fallen into. This story, impressed for six years on his mind, was never doubted, when the veil was thus rudely torn off that had so carefully concealed from him the disgraceful reality, more disgraceful indeed than I was myself aware of: for I had now for many years abstained from inquiring after that unhappy woman, whose annuity my steward regularly paid every quarter.

"'Francis, with an expression I shall never forget, turned towards me. His speaking eyes demanded an instant explanation. I feared he would have fallen at my feet; and clasping him in my arms I bade him bear like a man an insult which should never be repeated; then, unable wholly to refrain from expressing the indignation I felt, I spoke to Mrs. Maynard with more passionate severity than ever I had used towards her before; and hastened with my son from a scene of provocation to which I determined at that moment never again to expose him, whatever my now hateful bonds might bind me to endure. I immediately ordered my post-chaise, and with my son, his tutor, and our own servants, set out for London; giving my boy no time to hear the truth which at that moment I had not resolution to tell him. At the first post town,[169] however, another chaise was ordered for Mr. Warley; and then, my poor Francis and I travelled together, and I related to him the cruel misconduct of his mother; and saw, though I palliated rather than exaggerated every circumstance, that while he heard me in profound silence, every word I uttered sunk with fatal force into his heart.

"'"And does she still live, Sir?" said he in a tremulous voice,

"Does my mother—(Oh, God! how shall I ask it?)—does my mother still live, and live in infamy—in prostitution?"

"'What a question from a son to a father!—from such a son to a father feeling as I felt! I endeavoured to re-assure him, however; I told him, I hoped and believed that assertion originated only in the malice of Mrs. Maynard; for that I trusted, as his unhappy mother had a sufficient income, necessity could not, so mere constitutional vice would not, induce her to descend to this last wretched degradation; and that her annuity continued to be paid to the same person who had, from the first year of my divorcing her, always received it.

"'Francis forbore to ask any farther questions, and our journey was made in melancholy silence. I tried, but unsuccessfully, to speak on any other topic: the mind of my poor boy seemed wholly absorbed by reflections on what he had heard; and when we arrived at the house I inhabited in town, I beheld him with undescribable anguish. His countenance had lost its bloom, his eyes were heavy and sunk; he seemed half unconscious whatever I said to him; he ate nothing; and, as his chamber was adjoining to mine, I heard but too plainly, though I forbore to notice it, that he did not sleep during the whole of the succeeding night. I arose, however, before him; and concealing none of my fears or their sources from Mr. Warley, I consulted with him on what it was best to do; for, from my knowledge of the temper and disposition of my son, I foresaw the most fatal consequences from the wound his sensibility had thus received. Warley imagined, with probability enough, that the impression however deep would easily be erased from a young mind, to which almost every object beyond the paternal roof was new. He advised me to throw him as much as I could into scenes of innocent gaiety and dissipation for a few weeks, but never without either one or other of us, his father or his tutor, accompanying him.

I had many acquaintance[170] in town, (for a man of fortune can always command acquaintance,) at whose houses he would see variety[171] of characters. The public amusements he had seldom visited; and I concluded with Mr. Warley, that we should conquer in a short time the depression he now suffered under; and afterwards, as the Easter term would begin, he was to go to Christchurch,[172] of which college I had entered him a gentleman commoner some months before.[173]

"'In pursuance of this plan, I affected an ease of mind which I was very far from feeling. I endeavoured to appear to Frank as if having been long accustomed to our mutual misfortune; I had taught myself to consider it, without suffering more than I should have done had I known his mother had been dead; yet heaven is my witness with how much more anguish I always thought of her, unworthy as she had proved herself, than if I had known she no longer inhabited this world! But I dared not, while I persevered in this plan, flatter myself it was successful. My son went wherever I told him amusement was to be found, and whither I seemed to wish he should go; but nothing appeared to amuse him, or to have any power to detach him from the sad subject which occupied his thoughts, corroded his heart, and I thought was visibly undermining his health.

"'After we had been about three weeks in London, during which time Mrs. Maynard never deigned to make in writing any apology for the conduct that had driven me from the country, it happened that I dined with a party of gentlemen, where, as I knew the conversation would turn wholly on politics and on party disputes, which at that period ran very high, I thought my son would find rather fatigue than amusement; it was settled therefore that he should dine at home with his tutor, and afterwards go to a new play in which a celebrated actress performed her part so admirably, that during the three or four nights it had been performed, the house had been greatly crowded. I promised to meet them there; but it was late before we arose from table, and still later before my friends would suffer me to go. At length I reached the theatre; but the play was over, and even half the entertainment[174] passed. I went into an upper box, and surveyed the house; but I could not distinguish those of whom I was in search. I crossed to the other side, but still could not perceive them; and I concluded, as it had often happened before, that my young man, satisfied with the play, had returned home before the afterpiece began. It was now closed, and I was making my way out with the crowd, when every body was stopped in the lobby by a number of persons assembled round two men who were quarrelling, and, as it was understood, insisting on fighting about some women of the town.[175] The tumult became so great that the sentinels[176] were called, and I saw sticks and bayonets brandished about, and heard the oaths of the men and the shrieks of the women, with a degree of disgust that urged me to hasten from this scene of vice and noise; when pressing near the disputing parties to reach the door, I heard—Oh, memory! thou wert but too faithful!—I was struck by the tone of a voice which, though seven years had passed since I last heard it, still made my heart vibrate. I stepped forward, and I saw a face—faded indeed! and changed. The features were disfigured by bad habits, and the complexion polluted by art;[177] but it was the face on which I had gazed so often with rapture. Alas! I saw before me in one of the objects of ruffianly contention my once-loved lamented Fanny. She was appealing to strangers for protection against the insults that some of the men had offered her, and which others were now trying to resent; but the people she was speaking to treated her with scorn and derision, and at that moment, for it was all momentary, a blow was levelled at her from one of the contending parties. I saw it about to fall on her; and receiving it on my shoulder,

I involuntarily clasped my arms around her; and either from my appearance, or rather because a humane action, for whosoever exerted meets with applause from any assembly of English people, the spectators gave me way, and I bore her to a seat. She knew me, and fell senseless into my arms.

"'The crowd was soon dispersed; the persons who had been fighting were carried away in custody. Few others felt any curiosity about the poor abandoned creature that had been one of the causes of quarrel; and the other women who had been parties in it were glad to escape: so that I soon found myself almost alone with this fatal object, the cause of all the calamities of my life; and, merciful Heaven! in what a situation did I see her!

"'The faded reality, the diminished and injured beauty of that form and face, which were so clearly represented by my heart to my imagination, was in my arms. I could have pressed it to my bosom;—but then came the idea of that perfidy, ingratitude, and degradation which had stained this lovely image, once so perfect; the recollection of the long years of misery succeeding those when my tenderness, my affection, should have secured all her gratitude and my happiness. No: it is impossible, by any form of words I can find, to describe what at that moment passed in my mind. I could now have rejoiced in the illusion that time only had dimmed the lustre of that eminent beauty; and by a sudden revulsion of my thoughts, I next meditated how to shake from me the worthless destroyer of my peace, merely performing towards her the duties of humanity as an unfortunate woman.

"'Thought is rapid under the domination of violent passions; and though hardly two minutes had passed, and Fanny still lay senseless in my arms, I had run over in idea all my preceding life, and brought my mind to the consideration of what I and what she now was. Some of the women who sell books and slight refreshments about the avenues of the theatre now came up, to propose services which I had not recollection enough to ask. I offered them money to procure help; I stammered out some unconnected sentences; but I was myself almost as much in want of assistance as the fragile and apparently half dead object I supported, when suddenly I saw before me my son! Imagine the strange impropriety of the situation in which he beheld me; the impossibility of my accounting to him for it. . . . "Sir," cried my poor boy, astonished at my confusion, "we have sought you the whole evening." He thought not at that moment of his mother; he only blushed to believe that his father had forgotten in his own person that propriety of conduct he had so earnestly enforced towards himself. Divided, torn, distracted by so many contending sensations, I felt my head grow giddy, and I was tempted to rush into the street, and like a maniac proclaim aloud the insupportable anguish of my bursting heart.

"'The pale countenance of Frank, (for mine, when he looked at it steadily, was not that of a man engaged in a transient intrigue) his trembling hand as he grasped mine, recalled in some degree my scattered senses. But how could I so shock him as to tell him the truth?—How could I say, "This woman whom you see, and who is evidently one that subsists on the casual profits of prostitution, is she who bore you!" My heart recoiled. I bade him in almost an angry tone leave me. It was very unusual, indeed, for Frank to hear from *me* a word that sounded harshly in his ears. At that instant, however, Mr. Warley appeared. I beckoned to him. The women who had surrounded us had by this time interposed, and supported the sad object of my solicitude. I left her to their care, while I seized Warley's arm; and briefly communicating to him the miserable truth, I besought him to carry my son from a scene I could with difficulty support myself.

"'Mr. Warley approached him, and after a short conversation they retired together; but I saw, with dread and amazement, the look which my unhappy son cast toward me, and then toward his mother. Never, no, never will the expression of his countenance at that moment be erased from my memory. I was relieved, however, by seeing him depart with his tutor, though I was convinced that he was not, nay, I hardly wished he should be, deceived, as to the person with whom he left me.

"'Consideration for him—pity, and even the weakness of a more tender sentiment—all urged me not to abandon the creature whom, though I could not restore her to honour and to peace, though she could never more be mine, I might at least rescue from the horrid destiny to which the career she was now in would infallibly lead her. I traversed the room where I was with hurried steps, endeavouring to summon my powers of endurance, that I might not in such a place expose either her or myself. In the mean time she recovered her senses, and all that had passed instantly occurred to her. She looked towards me, anxiously dreading to know whether the man who had once so adored her, and whom she had so irreparably injured, would not, however, be withheld by a momentary impulse of pity from those reproaches which her too busy conscience told her she so well deserved. I drew near her; the beloved name of Fanny rose involuntarily to my lips; but I checked myself, and, addressing her as a stranger, desired to know if I could be of any service to her in conducting her safe home. She turned her lovely eyes to me with a look most expressive! and attempted, but could not answer me. Uncertain what to do, hardly knowing what I did, I hastily paid the women who had assisted to recover her, and supported her (for she seemed hardly able to walk) down stairs, where my chariot[178] was waiting. I placed her in it, and followed her, without recollecting how improper and even impossible it was for me to conduct her to my own house, and that I knew not, and even dreaded to inquire, her abode. On the repeated question of my astonished servants, whither I would go? I was compelled to ask her, where she lived? She gave me, in a voice hardly articulate, a direction to a street in the outskirts of the town. Thither I ordered the carriage to be driven. We proceeded in silence, broken only on her part by deep and convulsive sighs. A dirty-looking servant girl opened the door; and I perceived, when we entered the house (for my mind was now more collected,) that she was surprised at the appearance of her mistress, and still more at mine, whose manner resembled but little that of the people with whom she had been accustomed to see her associate. Our dialogue, when we were alone and she was a little restored, was short and energetic. I could not listen to the agonizing confession she would have made of her errors, her ingratitude, and repentance; or, listening for a moment, I was unable to answer. I thought, however, she did not know that had I been weak enough to have forgiven her perfidy and cruelty, and to have restored her to the place she once held, still there was an insuperable barrier between us; that another now possessed her place; and the child of another was to share with her son my fortune and affection: and this truth, little as she had deserved my consideration, I had not resolution to tell her. Strange, and even now most dreadful to look back upon, were the mingled sensations that then agonized my bosom! They were confused, they were terrible! Her immediate ease and comfort were, however, the predominant wish of my heart. I could not bear to see her in such a situation; liable to want the decencies of life, exposed to the licentious insolence of every wandering drunkard who knew the house to be of ill fame. But to express to her all I felt on this subject was, perhaps, to raise expectations I never meant to fulfil. With such resolution, therefore, as I could collect, I parted from her. I attempted to appear cold; and yet my heart smote me, and my voice faltered, as, bidding

her, "farewell!" I told her, that the recollection of what she
was when first our ill-fated acquaintance began, would make
me ever solicitous for her welfare; and that the next day she
should receive a letter from me which would explain my
future views. I ran through the streets from her lodgings to
my own house, without being conscious why I hurried along,
or able to determine on what I ought to do when I got there.
The idea of my son, from whom it would be impossible to
conceal the truth; the conduct I ought afterwards to observe;
all pressed on my mind with anguish for the debased situation of the once-loved creature I had just left—and I felt as if
the power of rationally considering any thing would never
again return to me.

"'Breathless and confused I reached my own house. I
asked hastily for Frank, and was told he was not gone to bed;
but feeling myself quite unfit to speak to him that night, yet
unable to rest without determining on something, I went to
my study, and there sent for Mr. Warley.

"'From him I learned that my unhappy boy had not the
least doubt who the person was whom he had seen with me;
and, indeed, had other evidence been wanting, the striking
resemblance between them could not have escaped him.
The account Mr. Warley gave me of the effect this discovery had on Frank made me shudder. I dreaded more than
ever to come to an explanation, of which, however, I saw the
necessity, and I passed the night in considering what I ought
to say to him, and how I ought to act towards his mother.
By the morning I had taken my resolution, and I sent for
him. Pale, dejected, unable to answer my anxious inquiries
after his health, he, after a moment, threw himself into my
arms, and burst into tears. "Oh, my father!" said he, "had I
never been deceived as to the unhappy person we saw last
night, Mrs. Maynard's cruel reproaches would not so deeply
have stung me, nor should I suffer what I do now." I felt at

that moment a proof that even those deceptions which are
called pious frauds are wrong; yet I was ignorant myself of
the situation of the wretched mother, though I knew enough
to wish her existence might be concealed from her son. It
was now, however, no time for me to repent of the past; it
was necessary that I should consider only the future; and I
summoned courage to enter on the subject, and to relate to
Frank all that had happened, of the ostensible circumstances
of which I found he had a clear recollection, though he was
hardly eight years old, and though so much pains had been
taken to deceive him. He remembered the abrupt departure
of his mother; he remembered my passionate agonies; and
had thought it strange, that after some time, when he was
told his mother was dead, I seemed less affected than I was
when she left me. He had at that early age an idea of death,
but none of those disagreements which had been assigned as
having caused, what he for some time believed would be, a
temporary absence.

'"While I related to him the truth, he sat with his arms
thrown on a writing-table that was before him, and his face
hid by his hands. He was silent. I could hear that he suppressed his sighs, and struggled with the painful sensations
that agitated his bosom, especially when I was obliged to
touch on the circumstances of premeditated ingratitude,
which had so aggravated the faithless conduct of his mother.
I paused—I had finished this dreadful explanation, and my
poor boy lifted up his head, and fixed his eyes on mine with
an expression so full of mingled emotion, that I shall never
cease to remember it. "Sir!" said he, his voice trembling so
much as to be almost inarticulate, "your injuries have indeed
been great;—but—she who has injured you is—still *my*
mother!—Will you abandon her to a course of life such as
she is now in?" . . . . . I will not be again so minute in relating our conversations. You now understand enough of our

dispositions to imagine what they must have been! Before I could execute the engagements, now made to my son, it was necessary to know, if she to whom they related, and who had I found taken the name of Saville, would on her part enter into my views; and, while I should consider her as a sister, relinquish for ever a way of life so disgraceful to those connected with her by more than human ties, and which no human laws could dissolve. I had, it is true, seen appearances of remorse and repentance, but they might be only the consequences of sudden surprise and shame.

"'I found, however, the next day, that there was every reason to believe her perfectly sincere. She deplored her fatal infatuation, and gave me such proofs of the villainous arts of her seducer, as though they could not exculpate her, greatly lessened her crime. He had abandoned her in a foreign country, taking with him every thing he could obtain from her in money and jewels, under pretence of carrying on some of those schemes which were to raise him to unbounded affluence; and on the same fallacious ideas had prevailed upon her to make over her annuity in such a way, as that its alienation might be concealed from the persons who paid it quarterly on my behalf.

"'I have already been too minute. Let me, therefore, hasten to relate not my conversation with my son, or his subsequent interview with his mother; I must leave those scenes to your imagination, since I have no power to dwell upon them. I took a small but elegant detached house for that ill-fated woman, in a village some miles from London; whither, having discharged all her debts and her servant, and concealed her abode as much as possible by changing her name, she removed. However convinced of her penitence, it never was my intention to see her after this arrangement; but I permitted my son to visit her alone, and I took other means than by questioning him to assure myself of the propriety of her conduct.

"'Having, therefore, satisfied myself in having done all that the duties of humanity required of me; and flattering myself that Frank, though still very much dispirited, had conquered the effects of the shock this occurrence had given him, I returned to consider his future destination, and in about a fortnight named to him the necessity of his preparing for Oxford. He changed countenance while I spoke, and, when I paused, said, "I have never yet disobeyed my father, nor would I in any other instance for a thousand worlds; but not even my fear of offending him, which I protest is little inferior to that of death itself, will induce me to go to Oxford."

"'I anxiously inquired the reason of a resolution so extraordinary. He endeavoured to evade the question; and when he found that was not to be done, he entreated me to ask Mr. Warley.

"'That worthy man, with every expression of the truest concern, put into my hands a letter, which a day or two before my son had received from the woman who now bore my name, and was called my wife. It was to inform him, in the most bitter and sarcastic words, that *my* infamous secession from her and from honour, to take back a harlot, and set all decency at defiance, was well known; that her family (she piqued herself upon her family) were about to obtain justice for her; but that in the mean time she could not but congratulate him on the fortunate and creditable circumstances under which he was about to begin his studies at Oxford, where he might be assured the respectability of *both* his parents was already well known.

"'Mr. Warley saw my lips tremble with rage, and heard, as I would have answered him, my voice inarticulate and choaked. He attempted, but in vain, to appease me; the tumult, the agony of my soul, only increased by his remonstrances. I called Heaven to witness, that the monster (for woman I

could not call her) who had thus endeavoured to wound me
through my son, I would never again live with, never meet
but with the purpose of parting with her for ever! My poor
unhappy boy entered my apartment at that moment, and his
countenance had instantaneously the effect of restoring me
to some command over myself. I saw, that while it was necessary to check the expressions of that pain this inhuman conduct had inflicted, I should yet hurt him, if I appeared not to
feel it acutely. Affected in a manner of which it is impossible
to convey an idea to another, by the look, the manner, the
silent misery of my son, I was compelled to shorten our conversation; and leaving him with Mr. Warley, who had always
great influence over his mind, I went out under pretence of
business that admitted of no delay, and took my way to the
Park, which was only at the end of the street, in hopes that
the air and a short conference with myself would abate the
perturbation of my mind, which now was hardly short of
phrensy.

"'After some hours I became calmer; for I had now formed
a plan for securing, as far as it might yet be done, my own
tranquillity in another country—after having provided in
this, for the support of the poor penitent, who, though no
longer my wife, depended for her subsistence on me, and
left Mrs. Maynard and her daughter in such a situation, as
to pecuniary concerns, as should on her part preclude every
just complaint, I determined that I would accompany my son
to pursue his studies at Lausanne,[179] at that time much frequented for the purposes of education: and I flattered myself
that his mind would gradually regain its tranquillity; that his
youth, and facility which all innocent and rational pleasures
might there be enjoyed,[180] together with his being removed
from the scenes where he had so cruelly suffered, and from
the intercourse of all those in whose opinion he conceived
himself disgraced, would give another turn to his thoughts,

and restore him to me such as my excessive affection for him had from his infancy represented to me that he would one day be.

"'This plan, which, the longer I considered it, offered new advantages, served to tranquillize my mind for some days, though I saw that my poor Frank became more and more melancholy and reserved. I spoke to him of my project. He acquiesced, but without the slightest appearance of being pleased. I even began the preparations for our journey, and sent for the lawyers, whose advice was necessary to settle the disposition of my fortune in my absence. Frank saw all this going on without any remark: it seemed as if, too certain of being miserable every where, he was indifferent as to place. I became, however, very uneasy, and particularly when I observed, that on those days when he had visited his mother his dejection was visibly increased. I had permitted him to see her once or twice a week; but I never went with him, or held any communication with her but by letters which he carried; and on these occasions he went alone on horseback, lest his servants should guess to whom those visits were paid.

"'They were usually made in a morning, and he returned to dress for dinner about four o'clock: but one day, when he had told me he was going thither, I waited dinner for him till five, till six, till seven. He came not. I began to be uneasy, yet appeased my first inquietude by supposing, that as the spring was advancing, and the evening fine, he might have been induced to dine with his mother, and ride home by moonlight. Time however passed, and he was still absent. I could perceive that Mr. Warley's inquietude was as great as mine; and he proposed to go himself to the village where we imagined he had been, to inquire what detained him. To this I eagerly agreed, and he went off instantly in a hired chaise. But when I had no one either to hear my conjectures, or offer others, I became more intolerably wretched, and utterly unable to support the apprehensions that now every moment increased. I went down therefore with an intention to follow Warley; when, as I opened the door of my house, a post-chaise stopped before it. I sprang forward, hoping to see my son. Gracious God! it was not Frank, it was his mother!

"'She knew me by the light of the lamps, and, in a voice of such wild fear as I cannot describe, asked me for him. "Is my son here?—*is* he here?" In tenfold[181] astonishment I answered, "No: has he not been with you?"—"He was—he was with me;—but—some dreadful accident has happened. If you have not seen him—he is dead!—murdered!—I shall never, never behold him more!"

"'I cannot tell you what I felt at that moment: an obscure recollection of agony is all that now remains on my mind. My servants, who soon assembled round the chaise, took out the half-frantic woman; and I had, after a moment, enough presence of mind to entreat her to tell me what cause there was for the frightful apprehensions she entertained. With difficulty I understood, that Frank had, at her entreaty, as he was so soon to take a long farewell of her, dined with her; that they had afterwards walked out together for about a mile, and perceived that they were followed by a person who had the appearance of an officer. They turned. He passed them in a very rude and insulting manner, and repeated the same insolence twice before they returned to the house; so that it was with great difficulty she could persuade my son not to resent it. She believed, however, that she had prevailed; and flattering herself that after a while the stranger would go his way, she detained Frank as long as she could; but that between seven and eight o'clock he went to the inn where he usually put up his horse, and, as she imagined, had returned to me. At night, however, her maid, who bought milk at this inn, which was also a farm, came suddenly back, and told her mistress, that the young gentleman who had dined there had had a quarrel with another whom he saw in the inn-yard; that after having, as the people told her, very high words, both had mounted their horses and rode towards London together, for the purpose, as it was understood, of fighting a duel immediately on their arrival there. "Who was the man?" cried I: "Give me some means of finding him; it may not yet be too late."—"None knew his name," replied the miserable mother; "they knew only that he had been there two or three times asking questions relative to me and to my son."

"'I must shorten the detail of scenes that kill me even in retrospection. While I yet was considering whither I could go, or what I could do, and my servants were engaged in administering to the unhappy and self-accused woman, a loud rapping at the door made me hurry down myself. Mr. Warley entered, and, grasping my hand, attempted to speak, but could not. "You have found him then?" cried I. He went into the parlour, sunk into a chair, and I saw by the convulsive working of his features that he was endeavouring to acquire resolution to give me a confirmation of my worst fears. "It is now," said he in a tremulous voice, "the time when you are called upon to exert your fortitude. Your son———"

"'"Is dead!—Is it so?"

"'"Would to God I could say it was not! I have seen him— dead! I had not the satisfaction of receiving his last breath!"

"'Whosoever having human feelings has undergone such a calamity as that which now fell upon me, even when a long and hopeless illness has prepared them for it, will know how to imagine what were my sufferings. To describe them would be to attempt torturing you and myself. I was for some hours in a state of distraction; and when exhausted nature could endure these violent emotions of the mind no longer, I sunk into insensibility; from which I was awakened only by the horror I felt at being told Mrs. Maynard and her daughter were in the house. There also had remained, because she was not in a condition to be moved, the most wretched of women and of mothers. With recollection, resentment towards Mrs. Maynard returned; yet I did not then know that she had levelled the instrument of death against the breast of my son.

"'I peremptorily refused to see her, and ordered her and her daughter instantly to quit my house. It was with infinite difficulty, and not without applying to some of her relations, that Mr. Warley prevailed on her to comply. I then learned the cause of the cruel event I deplored.

"'Mrs. Maynard had heard that I had received back my first wife; that I had even taken her from a life of public prostitution; and though she was not yet established at my house in London, that I supported her in splendour a few miles from it, where I, as well as my son, constantly visited her. To ascertain the truth of this, Mrs. Maynard could think of no better expedient than engaging her brother,[182] Gordon Hamilton, a young man who had been ever since her marriage on foreign service, to act at once as her spy and the avenger of her quarrel. He left my house in Dorsetshire, where he had been deeply impressed with the supposed injuries of his sister, and did not distain to employ persons to watch what passed at my house in town. There they gained no intelligence, but they set themselves to follow both me and my son wherever we went. He was soon traced to the village where was the habitation of his mother; yet when Gordon Hamilton saw her, she appeared to him too young to be the person of whom he was in search. Not, however, to be deceived, he engaged in his next inquiry an acquaintance of his to accompany him, who had known the unfortunate Fanny during the time she had been avowedly living on the wages of infamy. This man, profligate, unprincipled, and unfeeling, immediately acknowledged, and, having followed her on one of her solitary walks, had insultingly accosted her. Hamilton having then no farther doubts had waited from day to day about the village, meaning to accost me or my son. I never went thither, and he was soon tired of expecting me. Yet was he not at all convinced that any part of what his sister had heard was exaggerated; and on receiving a letter from her, reproaching him with the coldness and indifference with which he bore the cruel affront my conduct was to his family, he had called at my door, inquiring for me; when the servant, an ignorant boy, whom he questioned, and who had received general orders to deny me, had told him I was gone out of town; and on his asking if it was to Beckenham,[183] the village where the object of his jealousy resided, the boy answered "Yes," merely to be dismissed from his eager importunity. Thither, therefore, the hot-headed ruffian hurried, and, missing me, had followed and insulted my son when walking with his mother; then repairing to the inn, he waited till Frank was mounting his horse to return to town; when he went up to him, and after a few words they went together into a field, where my son was seen to strike the other—when the people of the inn-yard interfered, and separated them, but senselessly suffered them to depart together for London. They repaired to a tavern, from whence Hamilton went for his pistols. They fought; and my unhappy son fell, and died upon the spot. His murderer instantly absconded.

"'The body of my poor boy was brought to my house, and three days had elapsed before I was capable of hearing these particulars, or of giving any orders. With returning reason all the horrors of my destiny rushed upon my mind. I had lost the only being that had animated my existence, the sole object of my care and tenderness; and after years in which his delicate health had kept me in constant solicitude, he was snatched from me by the act of a vindictive monster, at the very period when his virtues and his affection were to repay me for all the sufferings of my preceding life.

"'Oh! how cruelly to me was aggravated the anguish of

the parent bending over the cold remains of an only child,[184] when I reflected on the character of him whom I had lost, and the circumstances with which his loss was attended! I have dwelt on this cruel period already too long. I feel even at this distance of time, that it is impossible for me to proceed without suffering again all the horrors of the moment. Vengeance alone occupied my mind as soon as I could think steadily, and I determined to pursue over the world the villain who had destroyed me; but my task, before I could set out to gratify the only sentiment I now felt, was not ended. The poor unhappy mother of my lost son, heart-struck, and overwhelmed at once by grief and remorse, was sinking fast into the grave. If I could have forgotten how very dear she once was to me, it was impossible that her being the mother of him I deplored could for a moment escape my memory; and I seemed to be fulfilling his last wishes, while I sought with the tenderness of a brother to soothe and console her. Yet the sight of her served but to deepen my anguish; and often when I have tried to assume before her some degree of fortitude, I have only mingled my tears and groans with hers, and each has aggravated the sufferings of the other. The unfortunate woman lingered almost two months, and then died in my arms.

"'The misery that had fallen upon me; the death of her whom she considered her rival; nothing seemed to appease the deep and inveterate hatred of the woman who now bore my name. She attempted to force herself and her daughter into my presence; but such were my dread and abhorrence of her, that I know not to what unmanly and savage excesses the sight of her might have transported me; and while I considered that the little girl was hers, and would by my son's death succeed to my whole fortune, unless I otherwise disposed of it, I sent for a lawyer, and, having made a provision of five hundred a year for the child, gave all the rest of my property in case of my death to one of my friends. Having made this arrangement, I hastened to Hamburgh, whither I was told the duellist or rather murderer had gone, to wait the success of those efforts his friends were making to obtain leave for him to return to Scotland, where he imagined he should be so protected that I should be compelled to drop all attempts to avenge the death of my son.—And certainly my conduct towards his sister, and the provocation that had been given him, were so misrepresented, that almost all of those who were once my friends, had learned to consider me as one of the worst of mankind; and such was the indignation which Mrs. Maynard's story had raised against me, among what is called the generality of the world, that, had I been disposed to have shown myself in public (which you will easily believe was far from my intention,) I should have incurred some hazard of personal insult. Such is the perverted state of society, (and that it was such has been, among many, one reason of my flying from it,) that I am sure nothing is more welcome to nine people out of ten, than to be told that a man or woman whom they either happen to know, or who is generally known, has been guilty of some crime for which they deserve to suffer by the public executioner. The avidity with which tales of defamation are received and propagated, the little satisfaction with which any one relates or appreciates honourable actions or meritorious conduct, has been one of those remarks that have most painfully convinced me of the depravity of my species. Rousseau was, towards the end of his life, undoubtedly insane—at least, so he appears to us even according to the account he has left of himself[85]—yet who can say that many of the injuries which affected him to the derangement of his reason, existed only in his own morbid imagination? Almighty and all-wise Creator and Judge of the Universe! is it thou that permittest thy rational creatures morally and physically to wound and destroy each other? and is man endowed with speech, only to become more fatal to his fellow than the lurking reptile or the prowling savage of the tropical regions?

"'You will not wonder, though I knew not all the clamour which was raised against me, that I knew enough to determine me never to return to London, or to associate any where with those whom I had formerly been acquainted with. My most immediate purpose, however, was to find the person who had robbed me of the being in whose life mine was wrapped—and as soon as I was able I hastened to the Continent.

"'No such person as he of whom I was in search was to be found at Hamburgh or Altona,[186] where I had been taught to look for him; and after a long search I ascertained, that Hamilton, being now emancipated from his father's authority, who had been dead two years, and doubting the possibility of his return to England, had sold his commission[187] under the King of his native country, and entered into the service of the Emperor of Germany;[188] in consequence of which he had about a month before been ordered into Bohemia. I followed him from place to place, and was within a few days, and then within a few hours, of coming up with his detachment. This intelligence quickened my speed. I arrived at Prague,[189] where the regiment was, as I understood, to be stationed; and. . . . . . I learned that Hamilton had that very morning fallen in a duel with one of the officers of the detachment, in consequence of some contemptuous treatment which the German conceived himself to have received from Hamilton. The aggressor then was punished by other hands than mine, and fell for an injury that was surely not by a million of degrees equal to that *I* had sustained from him. He was already among the dead, and I had been denied the opportunity of saying to him, "Thus didst thou——" Yet vengeance is a passion which is soon deadened in a generous mind. The wretched being whom I had pursued could not have restored to me my murdered child; and after a while I ceased to regret that he had died by other means.

"'I had now no passion to satisfy: I was without hope of pleasure and without pursuit of any other kind. My mind was all darkness and confusion; and even the lurid flashes with which the desire of vengeance had lit it up were extinguished. Existence became insupportable to me. I was among a people whose writings seem expressly calculated to promote suicide. Their books, even those of amusement, treat only of the effects of the most violent passions, and the catastrophe is generally self-murder. [190] On this I had steadily determined—and lingered less from unwillingness to quit a world of which I had so much reason to be weary, than to *feel* my own determination, and to know that the life I abhorred, it was always in my power to shake off. At this moment the friend to whom I had bequeathed the bulk of my fortune, and who had been in the West Indies during the last three years, suddenly appeared at Prague, whither he had followed me from England. I need not describe to you the power which the voice of a friend has over him who has yielded his whole heart to the torpor of despair. I could not altogether close mine against the zeal and the affection of a man, whom I had esteemed and loved from my infancy. I forbear to repeat the arguments with which he gradually won me from my gloomy purpose. I consented to travel with him, and we wandered round Europe, and visited parts of it little frequented by the English. But on me change of place failed to have lost its usual effect.[191] The cruel recollection of past wretchedness pursued me every where, and I found it impossible to obtain enjoyment in scenes where I had fondly projected travelling with my beloved boy, and where his pale image, such as I had beheld when I took my last farewell, and consigned him to the earth, was for ever present to my mind, whatever was passing before my eyes. My friend, however, would not appear to be discouraged. He persevered in those quiet, yet generous efforts, which, judging of me from the generality of mankind, would, he hoped, aided by the great soother of sorrow Time, reconcile me to life, and insensibly restore me to its enjoyment. In the midst of these noble exertions of the most honourable and disinterested friendship, he was seized with a fever at Rome, where, as he saw that place had rather more excited my curiosity than any other we had visited, he had prolonged our stay at the season of the *malaria*,[192] when it is deserted even by the natives who possess the means of removal.

"'I need not tell you with what solicitude I attended the sick-bed of a friend who had done so much for me. His danger incurred for me, and the anguish it gave me, convinced me I had something still to lose. I could not save him! *He* too died! He died, and left me alone in the world, which did not now contain one being interested for me, or for whom I felt any interest.

"'I attended the body of my dead friend to England: that seemed to be the only duty I now had to fulfil on earth. I saw his remains deposited with those of his ancestors; for, though he had very considerable property in Jamaica, he was the last of an ancient English family. I was his executor; and endeavouring most strictly to perform the directions given in his will, I remained some time at his family-house, sorting his papers, and destroying such as I knew he would not choose should be inspected by his heirs, to whom he was almost a stranger. Among these I found many manuscripts, as well as printed tracts, on the condition of the Africans and their state of slavery in the American colonies. Accustomed to consider these people as part of the estates to which they belonged, I had never properly reflected on this subject before; and when I now thought of it, I was amazed at the indifference with which I had looked on and been a party in oppression, from which all the sentiments of my heart revolted.

"'Determined no longer to indulge this guilty apathy, I found I had now an object which was not unworthy of engaging the thoughts of a reasonable being. As a considerable proprietor, I had I supposed the means of doing some good to this miserable race; and to do them good I devoted myself with all of that mind and of those powers which my own unexampled miseries had left me.

"'For this purpose I repaired to this island. Let me not dwell on what followed. If I was disgusted with the mere representation of scenes which I had never witnessed since I had made use of my reason, I found the reality of oppression, in which I was myself a party, utterly insupportable. But my endeavours at reformation were not only considered as the idle dreams of a visionary, but as being dangerous to the welfare of the island. I was not easily deterred by apprehensions of personal inconvenience, and I persevered, till the examples I gave of lenity to and emancipation of the negroes became so much circumstances of fear, that there was, I understood, a resolution taken to confine me as a lunatic; and my brother, the man born of the same parents,[193] who had from my infancy been my enemy, was to be put in possession of my estates. In a government remote from that of the parent state,[194] intrigue does every thing, and equity has as little to do as reason. The party against me increased every day in numbers and in acrimony. My seat in the council[195] I had long since resigned, and I was accused of fomenting the discontents among the black people, and of having communicated with the Maroons. In a word, my situation became extremely uneasy to myself, and worse than useless to the unhappy people whose condition it had been my purpose to ameliorate; for greater severities were often exercised on those in whose favour I had interfered, than if I had never pleaded for them the cause of humanity.

"'Repulsed, therefore, from my purpose, and disgusted with every system I had seen, I resolved to retire wholly from the world, and hide myself from the spectacle of human misery which every where empoisoned the scenes of nature, and made me abhor the species to which I belonged. As to give freedom to the people who were considered as part of my estate was not possible, and I knew, if the plans of my enemies succeeded, that they would fall into the power of my brother, who was reckoned the most severe and unfeeling man in the island, I determined to let my property on short leases, with a reservation as to the work to be imposed on the people, and liberty frequently to inspect them. Far from making one of them subservient even to my particular convenience, I did not keep a servant about my person, but, conveying a few necessities to the excavated rock among the mountains, took up my abode wholly there; a very few of the supplies of artificial life being sufficient for me, and those few easily to be obtained from persons whom I could engage among those who had been formerly in my service.

"'The insurrection among the people of colour,[196] which had been long frequent,[197] and only partially and for a time suppressed, now raged with more dangerous violence: but at that time, I mean on my first retiring to my solitude, their desire of vengeance towards Europeans was so far from being blindly indiscriminate, that, alone and defenceless as I was, I became the object of their respect and even affection; and the only danger I have incurred has been from my own countrymen, and among them those of my own rank; for they have more than once attempted to imprison me, under pretence that I have chosen such an unusual residence for the purpose of intriguing with the insurgents and fugitives, and abetting them in their sanguinary purposes against the landed proprietors of the island. As not the shadow of proof could be brought against me, but as it was on the other hand made evident that I had, on more than one occasion, thrown myself among them, restrained their violence, and induced them to return peaceably to their abodes in the mountains; these attempts and others, made at the instigation of my unhappy brother to prove me a lunatic, from my eccentric manner of life, have hitherto failed.'

"'They may not always fail,' said I[198] to my unhappy and singular protector; 'they may not always fail, for malice irritated by avarice is hardly ever weary: and you see, that the continued outrages of these unhappy people render even the suspicion of wishing them less wretched, a crime which may involve in very serious embarrassment those who are suspected. You have now met one relation, who, though none can make you amends for the cruel losses you have sustained, will find the greatest pleasure of *her* life in contributing to the comfort of yours. Need I add, that the delight of mine will be to assist her in paying this debt of gratitude, duty, and affection?'

"'I expected this proposal from you, Denbigh,' replied Mr. Maynard; 'and if any thing in the world could re-animate my sad heart, and give any value to my existence, it would be to see Henrietta and you happy: but, wounded as I have been, believe me, it is only in perfect solitude I find life supportable. As to danger from those who call themselves my enemies, I despise it: and, alas! Denbigh! where will he who ventures to dissent from established prejudices, and to controvert the maxims of policy which the tyranny of custom has established, that the strong may trample on the weak—where, I say, will he who dares do this, go and not find enemies?—My brother, unhappy man! has paid the forfeit of his violence and his crimes;[199] and for the rest of the people in power here, who have no motive for their enmity, but because I dare not act against my conscience as they do, I fear them as little as I love them. Fear! do *I* name fear? I who have sustained in my own person every degree of misery, and who have yet had courage to live? No, Denbigh! He who has learned as I have done to suffer has nothing more to dread!'

"I found," resumed Denbigh, "by the vehemence of his manner, that this was not a moment to press on my friend my wishes that he would renounce his solitary manner of life. In a solemn and lower tone of voice he again spoke:

"'For what, my friend, should I return into the world?— For domestic happiness?—Ah! no. However I may love Henrietta and you, and I believe I should love you very much, nothing can restore to me the son I have lost, and cruel recollection would force itself upon me in despite of all I could do to attach my mind to other objects; and to speak sincerely, it would seem almost a prophanation of my sacred affection to his memory, were I to wean my mind from its habit of thinking continually on him. This may not be philosophical, it may not be pious; but I am neither a stoic nor a divine. You must recollect too, that the woman who bears my name, and the daughter she brought me, are, in my opinion, impediments to my return to England, which no inducement could engage me to conquer. Towards the child I could not do my duty so well as those to whom she is intrusted; and the mother I have sworn never more to behold. The friend to whom I was the most attached is no more. A martyr to his affection for me, he lost his own life in the generous exertions he made to restore some value to mine. Would you have me seek in desultory society, in the common parties and pursuits of life, a remedy against the malady of the heart? All those parties and pursuits I have tried, when I was more capable of enjoying them than I am now, and I know their value well.

"'Of the emptiness and wearisomeness of what are called the pleasures of the town, every man is probably sensible long before he is five-and-twenty, and I never had any enjoyment in field sports: those two resources, therefore, afford me nothing with which I could beguile one hour of my remaining life. To me the gaming table and the turf[200] never presented any thing but spectacles of strange infatuation, ending almost certainly in repentance. In the conversation of men of letters I found, while I inhabited the world, the most amusement; but, since certain events which have long been foreseen have intermingled politics with every discussion, the republic of letters is so disturbed by party violence, and there is so much pedantry and pretence puffed[201] by political favour into fashion; while scurrility, disgraceful to those who think it can support any cause, is so disgustingly frequent; and taste is so totally annihilated by the blind virulence of mercenary writers, that I sickened amidst the societies that once delighted me, and since I left England I believe all this has grown worse. To such, therefore, I shall never return. No, my dear Denbigh! leave me to the solitude which alone is soothing to my heart. It will be doubly dear to me, since my residence in it has been the means of saving and serving you and Henrietta. Do not imagine that I shall ever forget you. Amidst the awful stillness of the night, when, leaving my sleepless bed, I frequently wander forth, and, gazing on the planets above me, ask of the Divine Omnipotence that pervades all nature, why he has placed me in a world where only anguish has been my portion, I will try to believe that evil, however heavily it has fallen on me, is only partial, and that good and happiness predominate in the general system. I will carry my imagination to you and Henrietta; and there will yet be in the world two beings on whom I can think with pleasure; but I will not by being with you shade your felicity with my gloom, or suffer your society to become necessary to me. I can here only indulge the habit of my mind with-out intruding on others; and as to the apprehensions you entertain of personal danger from the Maroons, believe me, Denbigh, these men, whom we call savages, have neither the blindness nor the ingratitude of the polished Europeans; and they will not injure him who has been, as far as his power extended, their benefactor. But were it otherwise, is it for me to fear death? for me, whose only gratification it is to converse in idea with the dead?

"'Start not, my friend, but hear me. Such is my weakness, that I delight in imagining the spirit of "my brave!,* my beautiful!"²⁰² revisits me. It may impress you with apprehensions of my insanity; but it will not excite *your* ridicule, if I repeat, *"that when I lie down to rest and the moon looks into my cave,"*†²⁰³ his shade²⁰⁴ often stands before me; the air sighs among the boughs, and it is his voice; I look up to the stars, and behold in those orbs of ethereal fire the habitations of souls so pure as his. But at other times——No, I will not relate to you my darker reflections; yet even *they* are preferable to what those that afflicted me in the world were, whenever a worthless or insignificant young man, and I saw but too many of them, was obtruded on me, I felt all the cruelty of my destiny; and my mind, recurring to what he was, my lost, my murdered boy! I have exclaimed, Wherefore should *such* an animal as that exist in high health, and my son be in his grave?

"Why should a dog, a horse, a rat, have life,
And thou no breath at all? Thou'lt come no more!
Oh, never, never, never!* ‡²⁰⁵——"

"'From this description of my feelings, which more than half the world would, I am well aware, call madness, you will judge, my friend, how unfit I am to return to a place in that world. It is among my rocks and trees, then, that I can indulge this weakness, if weakness it be; and there are times when I rise above it. When, alone in my cavern amid the mountains,

---

* The tragedy of Douglas. [Smith's note.]
† Ossian. [Smith's note.]
‡ Shakspeare. [Smith's note.]

the night-storm and land-wind threaten to dismantle them of their magnificent shades, and the rocks tremble to their centre; or, when I listen to the heavy waves bursting against the northern cliffs of the island; when the clouds that bear the thunder are gathering around me, and afar off at sea I mark the signs of an approaching tornado; then it is that I feel myself elevated, sublimed above this earth, and partake in some degree of the beatitude of those beings who dwell beyond the tempest and the earthquake. Disengaged from all that binds others to this planet, I rather court than fear the phenomena, which are likely to detach me from it physically, as already I am morally emancipated.'

"You will easily believe," continued Mr. Denbigh, "that after the close of this conversation I desisted from any further attempts to prevail on my singular and unhappy benefactor to accompany us to England. I now return to the sequel of my poor Henrietta's terrific adventures, which I will repeat as nearly as I can in the first person, and in her own words."

———————

The Story of Henrietta concluded.

"'On the evening,' said my poor girl, 'after I had written the last lines you have seen, my uneasiness was considerably increased by the appearance of Amponah, who seemed to be in the greatest agitation and uneasiness. Yet when I urged him to say, whether my father was coming, or what was the cause of his being so much affected, his confusion appeared to increase, and his answers, vague and contradictory as they were, struck me with more terror than if the objects of my dread had been clearly defined. To the two most hideous causes of fear, the arrival of my father and Mr. Sawkins, and an attack of the Maroons on the plantation, he added a third, by saying, that the Obi women had been in the woods

employed on their spells, and they discovered that some great
misfortune was about to happen to me, and would happen
if I did not immediately leave the house and take shelter in
some other place.

"'I cannot convey an idea of the effect which all this,
delivered in Amponah's strange jargon, had on me. His wild
looks; the interest he seemed to take in my safety, for which
it appeared as if his fears were so great as almost to deprive
him of his reason; all contributed to distract and distress me,
while there was not another person in the house to whom I
could communicate my apprehensions, or of whom I could
ask advice. Gasping for breath, I went to the window, and certainly heard noises enough among the woods and high lands,
to confirm what Amponah had told me, that an immediate
attack of the Maroons was to be feared. He assured me too,
that on more than one plantation, four or five miles off, the
buildings and canes had been fired, and that to the south-east
I might see the flames. He came in a few minutes afterwards,
in apparently increased terror, to tell me, that he had just
discovered that a much greater number of the people than
he had at first supposed were not only disaffected, but, irritated by the hard treatment they had received, waited only
the arrival of their master, to wreak their vengeance more
completely on his person than they could do on merely his
property. Oh! think, my dear Denbigh! the effect that all this,
which was indeed but too probable, must have on the mind
of your poor Henrietta!

"'I now for the first time thought of my father's presence
as desirable, since I could not imagine that in such an hour of
peril he would persist in concluding the detested marriage;
but Amponah, who saw that I caught at this hope, assured
me, that I might satisfy myself the preparations still went on,
and that a party of military were supposed to be on their way
to meet my father, and protect him and his guests from every

apprehension. Though this was a contradiction to some part of what he had told me before, the general impression of terror on my mind prevented my attending to minute probabilities; and the negro girl, who now waited on me, said all that was calculated to increase the agonies of fear which I suffered. On the other hand, Amponah, on whose faith and attachment I had the greatest reliance, and who was I believed much more intelligent than the rest of the negroes, proposed to me to escape. He said he could undertake to conduct me through the woods by a path so little known or frequented, that there would be no danger of my being met by any one, and that he would take a mule from the stable, and lead him round to a place beyond the wood, from whence he could conduct me in safety to the house of a lady he named to me; and then go himself to Mrs. Apthorp, who was not far off, and who would, to use the man's phrase, "be my good friend, and make peace with massa." The scheme was plausible; my situation was desperate; and to deliberate was, I thought, to hazard irrecoverable misery. I decided then to trust myself to the guidance of Amponah that very evening. Yet such was my terror and reluctance that I should have shrunk from this dangerous confidence, even after I had agreed to give it, had not a negro arrived with intelligence, as he assured me, that my father and Mr. Sawkins, with the man of the church who was to perform the ceremony, were at the plantation of one of his friends, only eleven miles off, and would be at the house before the noon of the next day.

"'As soon, therefore, as it was night, I crossed the garden with trembling steps, and found Amponah waiting for me without. He had a brace of pistols, and a dark lantern; and assured me, as falteringly I questioned him, that he had taken every precaution to secure my safety. It was soon too late to retreat, and, in a state of mind not easy to be imagined, I followed his steps through the winding and rough path of a

wood of cedar,[206] and other large and shadowy trees, where
it was soon totally dark, and even the silence of my conductor and his footsteps were now become objects of terror to
me. I spoke to him. He said we should soon come to the
place where he had left the mule; but there was something
in his manner that aggravated my apprehensions. I thought
he no longer spoke with his accustomed respect. He spoke
as if he felt that I was in his power. I had declined taking his
arm to assist me in walking; though I began to totter through
fear and fatigue, for the way seemed endless, and became
more rugged at every step. I was at length obliged to complain; for we had now passed what could not be less than
two miles, still going up or descending among the woods.
Just as I declared my doubts of being able to go any further,
we were in a sort of ravine formed by torrents of water in
the rainy season, over which a large tree was thrown to facilitate the passage when the torrent raged beneath. Here it was
absolutely necessary for me to suffer Amponah to assist me;
he almost carried me in his arms across. When we reached
the opposite bank, I disengaged myself from his hold; and
assuming the manner which I felt to be necessary, though
my heart sunk as I spoke, I ordered him to tell me exactly
how much farther we had to go. Instead of a direct reply,
the negro*[207] turned towards me; and suddenly throwing the
light of the lantern on his countenance, I saw his eyes roll,
and his features assume an expression which still haunts my
dreams, when fearful visions of the past flit over my mind.

"'He made a step or two towards me. I recoiled, and,
almost on the brink of the precipice we had just passed, no
idea but that of throwing myself into it occurred to me when
he thus spoke:

""'Missy, I tell trute now—I love you. I no slave now; I *my*

---

* What is here related is taken from a real event, though not happening
under similar circumstances. [Smith's note.]

master and yours. Missy, there no difference now; you be my wife. I love you from a child! You live with me: nay, nay, no help for it; I take care of that."

"'Thus speaking, he approached me, and all the horrors to which I saw myself liable were but too certain. Escape there was none; but the hollow we had passed was more than deep enough to have destroyed me in my fall; and stepping back as the wretch advanced, I seized a sapling that grew on the edge of the excavated rock; by which I held, declaring to Amponah, with a degree of firmness at which I am now astonished, that if he advanced another step I would throw myself down the precipice and perish. Trusting, however, to his strength and my weakness, he was advancing, and I prepared for the dark and desperate plunge, recommending my soul to the Being who gave it, when a volley of shot from I know not where levelled my assailant with the ground, and I fell half stunned, yet not insensible, at the foot of the tree to which I had clung.

"'I was immediately surrounded by men of various shades of colour; negroes, maroons,[208] quadroons, I knew not what. One among them, who was evidently their chief, advanced towards me, spoke to me in English, and, by his voice and manner, tried to re-assure me. All the recollection and presence of mind I could command did not, however, serve to give me any confidence of safety. I seemed to have been delivered from one evil, only to have fallen into another. The noises, the gestures, the eager manner of these strange people filled me with terror and dismay. The Maroon, however, who commanded them, and to whom they gave the title of *General*, appeared to have not only more authority but to be more humanized than the rest. To *him*, therefore, with a degree of resolution which now excites my surprise, I addressed myself. I told him who I was, and the cause which had compelled me to leave my father's house, and put myself

into the guidance of one of the negroes. The general, for so I
must distinguish him, received this information as not being
new to him. He said what he thought might tend to console
me, though it had a very contrary effect; and ordering his
men to cut down some boughs, and make a sort of litter,
which they effected in a few moments, I was placed in it; and
the general walking by my side with a pistol in his hand, they
began to ascend the mountain, near whose base I was when
this meeting happened. All this passed by the light of torches,
which had been produced and lit a moment after the appearance of this party of people.

"'Denbigh! I will not attempt to convey to you an idea
of what passed in my mind during this fearful hour; for it
was at least that before the cavalcade, of which I was so miserable as to form the principal object, arrived at the place I
shall afterwards describe. At the moment I was deprived of
all sense and resolution; for a number of women came out
from a dark cavern overhung with wood, to meet the persons
they had all the night been expecting. Their clamours and
strange noises were sufficient to have alarmed me: but, judge
of my consternation when I learned, by an harangue from
the general himself, which he delivered with an air of authority, as he commanded them to lift me from the litter, that he
had in the woods rescued a beautiful white woman from a
negro, and had brought her to be added to the number of
his wives.[209] He, therefore, as he was obliged to go out again
for some hours, directed them to take great care of me, and
cause me to take refreshment, and induce me to consider
myself as one of their number at his return.

"'Overcome with the variety of horrors I had undergone,
my mind could no longer resist personal fatigue; and when
two or three wild-looking female dark faces advanced, and,
taking me up among them, carried me into the cavern; I no
longer knew what happened, but sunk into total insensibility;

having only preserved my recollection long enough to know that the men, after calling for a supply of drink, again disappeared; a circumstance which would have lessened my terror, if the aspect of the women, and the orders I heard given, had left me any power to argue with my fears.

"'I remained many hours incapable of reflection, and then recovered from this half-conscious state, in which all I seemed to know was, that something very dreadful had befallen me, when to my opening eyes objects presented themselves which I shall never forget.

"'I was lying on the ground on a parcel of those blue and white rugs of cotton woven and dyed by the negroes. Above me, I saw the high rough arch of a rocky cavern; to which light was admitted only by the entrance at some distance, half obscured by foliage, and the evening was approaching. I raised myself on my elbow, and looked around me. I saw, at the entrance of the cavern, a group of negro and mulatto children; and near them, a little within it, three negresses or mulattos. One of the children observed me move, and exclaiming, "Buckra, buckra, live!"[210] the oldest of the women turned and came towards me. I never beheld so hideous, so disgusting a creature; and such was the dread with which I was inspired as she hung over me, that I was once more on the point of losing my misery in insensibility.

"'The fearful wretch seemed, however, to express a strange sort of satisfaction in seeing me revive. She beckoned to another who did not appear equally delighted, and bade her, as I understood by her signs, bring her something for me from another part of the cavern. This negress was a fat and heavy creature, her neck and arms ornamented with beads, strung seeds, and pieces of mother of pearl; and though there was an affectation of European dress, she was half naked, and her frightful bosom loaded with finery was displayed most disgustingly. Reluctantly, and eyeing me malignantly, she reached what the old woman demanded, and then, with an expression it is not easy to describe, withdrew, and seemed, as did her companion, anxiously to listen at the entrance of the cavern.

"'The elder woman now offered me something in a cocoanut shell,[211] which I put by, for I thought it impossible for me to swallow. But I soon found I had no choice. The menacing attitude and countenance assumed by the sorceress terrified me into immediate submission; and while she stood chattering over me, I forced myself to take what she held; which was, I believe, rum mixed with goat's milk. I prayed, as well as the confused and stunned state of my mind would permit me to pray, that it might be something which should speedily end my wretched existence. The third of the women was a mulatto, younger and less terrific to my imagination than the others: but her disposition seemed to differ in nothing from the fat negress; for, approaching me, as I had again laid myself down, and hid my face with one of my hands, she pointed out to her companions the bracelets I had on my wrists, which, together with a pair of small gold ear-rings, and a picture of my aunt tied to a riband round my neck, were all my ornaments. These they took away, and divided, I imagine, between them. The elder, soon after returning, took off my pockets,[212] in which there were two smelling-bottles,[213] a pocket-book, and an inlaid tooth-pick case. These things were set in gold; of which they seemed to know the value, and to be mightily delighted with them. My clothes were next examined; and a petticoat[214] of fine muslin[215] and a cloak of the same, in which I had been wrapped, were appropriated without ceremony; but my upper garment, which was a dark chintz,[216] seemed not to tempt them, and they left me in possession of it.

"'The old woman, who was, as I afterwards found, the general's mother, opposed this plunder of my trinkets and

clothes with all her power; but the other two, who were his
wives, seemed to hold her authority in contempt. After a time,
the two who were the general's wives went out together. The
old woman remained, and, after offering me every thing she
thought would most completely answer the directions she
had received from her son, of which I rejected the greater
part, she went to her bed, as I imagined, in another cave, or
at least in another and distant part of that where I was.

"'The children too, who had surrounded her, were all
gone to the places where they slept, and the cavern became
silent. I heard nothing but the sighing of the wind without,
and so perfect was the stillness, that I fancied it possible I
might escape; but, perhaps, only the exhausted state in which
I was, the weakness of my body affecting my judgment, could
have induced me to form such a scheme. I arose, however,
and creeping with difficulty to the entrance of the cavern, I
looked around me in a state of mind so confused and bewildered, that I cannot now distinctly relate what I then felt.
The sky above me was illuminated with myriads of stars.
There was that peculiar clearness and lustre in the blue arch
where they sparkled, that is seen only in these regions. My
spirits were revived: I breathed more freely, and my soul once
more resuming its powers, I was able to supplicate Heaven
for mercy and deliverance.

"As if the great Governor of the Universe had heard me
it was already at hand. I saw, coming from the ascent among
the trees, two female figures, in whom I soon recognized
the general's two wives. The younger of them immediately
approached me.

"'She inquired of me in a language which my solicitude
to comprehend her, taught me to understand whether it was
not contrary to my wishes that I was where I now found
myself.

"'I answered, that it was most undoubtedly so, and that

there was nothing I would not do to acquit myself of the obligation I should owe to the person who would deliver me from it.

"'After a short conversation, I found that this woman, long the favourite sultana of the Maroon chief, had no inclination to have another rival in his favour; and that, after a consultation with the other woman, who joined in the desire to appropriate this hero of the hills to themselves, the younger, who called herself Mimba Qua, had resolved to try my disposition to depart, or if I had shewn no such disposition, to murder me!—for though she did not say so, I perceived that such was the resolution these rival ladies had taken.

"'My agonizing eagerness to escape, however, was too unequivocal to leave them a moment's doubt of my sincerity. There was not a second of time to lose. The negress undertook to watch the old woman; the mulatto, to conduct me. My fears lent me strength. I followed, or was led by my conductress to the hermitage, whose inhabitant I have since found was my uncle! I will not attempt to describe my reception. You have seen him, you have heard him, and may imagine how such a man received, at the risk of his safety and life, a wretched young woman, of his own colour and nation, though he did not then know she was the daughter of his brother.

"'What happened at the cave of the Maroons, how the women contrived to divert the suspicions, or appease the anger of the general, or whether some attack of the troops sent against them prevented any pursuit, I had no means of ascertaining. I only know, that after remaining two days in my uncle's wild abode, a stay which greatly restored my strength, Providence in its mercy conducted you, my dear Denbigh! thither, and what followed I need not relate.'"

———

Here my friend Denbigh concluded the narrative of his wife's sufferings. They were married immediately, the governor serving Henrietta as a father at the ceremony; they embarked as soon as possible afterwards for England, where they have now been a few weeks only, and Denbigh is looking out for the purchase of an estate in England, having divested himself, though at some loss, of all his property on the other side the Atlantic.

Here then, my friend,[217] the eventful history closes. Of me you will hear farther from another country perhaps; for I meditate an excursion, of which I will not mention the particulars, because I have not quite decided upon them in my own mind, and know that at all events they will be too eccentric to obtain at least in the prospectus your approbation.

Adieu.

END OF THE SECOND VOLUME.

EXPLANATORY NOTES

1   "tout est bon . . . mais l'amitié est chose véritable":
    "Everything is well, provided one reaches the end of the day,
    that one sups and that one sleeps: the rest is vanity of vanities,
    but friendship is a real thing." From Voltaire's letter to Madame
    la Marquise du Deffant, 24 April, 1769. See *Recueil des lettres de
    M. de Voltaire 1769-1770*, vol. 13, in *Oeuvres completes de Voltaire*,
    vol. 80 (L'Imprimerie de la société littéraire-typographique,
    1785) 103.

2   the first settlement of the island: Jamaica was first colonized
    by the Spanish arriving with Christopher Columbus in 1494,
    at which time the island was inhabited by a people called
    Arawaks or Tainos. Denbigh however probably refers to the
    British conquest of Jamaica in 1655.

3   residence alone . . . his people contented: Absenteeism was
    a major issue in the debate over slavery at the time Smith was
    writing *The Story of Henrietta*.

4   common mode of education . . . Italian and French: Like
    Mary Wollstonecraft, Smith was critical of the superficial edu-
    cation given to women at the time, apparently speaking from
    her own experience (see the introduction).

5   The only son: Smith apparently forgets that Henrietta's father
    is supposed to be an only son when she later introduces his
    younger brother, George Maynard, in the story.

6   ten years old: another inconsistency with the story told by
    George Maynard later on, in which Henrietta's father is said to
    be at Oxford when his younger brother is almost eighteen (p.
    83-84).

7   quadroon . . . negro: "quadroon" is a racial term formerly
    used of a person of one-quarter black ancestry. At the turn of
    the nineteenth century, when Smith was writing, many words
    now considered offensive or obsolete were used as a matter of
    course to describe a person's appearance or ancestry.

8   By a variety . . . other children: it was not unusual for

Europeans visiting or residing in the West Indies to keep mistresses of color, even though the practice was condemned in the metropolis and among writers on colonial customs (see the introduction).

9   **Mr. James Maynard, the young heir:** The 1800 London edition gives the family name here as Denbigh, which was corrected to Maynard in the errata list included in some of the copies of volume two of *The Letters*. Smith seems initially to have intended the name Denbigh for the family of Henrietta's father; but when she finally settled for Maynard, giving the name Denbigh instead to the heroine's fiancé, the revision of the names was never carried out completely before printing. The errata list corrects some of the mistakes, but not all; those not corrected by Smith have however been so in the present edition (see the List of Emendations in the Note on the Text).

10 **the fever:** Probably a reference to the yellow fever, of which there were several outbreaks in the Americas from the seventeenth century onwards.

11 **I had met . . . at Pezena's:** Pézenas is a town in Languedoc-Roussillon in southern France. The meeting referred to here has not been mentioned earlier in *The Letters of a Solitary Wanderer*.

12 **nonage:** being legally under age.

13 **Portsmouth:** town in Hampshire on the south coast of England, and since the middle ages an important seaport and naval base.

14 **sloop:** a sailing-vessel with just one mast.

15 **his dam:** here, the devil's mother (a scornful epithet, now obsolete).

16 **jiggeting:** fidgeting.

17 **hearing perpetual changes rung . . . decorum:** hearing these words repeated over and over again in various ways.

18 **'rather in sorrow than in anger':** Shakespeare, *Hamlet*, I.ii.231-232 ("more in sorrow than in anger").

19 **the Argonaut:** the ship is named after the Argonauts in Greek mythology, who sailed with Jason in the ship Argo to find the golden fleece.

20 **the South Sea:** the South Pacific Ocean.

21 **victuallers**: ships carrying provisions for overseas troops.

22 **St. Helena**: an island in the South Atlantic Ocean, fortified and colonized by the British East India Company from the mid-seventeenth century to 1833.

23 **the Madeiras**: the archipelago of Madeira, in the Atlantic Ocean some 440 miles (c. 720 km) west of Morocco, an important stop for taking in provisions for ships about to cross the Atlantic from Europe to the Americas.

24 **Fonchiale**: Funchal, capital of the Madeiras.

25 **prevention**: presentiment.

26 **foul**: overgrown with seaweed and barnacles and hence performing badly (see *OED* 6.c.).

27 **a very indifferent sailer**: her sailing capacities were poor.

28 **dead-lights**: porthole shutters used for stopping water from entering the ship.

29 **leagues**: a marine league, a unit of distance equaling three nautical miles.

30 **it fell a dead calm**: "it" was formerly used where modern British English has "there" (see *OED* sense B.2.b).

31 **Port Royal**: formerly a vital port city and naval base at the mouth of Kingston Harbor, Jamaica, destroyed by an earthquake in 1907.

32 **two sail to leeward**: two sailing ships sighted on the leeward side (the side of the ship turned away from the wind).

33 **they were . . . enemies**: Britain was at war with revolutionary France from 1793.

34 **French privateers**: during the 1790s war with France, British ships sailing the Atlantic had to watch out for privately owned warships, authorized by the French government to attack and capture enemy ships.

35 **Rochfort**: Rochefort, a town and naval port in south-west France on the Atlantic coast.

36 **cartels** : cartel-ships, used in war-time to exchange prisoners between two hostile powers.

37 **Government packet**: a packet boat sailed a fixed route between two ports at regular intervals in order to maintain a mail service, and it also took goods and passengers.

38 **a glass**: a spyglass, a telescope.

39 **'the rear of night'**: From Homer's *Odyssey* (XIX.500), translated by Alexander Pope, W. Broome and Elijah Fenton in 1725-26.

40 **high latitudes**: as Henrietta is close to the equator, latitudes are low, not high (being zero degrees at the equator and ninety degrees at the poles).

41 **glancing**: gleaming.

42 **many-coloured dolphins**: the reference is to a fish (and not to the sea-living mammal) feeding on flying fish, at the time popularly called dolphin, or dorado (*Coryphæna hippuris*). Known for its beautiful colors when out of the water, it was praised in the often anthologized lines by Richard Blackmore (1654-1729): "As when a Dolphin sports upon the Tide, / Displays his Beauties, and his scaly Pride; / His various-colour'd Arch adorns the Flood / Like a bright Rainbow in a wat'ry Cloud; / He from the Billows leaps with gamesome Strife, / Wanton with Vigour and immod'rate Life."

43 **I tried to remember . . . their faculty of flying**: The plight of the poor flying fish was a popular metaphor for persecution in the eighteenth century. D. L. Macdonald, the editor of the Pickering & Chatto edition of *The Letters of a Solitary Wanderer*, suggests three possible sources for Henrietta's reflections: Joseph Addison's letter on transmigration in the *Spectator* 343 (April 3, 1712); Oliver Goldsmith's letter cx in *The Citizen of the World* (1762); and "The Flying Fish" in the second volume of John Aikin's and Anna Letitia Barbauld's *Evenings at Home, or, The Juvenile Budget Opened*, vols. 1-6 (1792-96). Another possible source might be Voltaire's essay on Venice in *Questions sur L'Encyclopédie* (1770-74), where the metaphor is used to describe the plight of the Venetians, defending their liberty against the emperors of Greece in the east, and the German emperors in the west. In the English translation, reproduced e.g. in *The Monthly Review*'s appendix to vol. 48 (1773): 530-531, and in *The London Magazine, or, Gentleman's Monthly Intelligencer* 42 (1773): 393, Voltaire's lines read: "I here think I see a poor flying fish, pursued at the same time by a falcon above and a shark below, and escaping from both."

44 **the Emily**: the ship in which Denbigh travels.

45 **Captain More**: the captain of the Argonaut (owned by Henrietta's father).

46 **hims**: his [ship]. Juana is represented as speaking Jamaican English, developed from the language of English-speaking colonists into which were mixed elements from the various African languages spoken by slaves born in Africa.

47 **captain Ramsay**: the captain of the ship of war from which the surgeon comes to visit on board the Argonaut.

48 **'answer neglectingly they know not what'**: Shakespeare, *King Henry the Fourth*, Part 1, I.iii.51 ("Answered neglectingly, I know not what").

49 **Kingston**: The largest town in Jamaica since 1716, and its official capital since 1872. Situated on the south-eastern coast of the island, Kingston has a natural harbor protected by a long sandspit, at the end of which is the small town and former naval base Port Royal.

50 **managers or agents**: slave labor on Jamaican estates was hierarchically organized. If a proprietor did not reside in the island himself, he left the overall responsibility for his estates to a superior agent, called an attorney. Under the attorney there was an overseer or manager for each estate, usually a white creole or lower-class European. The overseer had under him a number of drivers, who were usually slaves, each of whom were responsible for the work of a gang of slaves.

51 **post-chaise**: a closed carriage with four wheels, carrying passengers or mail, and drawn by horses controlled by a postilion riding one of the horses.

52 **pleased to revisit her native land**: in view of *Somersett's Case*, a decision of the English Court of King's Bench in 1772 which declared that slavery was unlawful in England, and that all slaves residing in the country were thus emancipated, Juana's pleasure at going back to Jamaica and slavery may not seem wholly uncomplicated.

53 **Horton's . . . near the sea**: Smith is vague and sometimes confused about Jamaican geography. Horton's is said to be situated about thirty miles from Kingston, though in which direction is not clear except that it does not seem to be north, as

Henrietta is later said to be transferred from Horton's to her father's "estate on the northern part of the island" (p. 42).

54 **an odd sort of dialect . . . spoken in England**: Although women in Henrietta's sisters' position might get some experience of the manners and language used by people born or educated in Britain, their dialect would still be that common to people born and bred in the island.

55 **a mestize**: mestizo, a person of white and Native American descent.

56 **creoles**: in eighteenth-century West Indian usage, people native to the West Indies. White creoles were thought by writers like Edward Long and Bryan Edwards to have developed certain characteristics over time, peculiar to themselves (see the introduction).

57 **Maroons**: the Maroons in Jamaica were descended from African slaves who had escaped to the mountains when the British took over the island from the Spanish in 1655. Intermarrying with such native Arawaks as had survived the Spanish occupation, their number was added to by runaways from British plantations. They fought the British colonists until treaties were reached in the late 1730s, when they were granted the right to their own communities with certain limited self-government.

58 **for whose slave my father designs me**: For Smith's use of the slavery metaphor for marriage, see the introduction.

59 **pens**: a pen is a country estate, esp. one for breeding cattle, hogs or poultry; also an enclosure for such livestock.

60 **trute**: [the] truth. RP /θ/ is often pronounced as /t/ in Jamaican English.

61 **a vidow lady**: the spelling "vidow" for "widow" is presumably not a printer's mistake but rather an example of Smith's attempting to reproduce Jamaican English. In the mid-twentieth century Cassidy & Le Page recorded the use of /v/ for RP initial /w/ "in occasional archaic speech" in Jamaican English (lx), and Smith, writing one hundred and fifty years earlier, may well have come across or heard of this use.

62 **'Tel est notre plaisir'**: car tel est notre plaisir (for this is our will, or, literally, for such is our pleasure) was the phrase

traditionally concluding monarchial edicts in autocratic France before the revolution.

63 **to repeat**: to enunciate in a formal manner.

64 **visible on his countenance**: as was not uncommon at the time, Henrietta believes in physiognomy, *i.e.*, the idea that people's characters showed on, and could be assessed from, their faces.

65 **to plight**: to pledge.

66 **palmetos**: palmettos, palms with fan-shaped leaves, esp. of the genus *Sabal*.

67 **mountain cabbage**: a West Indian palm tree with edible terminal buds. Now known under various Latin names, the mountain cabbage in its Jamaican version is termed *Euterpe oleracea* by Cassidy & Le Page, while Edward Long called it *Palma caudice æquali* (3. 744).

68 **Jacobin principles . . . a reformer**: the term Jacobin was popularly applied to people in France supporting the 1789 revolution, and came also to be applied to radicals and liberals in England by their adversaries. Especially after the 1791 revolution in Haiti, people wishing to reform the conditions of the enslaved were regarded with equal suspicion by slaveholders in the Caribbean colonies, as were the "Jacobins" in England.

69 **a woman should acquire fixed principles . . . wretched**: This is just one of many places where Smith makes her characters speak out against the passive and helpless roles assigned to women at the time.

70 **a myops**: a myope, that is, a shortsighted person.

71 **'I like this rocking of the battlements'**: Edward Young, *The Revenge: A Tragedy* (1721), I.i.4.

72 **St. Jago de la Vega**: the former capital of Jamaica, now called Spanish Town.

73 **'the pelting of the pitiless storm'**: Shakespeare, *King Lear*, III. iv.29.

74 **boiling-houses**: the mills on sugar plantations where the cane juice was boiled and converted into raw sugar.

75 **mountain palms**: the same as mountain cabbage, see note 67.

76 **plantains**: tree of the genus *Musa*, related to bananas.

77 **Indian landscape**: i.e., West Indian.

78 **shaddocks**: the shaddock is a large citrus fruit, also called

pummel, pomelo and pompelmoose. It was brought to the Caribbean (to Barbados) from the South Pacific by a Captain Shaddock, from whom it got its name.

79   **the mountains . . . tower to the clouds**: almost all of the inland part of Jamaica is hilly, but Smith is presumably referring here to the Blue Mountains, a thirty-mile long mountain range dominating the windward (eastern) third of the island, its highest peak reaching 7402 ft (2256 m).

80   **mahogany**: the tree *Swietenia mahagoni* and its wood (Cassidy & Le Page). Long discusses it in detail, although under other Latin names (3. 842-844).

81   **ceiba**: the West Indian silk cotton tree (see Long 3.736-738).

82   **Indian fig**: hardly an immense tree, the Indian fig as described by Long as growing in Jamaica is a cactus, of whose several varieties he particularly mentions two: the prickly pear and the cochineal-cactus (3.731-734).

83   **the Maroons . . . excited so much alarm**: probably a reference to the outbreak of the so-called Second Maroon war, between the British and the leeward Maroons of Trelawny Town in western Jamaica, in 1795-96. The windward Maroons in the eastern part of the island did not take active part in this rebellion, but were reported to make preparations for war in the Blue Mountains, in case they should be attacked by government troops (Campbell 221, 239).

84   **depredations**: ravaging, plundering.

85   **a sort of corridor that goes round the house**: called piazza in Jamaican English.

86   **gombay**: a drum, played with the hands.

87   **shell**: the spiral shell of a conch (a mollusc, esp. of the larger gastropods), which when blown served as an instrument of call in the Caribbean.

88   **knockers**: a species of cockroach (see W. Adams, *The Modern Voyager and Traveller through Europe, Asia, Africa, & America*, vol. 3 [London, 1828] 433).

89   **ground dove**: the smallest dove in Jamaica, living on the ground, *Columbigallina passerina* (see Cassidy & Le Page, and also Beckford I.366).

90   **fire-flies**: insects emitting phosphorescent light.

91 **Obeahs**: Obeah men and women, or Obis, were persons among the Jamaican enslaved who practiced Obeah, a diasporic religion of West African origin.

92 **witches . . . cauldron**: Cf. Shakespeare, *Macbeth*, IV.i.

93 **severe punishment**: because Obeah was believed to play an active role in slave rebellions, it was made a capital offence in Jamaica after the 1760 Tacky rebellion.

94 **darkness visible**: John Milton, *Paradise Lost* (1667), Book 1.63.

95 **till she again resumed the pen**: she does in fact *not* resume the pen, but tells the rest of her story orally to Denbigh, who then repeats it to the Wanderer (p. 138).

96 **the date of this last letter**: no dates are given in the text of the novella.

97 **an epidemical complaint**: there was a serious outbreak of yellow fever in Jamaica and other Caribbean islands in 1793-94.

98 **the Assembly**: the House of Assembly, elected by the white settlers, was one of the two bodies of the Legislature in colonial Jamaica, the other being the council appointed by the governor.

99 **residence . . . to which Henrietta had been first carried**: *i.e.*, Horton's. Now said to be on "the other side of the island" from Kingston, where Denbigh makes his inquiries, its location might be on the leeward (westward) side of Jamaica (since presumably not on the northern side, cf. note 53 above).

100 **the overseer**: see note 50.

101 **ship-mate**: African slaves, transported in the same ship during the so-called Middle Passage from Africa to the Americas, developed new relationships with each other, which in Jamaica became equivalent to those of biological kinship and sometimes continued for generations (see S. W. Mintz & R. Price, *The Birth of African-American Culture* [Boston, c. 1992]).

102 **The manager . . . chief deputy**: see note 50.

103 *sangarie*: a cold drink of lemon water and red wine.

104 **a legal prostitute**: a metaphor for marriage used by Mary Wollstonecraft in her *Vindication of the Rights of Woman* (ch. 9), and one which Smith herself would later use about her own marriage in a letter to a friend (see the introduction).

105 **the blue mountains . . . the Maroon insurrection**: Smith may

be confusing the geography here. For notwithstanding the preparations made by the windward Maroons to defend themselves against government hostility (see note 83 above), the seat of the 1795-96 Maroon war was not the Blue Mountains, but the country around Trelawny Town (now Flagstaff) in the Cockpit mountains in the western part of Jamaica.

106 **Maroons and blacks:** Like Bryan Edwards, who distinguishes the Maroons as more physically fit than "any other class of African or native blacks" in Jamaica (*Observations* xxxix), Denbigh speaks of the Maroons as a people different from other "blacks."

107 **fastnesses:** strongholds.

108 **Indian nakedness:** naked like a native of the Americas, possibly a specific reference to the supposed Arawak ancestry of the Maroons.

109 **look of ferocity . . . rolling in its deep socket:** the image of rolling eyes is an alienating racial stereotype formerly found in European descriptions of Africans.

110 **mackaw:** macaw, a large tropical American parrot.

111 **laced hat:** a hat with braids of gold or silver, often used as part of a military uniform.

112 **sweet sop:** also called sugar apple, the fruit of a tree, *Annona squamosa*.

113 **bolls:** boles.

114 **parroquets:** a parakeet is a small parrot.

115 **mangroves:** various tropical trees and shrubs, growing in swamps and other areas liable to be flooded with salt water, and having aerial roots.

116 **caves so frequent in these mountains:** there are plenty of subterranean caverns in Jamaica, esp. in the Cockpit country in the western part of the island. During the 1795 war the Maroons used them as hide-outs, "almost inaccessible to any but themselves," Edwards writes (*Observations* lx). In a rather different vein, Beckford includes a long contemplation on "the solemn ideas that arise from the investigation of caverns" in his account of Jamaica (1.242-249).

117 **giant bats:** Edward Long writes of bats living in caves in Jamaica (3.848), but Denbigh's observation may also be inspired by the

"Giant-bat, with leathern wings outspread" that figures in Anna Seward's "Elegy on Captain Cook," published in several journals in 1780 and later anthologized.

118 **the inward apartment of Robinson Crusoe**: the walled-in cave in which Daniel Defoe's hero in *The Life and Adventures of Robinson Crusoe* (1719) takes shelter when stranded on a desert island.

119 **cassada**: variant spelling of cassava.

120 **phrensy**: frenzy, mental derangement.

121 **conchs**: see note 87 above.

122 **gomgom**: the *OED* (citing amongst others Smith's *Henrietta*) explains the gom-gom as being a hollow iron bowl, or a series of such, struck with an iron or wooden stick. This is probably the meaning Smith intends it to have here, although English journals in the 1760s also mention an African string or wind instrument called the "gom gom."

123 **a language . . . borrowed from the negro English of the colonies**: The Maroons, descending from slaves held by the Spaniards, and living fairly isolated in the mountains, may as late as the turn of the nineteenth century have spoken a language considerably different from the Jamaican English otherwise spoken in the island. Smith may be drawing on Bryan Edwards here, who describes their language as "a barbarous dissonance of the African dialects, with a mixture of Spanish and broken English" (*Observations* xxix).

124 **[à] *pas de loup***: stealthily.

125 **capot**: capote, a long cloak or mantle, often with a hood.

126 **dark lantern**: a lantern with a sliding device to conceal the light.

127 **pimento tree**: *Pimento dioica*, also called the allspice tree because of its aromatic berries.

128 **wild oranges**: though growing in a wild state, oranges were not indigenous to the Caribbean but brought there by the Spanish, being originally from tropical Asia.

129 **tamarind**: the tamarind tree, *Tamarindus indica*, introduced into the West Indies after its colonization by Europeans. Its seeds, contained in brown pods, are used in cooking and for medicinal purposes.

130 **hogsheads**: large wooden barrels.

131 **Harrow School**: a famous English public school.

132 **the rudiments of Latin**: Latin was a standard part of the cur-
    riculum in all British public schools in the eighteenth century.

133 **my mother (whose name I was to take)**: George Maynard,
    wearing the same surname as his brother, did obviously *not*
    take his mother's maiden name, but kept his father's family
    name.

134 **shag, fag, skip**: a shag is "a low, rascally fellow" according to
    the *OED*, which quotes Smith's sentence here as evidence; a
    fag is, according to the same source, "a junior who performs
    certain duties for a senior" in English public schools; and a
    skip is likewise some kind of valet or servant.

135 **my majority**: at this time the age of majority was twenty-one.

136 **Gretna Green**: a village on the Scottish border where English
    couples could marry according to Scottish law without the
    parental consent required for minors in England.

137 **unable . . . to suckle her infant**: The custom among the
    upper classes of hiring a wet nurse for the convenience of the
    mother was becoming an issue after the enormous success of
    Jean-Jacques Rousseau's *Émile* (1762), where he urged mothers
    to breastfeed for the sake of their children's health. The influ-
    ence of Rousseau is evident also in other places in *The Story of
    Henrietta*, *e.g.* in the title Smith gave to her collection of stories
    supposedly gathered by the Wanderer, which echoes that of
    Rousseau's *Reveries of a Solitary Walker* (1782).

138 **St. James's**: an area in the City of Westminster, London. Smith
    herself was born in her father's town house in King Street, just
    off St. James's Square, and very close to St. James's Palace, the
    monarch's London residence in the eighteenth century.

139 **in the *mezza voce***: (Ital.) in a soft voice, lit. in a half voice.

140 **garden chair**: a chair on wheels or small carriage, used by
    invalids, elderly people, or children, for drives around garden
    paths.

141 **a 'plentiful lack of wit'** : Shakespeare, *Hamlet*, II.ii.198.

142 **members of parliament . . . seats**: before the parliamentary
    reform in 1832, landowners in depopulated constituencies
    with very few voters, so called rotten boroughs, could use

their influence to have a candidate of their own choice elected for parliament.

143 **half and bye words**: half words and bywords, i.e., half-spoken words seemingly hinting at something, and derisive epithets.

144 **that disposition . . . attributed to West Indians**: cf. Edward Long writing that the white creoles "are liable to sudden transports of anger; but these fits, like hurricanes, though violent while they last, are soon over and subside into a calm" (2.265); and William Beckford, also generalizing, claiming that the "warmth of temper" of "the West-Indian [. . .] is not followed by a coolness of judgment; but then I have seldom known the heat of passion conduct him to revenge" (2.375).

145 **prolixity**: tedious lengthiness.

146 **prison**: that is, a debtor's prison, of which Smith herself had sorry experience having accompanied her husband to one for several months in 1784.

147 **Sheriff's officers**: bailiffs, officers of justice who make arrests, and make sure that court orders and sentences are carried out.

148 **exigence**: emergency.

149 **the English funds**: the stock of the national debt considered as a mode of investment.

150 **personals**: personal property.

151 **a rubber or a pool**: terms relating to card games. A rubber is a set of three (sometimes five) games; a pool is a game where the stakes are combined into a collective pot to be won.

152 **dowagers**: a dignified elderly lady.

153 **consumptive patients**: the little girl apparently suffers from tuberculosis (often called consumption), an infectious disease common in Europe in the eighteenth and nineteenth centuries. Presumably this is also the "pulmonary complaint" referred to by Denbigh as having killed Henrietta's aunt (p. 9).

154 **Bath**: spa town in Somerset, south-west England, and center of fashionable society in the eighteenth century.

155 **considered as desperate**: thought to be beyond recovery.

156 **the admirable Crichton**: sobriquet referring to James Crichton (1560-1582), known for his various talents and mastery of many different fields of learning.

157 **creditor**: an error; as Mr. Halwyn owes George Maynard, he is his debtor.

158 **moppet**: an empty-headed, silly woman.

159 **children**: strictly speaking, Fanny had only one child alive at the time of her elopement, as her daughter had recently died.

160 **divorce**: divorces were rare in eighteenth-century England, as the costs were enormous, amounting to several hundred pounds. A very wealthy man could however divorce his wife on the grounds of adultery (whereas up until 1857 it was more or less impossible for a woman to divorce her husband).

161 **her syren voice**: her alluring voice. The sirens were creatures in Homer's *Odyssey* who had the power of drawing sailors to destruction by their song.

162 **Buxton**: spa town in Darbyshire.

163 **a father and three daughters**: later in the story Smith also introduces a brother (see p. 125).

164 **Hamilton . . . the noble family of that name**: a family of Scottish nobility.

165 **settlements**: the marriage settlements, the legal arrangement by which property for an intended wife and sometimes children of an intended marriage was secured.

166 **Frank**: short for Francis.

167 **was then seventeen**: the 1800 first London edition prints Frank's age as fifteen, but this was changed to seventeen by Smith in the errata list included in some copies of that edition. This is however a mistaken correction, as everything else in her text points to Frank being indeed fifteen at the point in the narrative when this remark is made. For, as is said later in George Maynard's story, if Frank had been told for six years that his mother had died away from home (109) ("impressed for six years"), and seven years had passed since Fanny left her husband (112) ("seven years had passed since I last heard it")— an incident that occurred when Frank was barely eight (118) ("though he was hardly eight years old")—this would clearly make him only fifteen rather than seventeen.

Likewise, as Frank is said to be ten when his father remarries (103) ("who was now in his eleventh year"), he would be twelve or thirteen when his half-sister is born (107) ("in the

third year of our marriage, she bore a daughter"), which
would make him fifteen, and not seventeen, at the time when
his sister is two (108) ("now above two years old") and his step-
mother turns against him.

168 **prevent:** anticipate.

169 **post town:** a town where travelers could change or hire new
horses.

170 **acquaintance:** here a collective noun, used as plural (cf. *OED*
sense 3).

171 **variety of characters:** an old-fashioned usage without article,
see *OED*, sense 5.b.

172 **Christchurch:** a college of Oxford University, founded in 1546.

173 **gentleman commoner:** paying undergraduate students at
Oxford were called commoners, among whom there formerly
existed various ranks. A gentleman commoner enjoyed certain
privileges and paid higher fees than the ordinary commoners.

174 **entertainment:** in late eighteenth-century theatre perfor-
mances in Britain, the main play was usually followed by a
so-called afterpiece, a short entertainment which could for
instance be a one-act play or a pantomime.

175 **women of the town:** prostitutes.

176 **sentinels:** guards or watchmen, before the formation of the
Metropolitan Police in 1829.

177 **polluted by art:** defiled by cosmetics.

178 **chariot:** a carriage having only back seats, drawn by four
horses.

179 **Lausanne:** town in Switzerland, on the northern shore of
Lake Geneva.

180 **his youth, and facility which all innocent and rational pleasures might there be enjoyed:** something seems missing in
this clause, which might read better as: "his youth, and [the]
facility [with] which . . . ."

181 **In tenfold astonishment:** in immense astonishment (ten times
greater than might be normally expected).

182 **her brother:** first mention of the second Mrs. Maynard's
brother.

183 **Beckenham:** at the end of the eighteenth century a small vil-

lage south east of London, now part of the Greater London area.

184 **an only child**: at this point George Maynard disregards the fact that he also has a daughter by his second wife.

185 **Rousseau . . . the account he has left of himself**: The work generally mentioned as betraying Rousseau's mental decline was the volume entitled *Rousseau Juge de Jean-Jacques* (1780), where his persecution mania, made worse by his stay in England, is quite evident. As Smith, like Rousseau, had experience of feeling injured and persecuted, she has George Maynard make the point that such feelings may not always be signs of madness.

186 **Altona**: a town on the Elbe, close to Hamburg and now a part of that city.

187 **sold his commission**: a commission was the authority entrusted to an officer in the army; in the eighteenth century it was common for officers to purchase their rank, and hence to sell their commissions if they wanted to leave.

188 **the Emperor of Germany**: the Emperor of the Holy Roman Empire, which was finally dissolved during the Napoleonic wars, but in the late eighteenth century a decentralized state composed of a number small states and city states, among them Bohemia, Austria, Brunswick-Lüneburg, Prussia and many others. The emperor referred to by George Maynard would have been Joseph II (reigning 1765-1790).

189 **Prague**: Situated on the Moldau river in Bohemia, Prague was part of the German empire at the time George Maynard arrived there.

190 **whose writings . . . the most violent passions**: the reference would be to the *Sturm und Drang* movement in German literature in the 1770s, and especially to Goethe's *The Sorrows of Young Werther* (1774) and its suicidal hero.

191 **failed to have lost its usual effect**: the sentence confuses two phrases. It ought either to read "failed to have its usual . . . ," or, "had lost its usual . . . ."

192 *mal-aria*: malaria, literally meaning bad air, a disease spread by mosquito bites but formerly thought to be caused by the unhealthy atmosphere in swamps and marshy areas. Malaria

had been endemic to Rome for centuries, its most active season being in the summer.

193 **my brother, the man born of the same parents**: cf. note 5, where Henrietta's father is said to be an only son.

194 **the parent state**: *i.e.*, Great Britain.

195 **the council**: one of the two bodies of the legislature in colonial Jamaica, the other being the House of Assembly (cf. note 98 above).

196 **The insurrection among the people of colour . . . on my first retiring to my solitude**: George Maynard is apparently not referring to the ongoing 1795 Maroon rebellion, but to an earlier uprising. The Tacky rebellion of 1760 would have been before his arrival in Jamaica, but there were other revolts in Jamaica during the following decades, for instance that led by Jack Mansong, known as Three-fingered Jack, in 1780.

197 **had been long frequent**: had been recurring often during a long time.

198 **said I**: Denbigh breaking into George Maynard's narrative.

199 **My brother, unhappy man! has paid the forfeit of his violence and his crimes**: The intimation is that Henrietta's father is dead, although we can only guess how, due to the gap in the printed text (see p. 80).

200 **the turf**: metonym for horse-racing (taking place on a grassy track).

201 **puffed**: inflated, promoted or praised with empty words.

202 **"my brave! my beautiful!"**: John Home, *Douglas: A Tragedy* (1757), V.i.254 ("My beautiful! My brave!").

203 **"that when I lie down to rest and the moon looks into my cave"**: a slightly paraphrased line from *The Battle of Lora: A Poem*, included in the 1765 two-volume edition of *The Poems of Ossian*, allegedly translated by James Macpherson (1.170: "when thou liest down to rest, and the moon looks into thy cave").

204 **his shade**: his disembodied spirit.

205 **"Why should a dog . . . never, never!"**: Shakespeare, *King Lear*, V.iii.305-307.

206 **cedar**: Jamaica cedar tree, *Cedrela odorata* (Cassidy & Le Page). Long mentions two species of cedarlike trees growing in Jamaica, the Barbadoes Cedar (*Cedrela foliis majoribus pinnatis,*

ligno levi odorato) and the Bermudas Cedar (*Juniperus foliolis inferioribus ternis*) (3. 835).

207　**a real event**: this event has not been identified.

208　**negroes, maroons**: Like Denbigh (see note 106), Henrietta categorizes the Maroons as a separate group of people from the African-Caribbeans.

209　**added to the number of his wives**: Smith may have relied on Bryan Edwards here, according to whom "[p]olygamy . . . with their other African customs, prevailed among the Maroons universally. Some of their principal men claimed from two to six wives, and the miseries of their situation left these poor creatures neither leisure nor inclination to quarrel with each other" (*Observations* xxx).

210　**buckra**: a white man or woman.

211　**cocoa-nut**: coconut.

212　**took off my pockets**: pockets were not always sewn into the clothes; women would instead wear separate pouches or small bags tied around their waist or otherwise tucked away on their person.

213　**smelling-bottles**: a small phial containing a preparation of ammonium carbonate (smelling-salts), having a restorative effect on people feeling faint or suffering from headaches.

214　**petticoat**: in the eighteenth century a dress or skirt, often decorated, showing beneath another dress or gown as part of the overall costume, hence not as now a piece of undergarment.

215　**muslin**: very thin and light cotton fabric.

216　**chintz**: closely woven cotton fabric, originally imported from India, often glazed, and with patterns printed in many colors.

217　**my friend** : the addressee of the Wanderer's letters, in which the stories of Denbigh, Henrietta and George Maynard are told.

Printed in the USA
CPSIA information can be obtained
at www.ICGtesting.com
JSHW031206040823
45811JS00005B/227